She was beautiful.

Kate stood before him, a look of vulnerable defiance in her eyes as he drank in the shape of her. As he stared at her, soft color rose in her cheeks, and she crossed her arms in an involuntary gesture, trying to shield herself from the intensity of his gaze.

Cullen clasped her wrists, pushing her hands to her sides. Then, his gaze locked with hers, he reached out, testing the incredible softness of her flesh. He kissed her then, coaxing her lips apart with gentle persuasion as he slid his hands to her back.

It was all he'd remembered, all he'd known it would be, something he knew he could never get enough of. Kate was more than just another woman.

You're falling in love with her.

The voice in his head whispered what his heart had refused to admit.

Dear Reader,

Have you ever been so excited after reading a book that you're bursting to talk about it with others? That's exactly how I feel after reading many of the superb stories that the talented authors from Silhouette Special Edition deliver time and again. And I'm delighted to tell you about Readers' Ring, our exciting new book club. These books are designed to help you get others together to discuss the brilliant and involving romance novels you come back for month after month.

Bestselling author Sherryl Woods launches the promotion with *Ryan's Place* (#1489), in which the oldest son of THE DEVANEYS learns that he was abandoned by his parents and separated from his brothers—a shocking discovery that only a truly strong woman could help him get through! Be sure to check out the discussion questions at the end of the novel to help jump-start reading group discussions.

Also, don't miss the other five keepers we're offering this month: *Willow in Bloom* by Victoria Pade (#1490); *Big Sky Cowboy* by Jennifer Mikels (#1491); *Mac's Bedside Manner* by Marie Ferrarella (#1492); *Hers To Protect* by Penny Richards (#1493); and *The Come-Back Cowboy* by Jodi O'Donnell (#1494).

Please send me your comments about the Readers' Ring and what you like or dislike about what you're seeing in the line.

Happy reading!

Karen Taylor Richman,
Senior Editor

Please address questions and book requests to:
Silhouette Reader Service
U.S.: 3010 Walden Ave., P.O. Box 1325, Buffalo, NY 14269
Canadian: P.O. Box 609, Fort Erie, Ont. L2A 5X3

Hers To Protect

PENNY RICHARDS

Silhouette®

SPECIAL EDITION™

Published by Silhouette Books

America's Publisher of Contemporary Romance

SILHOUETTE BOOKS

ISBN 0-373-24493-2

HERS TO PROTECT

PENNY RICHARDS

also has written under the pseudonym Bay Matthews and has been writing for Silhouette for sixteen years. She's been a cosmetologist, an award-winning artist, and worked briefly as an interior decorator. She also served a brief stint as a short-order cook in her daughter-in-law's café. Claiming everything interests her, she collects dolls, books and antiques, and loves movies, reading, cooking, catalogs, redoing old houses, learning how to do anything new, Jeff Bridges, music by Yanni, poetry by Rod McKuen, yard sales and flea markets (she loves finding a bargain), gardening (she's a master gardener) and baseball. She has three children and nine grandchildren and lives in Arkansas with her husband of thirty-six years in a soon-to-be-one-hundred-year-old Queen Anne house listed on the National Register of Historic Places. She supports and works with her local garden club, arts league, literacy council and Friends of the Library. Always behind, she dreams of simplifying her life. Unfortunately, another deadline looms and there is paper to be hung and baseboards to refinish.…

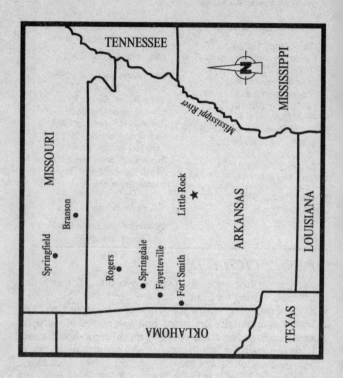

Prologue

The slightest rustling of leaves alerted Cullen McGyver that he was no longer alone. He sat straighter in the swivel chair atop the ten-foot-high tree stand. His gaze panned the fringe of woods to his right before traveling down the logging road that disappeared around a bend to his left.

The buck stood at the edge of the rutted, rock-strewn road, knee-deep in grass left brown and brittle by subfreezing temperatures. Like Cullen, the buck was statue still, listening. His massive rack—at least twenty inches wide and ten perfect points—looked too heavy even for his thickly muscled neck.

Muy Grande, Cullen thought, a satisfied smile curving his mouth. The elusive, phantom buck whose infrequent, random sightings and narrow escapes from many shells and bullets had, through the years, become the deer hunters' equivalent to the fisherman's ''one that got away'' tale. Many of the people who hunted on the three-thousand-acre McGyver deer lease had had at least one encounter with the big buck who somehow managed to outmaneuver, outrun or outsmart them all.

Moving with purpose and yet with an unbelievable stealth, the buck came straight toward Cullen, intending to check out the scrape, which was almost directly beneath the stand. Cullen was a good shot and had killed his share of deer from this very spot, but he had no intention of using the .30-30 that lay within arm's reach. It was enough to sit and admire the forest king's magnificence. Besides, he hadn't really come to hunt; he'd come to escape the lingering outrage of a spousal abuse case that had ended that morning.

As chief prosecutor, he had gained a conviction, and Rodney Perry was on his way to the big house for a spell. Unfortunately, in Cullen's estimation, a lifetime behind bars wouldn't be long enough for what Perry had done to his family. It would take time for the memories of the horrors he'd brought to public attention to slip away to the place in his mind where he banished those things too painful to deal with—the horrors of what men did to each other on a daily basis, the futility of knowing that anything he did to ease the pain of victims would never be enough...Joanie's death and the improper way he'd handled his grief.

The muted sound of a rifle shot from somewhere beyond the hills dotted with waist-high pines rolling toward the horizon brought him out of the morass of his thoughts. The buck froze again, listening...waiting.

From the dark heart of the forest came the unmistakable bleating of a doe. The rut was well underway, and if the buck was likely to make any errors in judgment, it would be now, while he was being ruled by his hormones instead of the wary intelligence that enabled him to survive autumn after autumn.

The buck snorted, gave a final look around and disappeared into the thicket where the sound had come from, unaware—or perhaps uncaring—that danger in the form of one of the many hunting members and not a willing lady might be lurking in the deepening afternoon shadows.

Cullen leaned back in the chair and let the breath he hadn't realized he'd been holding ease from him. He wouldn't tell any of the other hunters what he'd seen. He'd never hear the end of it for not taking the shot. But bagging the buck wasn't that important. There were some things meant to be kept to oneself, just as there were some things not meant to be harmed. Like the Perry family and just maybe a big buck who'd earned the right to a little pleasure for having escaped a bullet for so many years.

Cullen poured himself a cup of coffee from the thermos he'd brought along and let his mind wander. Because of his high profile in righting many of the wrongs in Arkansas, his name had been bandied about by the state movers and shakers as a possible candidate for U.S. senator. He was flattered, and a part of him was excited about the possibility of having the opportunity to serve the state in a more meaningful way. Another part of him wasn't sure if he'd like the lifestyle changes a win would demand. Meghan, his twin sister, told him he wasn't ambitious enough.

He responded by telling her that she was ambitious enough for them both and that his ambition was to be the best prosecutor he could be, to get and keep the bad guys off the street. Just because one job was higher profile or deemed more prestigious than the other didn't mean it was any better. Plus, with the political climate in the country so polarized, a scandal around every corner and PAC money influencing almost every decision made in Washington, he wasn't sure he wanted to be part of that scene. No doubt the job would play havoc with his hunting, not to mention the closeness he shared with his sister and her family. Next to his job, they were the most important things in his life since he'd lost Joanie.

The faraway drone of a small airplane reminded him of civilization. He should get back to Little Rock soon. He'd promised Elizabeth Longstreet, his brother-in-law's younger sister, that he'd take her to see Nancy Kerrigan et al at the Alltel Arena. It had sounded like a good idea when they'd made the date two weeks earlier. Liz was pretty, available, smart and single-minded in her pursuit of him. Cullen had rebuffed her so often he had begun to feel guilty.

The last two years he had made a conscious effort to put the past behind him and move on with his life, which included dating, even though he hadn't had a date in weeks. Not that there hadn't been opportunities. One of the problems with being considered one of the most eligible men in the city, if not the state, was that older women kept trying to fix him up and younger women kept coming on to him no matter how disinterested he might seem. Meghan claimed it was his very disinterest that made him so desirable. It wasn't that he didn't want to find someone. Being single meant coming home to a dark house. Solitary meals. Long, lonely nights. An empty bed. If finding a woman to share his bed was all he was looking for, life would be simple. But he wanted more. He wanted to find someone to share the rest of his life with. Like the big buck, he knew the elusive woman was out there, but so far he hadn't caught a glimpse of her.

A random thought escaped the dark corner of his heart where he'd banished it. A woman with long red hair whose very presence aroused him. *Forget her!* Good advice. Thinking of her inevitably brought on a depression rooted in guilt.

Think about Elizabeth. Also good advice, considering the way the shadows were lengthening. He glanced at his watch. Time to go. By the time he walked to the cabin where he'd left the Jeep and drove to town, it would be time to get ready for his date. Heaving another sigh, he replaced the cap on the thermos and reached for the rifle, wondering for the hundredth time why he'd agreed to the date.

Out of habit, he double-checked the rifle to make certain it was on safety before he started down the ladder. Then he grabbed the thermos and began his descent. He'd taken no more than two steps when he heard another shot, this one much closer. Almost simultaneously, he felt a stabbing agony rip through his left shoulder. With a cry that was as much surprise as pain, he lost his grip on the rifle, the thermos and the rung of the ladder. He was vaguely aware of the ground rushing up to meet him and the need to do something to break his fall, but a blessed darkness descended before he made impact....

Cullen awakened to a damp, musty smell. He opened his eyes and saw that a handful of stars was flickering in a bruised-looking sky. Taking short, shallow breaths—all he could manage with the pain holding his chest in a vise—he recorded three things with a sort of groggy awareness: it was almost full dark; he must have fallen from the deer stand; and he was going to be late for his date.

He started to sit up and fell back to the cold ground

with a cry of pure agony. A cold sweat broke out on his face. The ribs on his right side hurt like hell, and there was something wrong with his shoulder, too. Gritting his teeth, he raised his right hand and probed the aching, throbbing area, pulling away fingers smeared with blood. Memory came flooding back. He recalled hearing a nearby shot before falling. Obviously, he'd been the victim of some hunter's carelessness. He must have hurt his ribs in the fall, probably on the rotting stump he could feel pressing against his side. Best-case scenario, they were cracked. Worst case, they were broken, which meant that if he moved wrong he could puncture a lung— or worse.

He lay still, looking at the sky, trying to think the situation through while coping with the pain of his wounds. It was getting dark. No one knew where he'd gone. The temperature was cold and getting colder by the minute. The expected low for the night was well below freezing. As if to reinforce that thought, a chill breeze swept over the hilltop, rustling the pine boughs and sending a shiver through him. He flinched in reaction and was rewarded with another spasm of agonizing pain.

When the worst of it passed, he considered his options. As he saw it, he could gamble on the possibility of further injury by somehow getting up and walking to camp— how much blood had he lost, anyway?—or he could lie where he was and hope some other club member would stumble across him. Neither choice appealed to him, but they were all he had, since he'd left his cell phone in the Jeep to stop anyone or anything from interrupting his afternoon. After a bit more thought, he rejected the second scenario. Too many ifs and maybes. Besides, if he took that course, he'd be risking hypothermia and pneumonia.

Knowing there was really no choice, Cullen gritted his teeth and rolled to his side, groaning in agony. Levering himself to a half-sitting position with his good arm, he waited for the wave of pain and nausea to pass, then, using the rotting stump as an aid, eased himself to his knees. Eventually, he got his feet under him and began to weave down the trail that led to the cabin.

The short walk took twice as long as it should have, since there were times he had to stop and rest against a tree until his head stopped spinning. Finally, when he was beginning to think he'd gotten turned around in the darkness and might be lost, he saw the light on the porch of the cabin glimmering through the trees. In minutes, he staggered into the clearing, the keys to the Jeep already clutched in his numb fingers.

Getting inside was another ordeal, punctuated with waves of pain and nausea and curses. Once inside, he struggled to close the door and crank the engine, praying the heater wouldn't take long to warm up. He fumbled with the seat belt and finally gave up, shoved the gearshift into first and pulled onto the lane that led to the secondary highway, a mile away.

With his head swimming, Cullen approached the highway. A quick check told him nothing was coming from either direction. Holding the steering wheel with his left hand and clinging to consciousness with sheer willpower, he shifted gears and pulled onto the asphalt, pushing the speedometer needle to fifty-five despite the waves of dizziness that washed over him with increasing frequency.

Two zigzagging miles from the cabin, he forgot and drew a deep breath as he started around a sharp turn. Pain and a surge of darkness washed over him. In a haze of agony and encroaching unconsciousness, he gripped the steering wheel, unaware that he was over the yellow line. The lights of an approaching vehicle and the blaring of a horn brought him back with a start. Reacting without thinking, he wrenched the steering wheel to the right to get out of the oncoming vehicle's way. Too hard. Too much. Through the mist of pain, he saw the deep, tree-banded ditch alongside the highway rushing at him. *Slow down!* He slammed on the brakes. Too little, too late.

Before the Jeep went nose down into the ditch, a still-functioning part of his brain registered the fact that the brake pedal went all the way to the floor without any noticeable slowing of the Jeep's momentum.

Chapter One

Muted voices violated the sanctity of Cullen's sleep. A feminine, elegant scent teased his nostrils. Something warm and gentle brushed across his forehead. He forced open his eyes and encountered the blurred, smiling face of his twin sister. Meghan, a successful trauma doctor, was wearing street clothes, so she must have been called to his bedside from home.

As she brushed a tender hand over his hair, he noted the tears in her eyes. "You're awake."

"Sort of. What time is it?" His voice sounded rusty, as if it hadn't been used in a long time, probably because his mouth was so dry.

"Three a.m."

He tried to focus on Meghan's face. "Why aren't you working?"

"My night off."

He licked his dry lips. "And then you have to come in anyway."

"It's no big deal." Sensing his need, Meghan poured some water into a glass and offered him a drink via a straw. "Only a sip or two."

Cullen raised his head toward the straw. Amazing how even that small movement brought such agonizing pain. He grimaced and took a couple of sips, even though he wanted to drink down the whole glass. "What happened?"

Meghan's pretty mouth twisted into a semblance of a smile. "Maybe I should be asking you that question."

"What's that supposed to mean?" He was having difficulty not only forming his words but focusing on what she was saying. Pain medication, he reasoned.

"You have a gunshot wound in your left shoulder, just below the collarbone, probably from a rifle. You can thank your lucky stars it didn't hit any major organs or the shoulder joint."

Meghan recanted the list of his injuries in the unemotional, professional voice she used when dealing with her patients. "You also have a couple of cracked ribs on the right side from hitting the steering wheel when you went into the ditch. Of course, you weren't wearing your seat belt, so it's a wonder you aren't dead."

Muddled or not, Cullen was amazed at how quickly she went from professionalism to sisterly censure. By the time she'd finished her spiel, the detached tone had mutated to disbelief and irritation, which he knew was rooted in concern.

"No lectures, sis. I couldn't get the seat belt fastened, and besides, I didn't break my ribs in the Jeep accident. That happened when I fell off the deer stand, after I was...shot. May I have some more water, please?"

She held out the glass. "You were in the deer stand when you were shot?"

"Coming down, actually." He didn't miss the frown that flitted across her face as he took his drink of water. "I needed to get back so I could take Liz to see the ice show." He lowered his head to the pillow and closed his eyes, exhausted from the simple effort of raising his head and drinking from a straw. "I suppose she's ticked off."

"Actually, I believe she said something about your going to any length not to take her out," Meghan told him in a dry voice.

He moved his head back and forth on the pillow. Even that small gesture brought a wave of dizziness. "I don't want to hurt her, Meg, but—"

"You don't have to defend your feelings to me, Cullen, or to Dan," Meghan said. "Liz is a nice woman, but she isn't for you. That's no problem for either Dan or I."

He opened his eyes and tried to smile. "Good."

She regarded him steadily for several seconds. "What's going on, Cullen?"

Still groggy from whatever they had given him, Cullen tried to remember if she'd said something he'd missed. "What do you mean?"

"The sheriff's department's take on the incident is that you were hit by some careless hunter's bullet."

Cullen frowned, trying to think with the huge cotton ball that was once his brain. "That'd be my take, too." He slurred the words. "Why do I get the impression it isn't yours?"

Meghan shrugged. "If it had happened on the ground, I could buy it, but you said you were coming down from the tree stand. What kind of deer hunter aims up in a tree to make a shot at a deer?"

He frowned. "Maybe it wasn't a deer hunter. Maybe

he was hunting squirrel or coon.'' The comment came with no regard to whether or not the other two animals were in season.

Meghan raised her eyebrows in a gesture of disbelief. ''With a high-powered rifle? The hole in your shoulder wasn't made with a .22.''

Cullen passed his tongue over his dry lips. ''Are you suggesting…the shooting wasn't an accident?''

''I don't see how it can be,'' she said, shrugging.

''But…if it wasn't an accident, then you're implying someone wanted to harm me.''

''Kill you,'' she clarified in a no-nonsense voice.

''Who would want to kill me?'' Cullen asked, knowing even as he asked it that it was a stupid question. He could come up with a couple of names off the top of his head, and his fuzzy brain wasn't even working on all cylinders.

Meghan laughed. ''How about every slimeball you ever put behind bars, which anyone would admit is a pretty impressive list.''

''You have a point.'' He closed his eyes and thought a moment. ''No,'' he said, shaking his head. ''There has to be some other explanation.''

''Like what?''

''Like…'' He couldn't think of anything.

''Can't do it, can you? Face it, brother dear. What you can't accept is that not everyone out there thinks you're the greatest thing since sliced bread. Knowing you're the target of someone's warped sort of revenge or their perverted sense of justice is like facing a dreaded disease. Things like that don't happen to you. They happen to other people.''

She had a point. Actually, personal vendettas were carried out every day. The newspapers were full of killings, many executed for far less reason than being sent to prison. In fact, several of the people he'd put behind bars had been seeking their brand of revenge for some wrong—real or imagined—when they'd run afoul of the law. Meghan was right about something else. No one wanted to believe he was the object of someone's hate. And, when viewed from her perspective, the careless-hunter scenario didn't make much sense, unless…

"Maybe the hunter tripped and the gun went off. That would make the bullet go at a crazy angle."

Meghan thought about that for a moment. The expression in her eyes indicated that the idea held some merit. "Maybe," she agreed in a grudging tone.

"Mystery solved," he said, mustering a passable smile. She didn't look convinced, so he reached out and patted the hand resting on his bed. He didn't like to think about someone wanting to kill him. His shoulder hurt like Hades, and he was so tired…. "Go on home to your husband, Doc, and let me get some sleep."

"Okay." She leaned over, brushed a kiss to his cheek and raised the railing in place. "See you in the morning."

"Sure."

He watched as she scooped up her leather coat and bag from the chair and headed for the door. She was halfway out when she turned, her mouth open as if she wanted to say something.

Cullen held up a hand to silence her. "Too much TV."

She shook her head. "Too much ER."

"Local Prosecutor Victim of Hunting Accident." The story, along with a picture of Cullen McGyver, made lower right of the front page of the *Arkansas Democrat Gazette*. The man, sitting in a small room that smelled of medicine and leather, frowned as he read the account. He hadn't anticipated the accident making front-page news. Of course, he hadn't expected to miss his target, either—or for McGyver to survive the brake malfunction. Lucky son of a gun.

The man read the brief article, which told how Cullen McGyver had accidentally received a shoulder wound while hunting on his deer lease in Clark County and how, weakened from loss of blood, he had crashed his Jeep into a ditch as he'd tried to drive himself to the hospital. The piece went on to say that, despite his injuries, which included cracked ribs, the popular prosecutor was doing well.

The writer reported specifics about McGyver's unprecedented string of convictions and reported that his name had been mentioned in connection to a possible bid for United States senator. He had been transferred to a Little Rock hospital and would spend a short time recuperating before going back to work. There was no mention of where he'd be recuperating.

The hand on the newspaper tightened, crumpling the edge and distorting McGyver's photo. Cullen McGyver had ruined his life, destroyed him both financially and professionally by taking away his ability to work at his chosen profession, all in the name of justice and the pursuit of right and wrong. His star had been extinguished when it had barely begun to rise while McGyver's star climbed higher and higher, along with the state's respect and admiration.

Now there was talk of him running for the senate in a year. With his luck, he'd win, and even if he was sent to Washington, he'd try to legislate morality and ethics and tougher punishment for everything from drug dealing to smacking their dog with a newspaper. The American people were already legislated to death. While there was generally much ado about free speech, the government wouldn't be happy until it had stifled a man's most intimate thoughts.

A horse in a nearby stall snorted. Exactly, the man thought, as he unclenched his fist and smoothed the paper with infinite care. He reached for the scissors that lay on the table next to a cooling cup of coffee. What McGyver had done to him wasn't fair. He stabbed the likeness of his nemesis with the sharp point of the scissors.

Anyone could make a mistake in judgment. Accidents happened. As Cullen McGyver had found out.

Later that afternoon, Cullen, who was drifting in and out of consciousness in direct correlation to the frequency of his pain medicine, tried to divert his attention from the throbbing in his shoulder and the need for yet more of the pain medication by watching a gardening show. He was concentrating on the how-to of installing a water feature when the phone next to the bed rang.

Gritting his teeth against the pain, he turned slightly to his side and reached for the receiver, snapping a sharp hello.

"Hey, Cullen. This is Buddy." Buddy Perkins was a high school classmate who had kept Cullen's and Meghan's vehicles running since they were old enough to get a license. "How ya feelin'?"

Cullen managed a laugh, wondering why Buddy's usually cheerful tone was missing. "I've been better. And you?"

"Pretty good. I guess you know Meghan had the wrecker tow the Jeep over here, so I could assess the damages."

"I figured she would. So what's the verdict?"

"Well, for starters, the front bumper and right fender need replacing and the hood needs some work. Steve can fix that and touch up the paint. On my end, you need a new radiator and the brakes fixed.''

A fuzzy memory surfaced. One of slamming on the brakes as he went into the ditch. "Yeah. I tried to slow down before I hit the ditch, but the pedal went all the way to the floor.'' He gave a humorless chuckle. "I can't remember the last time I had new brake shoes put on.''

"It wasn't the brake shoes, hoss," Buddy told him. "You lost your brake fluid.''

"Oh.'' Cullen thought for a second. "A leak in the line?''

"I guess you could say that.''

Cullen didn't miss the irony in Buddy's voice. "What do you mean?''

Buddy sighed, a sound that said volumes about his state of mind. "It wasn't just a fluid leak, Cullen. Somebody cut the line.''

Cullen pushed around the food on his dinner tray and fought the need to administer more pain medication. He needed to be clearheaded to try to comprehend the full implication of the news Buddy had sprung on him. He was losing the battle with both goals when he heard a knock, and a familiar face appeared in the crack of the door.

Louella Stephens had been Cullen's secretary ever since he'd begun working as a prosecutor ten years before. In her early sixties, she was plump, pretty, pleasant and extremely smart. He often told her that if it weren't a conflict of interest, he'd marry her. Louella always replied that she wasn't sure he could keep up with her. Sometimes, watching her at work, he believed her.

"Hi.'' The round face framed by the salt-and-pepper hair wore a wide smile. Noting the barely touched food on Cullen's tray, Louella stepped into the room holding up a bag from a popular hamburger place Cullen frequented. She crossed the small room and leaned over to kiss him on the cheek.

"Looks like I timed it just right."

"That you did," Cullen said with a smile.

Louella removed the dinner tray and replaced it with the cheeseburger, an order of thick-cut, homemade fries and a chocolate milk shake. "Eat up."

"Thanks, Lou," he said, appreciating the effort but knowing he couldn't handle much but the milk shake. He took a sip. It was as good as he'd known it would be. He set down the drink and winced.

"Do they still tape up cracked ribs?" Louella asked.

"Nope. But they give you this nifty dispense-your-own-pain-medication gizmo. Sort of a trade out."

Louella smiled and straightened his sheet. "How long will you be out of commission?"

"I don't know what my doctor will say, but Meghan says I should be out of here soon. As she put it, it isn't as if I do any manual labor, and I can lie around at home as well as here. What's happening at the office?"

"Senator Falk called," Louella said, giving the sheet a final smoothing and sitting down in a chair next to the bed. "He and Senator Watson want to have a little talk with you really soon. They'd like to have you start raising some money for the election."

"I'll meet with them, but…I think it's a little early to worry about campaign finance," Cullen said, with a weary shake of his head. "I haven't decided for sure I want to run."

Louella looked at him over the tops of her half glasses. "It's a chance of a lifetime."

"I know, but I'm not sure I have what it takes to be a successful politician."

Louella smiled. "You have what it takes. And you have more than what it takes to make an appealing candidate."

Cullen gave her a questioning look.

"You still have a viable conscience," Louella said, patting his hand. "A rarity in the exalted arena of politics."

Cullen gave a half smile.

"Proctor lost the Kilgore case," Louella said, getting back to his request. When Cullen swore, she held up her hand and said, "I know, I know, but there's no sense your fretting about it. Martin said he was pretty satisfied with the jury for the Connelly trial, and I've had Margie working hard on the Jones case…assuming you'll be able to try it."

"I'll be able." Cullen wanted nothing less than life for Delbert Jones. Not only had he subjected his family to physical abuse for years, when his wife decided to leave him, he'd tried to kill her. He'd also wounded one of the policemen who'd tried to get him to surrender.

There was a sharp rapping at the door, but before Cullen could tell the visitor to come in, his sister swept into the room, wearing green scrubs and a look of wide-eyed disbelief. Ignoring Louella, she said, "I called Buddy."

Wonderful. "Hello to you, too, Meg," he said with the breathless voice that seemed all he could muster with the injured ribs. "I guess you didn't see Louella sitting there."

Meghan cast a fleeting glance at the older woman. "Hello, Louella," she said, then turned to Cullen. "Buddy told me about the Jeep, which is good, because I don't suppose you were going to."

"Actually, I was," Cullen said, reaching for the milk shake again. "But I didn't think it was worth bothering you in the middle of your day."

"Someone deliberately shot at you and then cut your brake line, and you didn't want to *bother* me?"

Cullen didn't miss the expression of alarm that flitted across Louella's face. "What do you mean someone deliberately shot at him?" she asked, finally snaring Meghan's attention.

Meghan gave a careless shrug. "It appears that someone tried to do him in."

"That's interesting. I have to confess the chance of that happening crossed my mind," Louella said. "Call me paranoid, but I guess I've just seen too much the last thirty years."

"He'd like to think it was an accident," Meghan said, cocking her head toward Cullen. "Some hunter's rifle went off accidentally, and out of three thousand acres, the bullet just happened to find him—ten feet up in a tree stand."

Louella gave a disbelieving snort. "Doubtful. What's this about the brakes?"

"Buddy told me that the brakes didn't fail. Someone cut the line and the brake fluid leaked out. Cullen could have been killed."

"But who would want to—" Louella broke off with a shake of her head. "Never mind. Stupid question."

"I called the sheriff's department and told them what Buddy said. They reluctantly agreed to look at the shooting from a little different perspective. They're going to talk to Buddy and they're supposed to be sending someone over to question Cullen."

"Good idea," Louella said.

Cullen, who'd been watching and listening to the two

women with both exasperation and fascination, said, "I'd really appreciate it if you ladies wouldn't…talk about me as if I weren't here."

"Sorry," they said in unison, but neither of them looked or sounded as if she meant it.

"So what are you going to do?" Meghan asked him, putting her fists on her slim hips.

"About what?"

"About the fact that someone is trying to kill you!"

"Assuming you're right, what can I do? I don't have any idea who it might be…and as we all know, the possibilities are legion. So what I'm going to do is go on with my life as if this really was a hunting accident."

"You're going to just continue to make yourself a target?" she cried in a disbelieving voice.

"What choice do I have?" Cullen asked, anger taking the soft edge from his voice.

"You could go somewhere and lie low for a while, just until the police figure out who this maniac is. He's bound to have left some sort of evidence."

"How do you find it on three thousand acres?" Cullen asked, reminding her of the reality of the situation. "What if they can't find any clues? Do I just withdraw from life? Hide out forever?"

The anger drained out of Meghan's eyes along with the starch in her spine. "No," she said, her voice little more than a whisper. "I suppose not."

She paced the length of the small room. "You could go to the farm for a couple of weeks," she suggested, a pleading look in her eyes.

Cullen opened his mouth to reject his sister's offer, but before he could say anything, she hurried to explain. "I understand that you can't stay forever, but you need some time to heal. You have everything there you need to carry on your work, and you can drive back to town when you have to be in court. Just until after Thanksgiving.''

The farm was the place in southwest Arkansas where he and Meghan had grown up. When their father passed away, he'd left it to them jointly. Meghan, who loved horses, raised Thoroughbreds there, entrusting their care to a farm manager who had a small house on the far side of the one-hundred-sixty acres. They both loved going back to relax but seldom had the time. It would make a great place to recuperate—or hide out—and she was right about the working conditions. It was just that he hated having some unknown someone calling the shots as to how he lived his life.

''No one would know where you are,'' she said in a coaxing voice. ''If you're out of the picture for a while, it might defuse the situation. And while you're there, you could compile a list of people you think might seriously want to harm you and give the cops some time to figure out who's out to get you.''

''She has a point,'' Louella said.

''I suppose,'' Cullen admitted grudgingly, raising his good hand to rub at his forehead. What he wanted was for them to go away. For it to all go away…the worry, the uncertainty and the aching pulse of the pain. What he wanted was to hit the little button and dispense some instant forgetfulness. But he wasn't the type who made a habit of dodging the unpleasantness of life, which is why this all rubbed him the wrong way.

''There's something else you might consider,'' Louella said with a thoughtful expression.

''What's that?''

She looked from Cullen to Meghan. ''A bodyguard.''

''No!'' Cullen snapped.

Meghan smiled and said, ''That's a great idea!''

"No," Cullen said again. "That's going too far. Besides, you said no one would know where I am."

"They won't," Louella said. "But it never hurts to have a backup plan."

"Come on, Louella! Besides being as obvious as a case of measles, I'd feel like a fool with some seven-foot wrestler type following along behind me everywhere I went."

Louella gave him a wide-eyed look of innocence. "Who says it has to be a seven-foot wrestler type?"

"What other type is there?"

"What about a woman?"

"Have you lost your mind?" Cullen snapped. "I won't hide behind a woman's skirts. I try to protect women, remember?"

"Of course I remember," Louella said with a serene smile. "But this woman doesn't wear skirts—at least not often—so that's no problem."

"Oh, great! So I have a female wrestler type following me around instead?"

"Of course not," she said with a comforting pat on his arm. "You have a point about drawing attention to yourself with a bodyguard, so the smart thing to do is have someone around who doesn't draw suspicion."

"And how do you do that?" Meghan asked.

"Hire someone the public will perceive as a woman Cullen is seeing socially."

"Like a fake girlfriend?" Cullen asked.

"Exactly. You're single. You date lots of women. Why not let the public think you've found someone special? If the world thinks you're romantically involved with her, they'll have no reason to think she's there to protect you."

"It makes sense, Cullen," Meghan said, her eyes gleaming with excitement.

"It's a ridiculous idea!"

"Do you have a better one?"

"Yeah," he said gruffly. "I'll take my chances."

"That's not an option," Meghan snapped, but he didn't miss the supplication in her eyes. "Twin brothers are hard to replace."

Cullen recalled how devastated he'd been at almost losing Meghan from a ruptured appendix when they were small. Even though they weren't identical, they were very close. "It won't work."

"We can try," she said, turning to Louella. "You have someone in mind?"

Louella nodded. "Kate."

"Kate? Your niece?" Meghan asked.

"Yes," Louella said, smiling.

"No." The two women looked at him, surprised by the harsh curtness of his voice. Cullen's voice held a grim finality. "Forget it. I will not have Kate Labiche as my bodyguard."

Chapter Two

The expressions of stunned surprise on Meghan and Louella's faces might have been comical under different circumstances. Cullen considered the definite possibility that he'd overreacted to Louella's suggestion.

"I thought you were happy with Kate's work when you used her before," Louella said, the look on her face going from surprise to concern. She doted on her niece, and Cullen knew that any slight Louella might perceive would be taken personally.

"I was happy with her work," he said, eager to cover up his mistake. "She did a great job rooting out who was behind that illegal oil-waste dumping."

"Then why are you so adamant about not using her for a bodyguard?" Meghan asked, frowning.

Cullen sighed. What could he say that wouldn't put him deeper into this particular hole? "Look, ladies," he said with the smoothness that seldom failed to sway juors, "I don't want a bodyguard. Any bodyguard. I especially don't want to use Kate because…well, because she's Louella's niece and there's the potential for danger. …wouldn't feel comfortable knowing something might happen to her." *Brilliant, McGyver!*

Louella gave a dismissive wave of her hand. "Don't forget that Kate was a police officer before she became a private investigator. She's a trained professional, Cullen. She can take care of herself."

"Louella has a point. A lot of P.I.s don't have the kind of training you can get from the police academy. I've never met her, but if Louella says she's good, she must be. I say we put our heads together and come up with some sort of employment package then have Louella give her a call and see if she's interested."

Cullen fought the urge to let go with a round curse. There was no way he could argue with something as basic as women's logic. He didn't want Kate Labiche around twenty-four seven. Couldn't take it. But it looked as if he was overruled…unless he wanted to come clean about his real reasons for not wanting to hire her. Even with his considerable persuasiveness, he doubted he could make either his sister or his secretary understand what had happened between him and Kate when he'd gone to New Orleans. He had only recently begun to understand it himself.

"What do you think, Cullen?" Meghan asked. "I really think it's important that we find someone who can go the extra mile, and Kate certainly seems that."

What did he think? He thought that his side ached and his shoulder throbbed and his brain felt as if it were wrapped in a piece of cotton batting. He couldn't believe that anyone seriously wanted to do him harm, but the evidence seemed to definitely be pointing in that direction.

"Give her a call," he growled with a dismissive wave of his hand as he tried not to think about a tangle of sheets and legs and long red hair. Kate, the third time they'd made love in one evening, even though he wasn't sure he was able…him teasingly telling her she needed to learn to pace herself. Kate. Arching her back and neck as he trailed kisses down her stomach. Surging up to kiss him, her teeth clamping gently onto his lower lip…and then her own as they strove for satisfaction together. Kate. Going the extra mile.

The faraway sound of a phone ringing nudged Kate from a very arousing dream. Without raising her head or turning over, she groped for the bedside phone, turned it on and dragged it to her ear, rasping a groggy hello.

No one answered. Instead, the phone rang again. Squinting sleepily, she levered herself to her elbows and looked around the bedroom. The ringing was coming from the front of her apartment, where the small dining room had been converted into a home office for Tracers, Inc. She punched off the bedside phone, dropped it onto the rumpled sheets and swung her feet to the carpet, pulling down the tank top that had ridden up during the night.

"I'm coming, I'm coming," she muttered, her long legs making short work of the distance from bedroom to dining room. As she reached for the receiver, she glanced at the leather-bound clock, a gift from her father when she'd opened her business. Almost ten. She frowned, grabbed the phone and pushed the on button. "Tracers."

"Katie?"

Kate's frown faded along with her irritation. No one but her dad and his sister called her Katie. "Aunt Lou?"

"Yes. How are you, honey?"

That depended, Kate thought. She dropped into the secondhand office chair and propped her elbow on the scratched oak desk, resting her forehead in her hand. It depended not only on which part of herself was in question but what day it was. Sometimes it depended on the hour of the day. "I'm fine, Aunt Lou. How are you?"

"Great. I tried calling your other number a couple of times the past few days, but I didn't get any answer, so I called James and he gave me your business number."

"I've been out of town, tracking down a birth mother." The frown returned. It wasn't like her aunt to be so persistent in trying to get hold of her. "Is everything okay, Aunt Lou?"

"Everything's fine. I called to see if you'd be interested in picking up a little extra job."

Does a bear sleep in the woods? New jobs were always welcome. "I've got a couple of things going on with missing persons and a couple of adoptees looking for birth parents, but I can probably work someone else in. Last month was pretty slim."

"You haven't been in business long enough for word-of-mouth to have really kicked in," Louella said. "It will."

Kate ran slender fingers through her long red hair. "I hope. It's hard being self-employed when you've always depended on a weekly paycheck."

"I'm sure it is. The job I have for you will pay extremely well."

That sounded good. Kate regarded the water in a glass sitting on a stack of papers, the remains of ice from some tea she'd left sitting there days ago. "So who's the skip?" With a shrug, she picked up the glass and put it to her lips.

"It isn't a skip, honey," her aunt said. "It's my boss."

Kate's heart stumbled, and the water she was in the process of swallowing went down the wrong hole. She heard her aunt's concerned questions over her choking and coughing.

"I'm fine." She finally managed to croak the words out. The thought process, which had come to an abrupt halt, returned with a single word. Boss. Which translated to Cullen McGyver. The hotshot prosecutor her aunt worked for. No doubt the esteemed Mr. McGyver needed some more out-of-town P.I. work for some other big criminal case he was working on.

Nothing unusual there. A lot of private investigators worked hand in hand with attorneys who needed their skills for a variety of reasons, and she'd done a bit of work for Cullen when she'd started her business. She knew he'd been impressed with the work she'd done for him since he'd sent her a generous bonus check. Evidently, she hadn't been nearly as good in bed, since she hadn't heard a word from him since she'd handed him her report and he'd left New Orleans.

Kate was a big girl who certainly knew the rules of the games men and women played, but she'd been fresh out of a divorce, feeling vulnerable and needing validation of her femininity. Cullen had done a fantastic job of leading her to believe he was sincere and that what passed between them those few stolen days was different. Special. That there was enough between them to build on. When it turned out to be a lie, she'd done what she did best—erected a protective shield around her heart and chalked the encounter up to experience. Now, just knowing that Cullen wanted to use her again—was that an unintentional pun?—brought back a rush of memories she thought she'd buried beneath two years of hard work and stubborn determination.

"Boss?" The word came out with a hard edge. "What does he need now?"

"He was injured in a hunting accident a couple of days ago."

Despite the animosity she felt for him, a rush of panic pushed aside Kate's initial anger. She schooled her voice to a tone approaching noncommittal. "Hunting accident? How badly was he hurt?"

"He has a shoulder wound and some cracked ribs where he fell."

Thank goodness, it didn't sound too serious, Kate thought, responding with a lazy drawl. "You've called the wrong woman. Let me remind you, Aunt Lou, that my nursing skills are rudimentary at best. I'm not much good beyond Mercurochrome, Band-Aids and aspirin."

Her aunt laughed, a hearty chuckle. "Cullen doesn't need a nurse, honey. He needs a bodyguard."

Kate sat up straighter. Bodyguard. The single word conjured up more memories, these far less pleasant than those of Cullen, memories she would prefer never to think of again. She and her partner in a standoff with one of New Orleans's bad guys. Raul face-to-face with an acne-studded, stoned-out-of-his-mind kid with a semi-automatic in one hand and a bag of crack in the other. Raul, his gun pointed at the kid, screaming for him to drop it, to put down the weapon. Herself, off to the side, out of harm's way, knowing she needed to do something but unable to pull the trigger on someone who was little more than a boy....

Her stomach roiled sickeningly, and a sudden depression rolled over her in huge waves. "I'm not a bodyguard, Aunt Lou. You ought to know that."

"Katie, Raul Santiago's death was—"

"My fault," she stated flatly.

"You were trying to be cautious, trying to give Raul time to reason with the boy."

"Yeah, well," she said, "I learned the hard way that you can't reason with someone with mush for brains."

"You were taught to respect life, Katie. Even though you knew you might have to take one in the course of your work, you can't be blamed for hesitating at the thought of doing it."

Kate closed her eyes and saw dirt hitting the top of Raul's casket. Heard the hollow thuds as it fell, the sound dropping into the muggy afternoon like a wrecking ball crashing into a building. Luz crying. The kids crying. Kate dry-eyed. Beyond tears. Grieved to the farthest corners of her soul.

"Try using that rationale with Raul's wife and kids."

Kate heard her aunt's sigh. "I know it's been a difficult couple of years for you, honey, but you have to move on. You have to stop blaming yourself and deal with what happened."

"I have moved on," Kate said, trying to interject some enthusiasm into her voice. "I gave up police work and became a private detective."

"Yes, you've moved on, but you haven't come to terms with what happened. Not really. You were a wonderful cop. You have talents that are going to waste tracking down deadbeat dads and skips."

"I like to think I'm doing some good," Kate said in a prim voice.

"And you are," Louella hastened to assure her. "But you're not making the best use of your abilities. You've got to come to grips with what happened and stop running from it."

"And just how do I do that?" Kate heard the irritation and challenge in her voice and hated herself for using the tone with her aunt.

Louella sighed again. "I can't say exactly, but I imagine it's sort of like getting back on a horse once you've been thrown."

Neither of them spoke for several seconds. Kate knew her aunt was right, but the pain of knowing she was responsible for someone's death was something she wasn't sure she would ever get over. She was certain, though, that it would be the height of foolishness to take on the responsibility for someone else's life, considering her state of mind the past two years. Nope. That was one horse she couldn't climb back on—could she?

Exhaling a sigh, she broke down and asked the question she'd been dying to ask. "And why does Cullen need a bodyguard?"

"All the evidence is beginning to show that the shooting wasn't an accident."

"All what evidence?" Kate asked, her heart giving another little lurch of fear.

"Cullen was in a tree stand in the middle of three thousand acres when he was shot."

"That's not impossible," Kate said, though her mind told her it was highly improbable.

"You're right, but it's been in the paper and on the news, and no one has come forward to say they were in the area when it happened. Cullen believes someone would have come forward if a rifle had accidentally discharged, especially if they knew someone had been injured and he's said there won't be any charges filed."

"You'd think," Kate said, her mind churning over the disturbing news her aunt had relayed. Though she'd often lain awake at night in the weeks and months after Cullen had walked out on her without so much as a goodbye, contemplating various ways of doing the dirty deed herself, she'd known it was only the pain of his betrayal that caused her uncharitable thoughts. The thought of someone actually hating him enough to try to kill him was incomprehensible.

"Is that it?"

"No. After Cullen regained consciousness, he walked back to the cabin and tried to drive himself to a nearby town to get some help. The brakes failed on his Jeep, and he wound up in a ditch. His mechanic says the line had been cut."

Kate frowned, and the worry gnawing at the edge of her mind took a deeper bite. That was pretty heavy evidence, circumstantial or not. She chewed on her lower lip in contemplation. There was no way she could deliberately put herself in a position where Cullen could have a chance to hurt her again.

The money is good.

The random, very pertinent thought came out of nowhere. Unfortunately, at this point in her life, money was important. Very. She'd had a bad couple of months and was falling behind on her credit cards. If it hadn't been for a bonus check she'd received from an insurance company months back, she wouldn't be in as good shape as she was…if you could call her current shaky financial position good shape. In fact, she was so far behind on her credit cards, she hadn't been able to use a couple of them when she'd been gone this past week, and without them to aid in her traveling, she couldn't survive.

Times were desperate, and desperate times called for desperate measures, like putting herself into a situation that held the potential for heartache.

"Does he have any idea who might be responsible?" she asked, hoping to get a better feel for what was going on.

"Any of a dozen or more people Cullen has put behind bars. He's a wonderful prosecutor, Katie," Louella said, her voice warming with enthusiasm and admiration. "Intelligent…"

Slick.

"Smart…"

Smooth.

"Savvy…"

A consummate liar.

"More important," Louella continued, "he cares about the victim."

"A real paragon, huh?" Kate said, unable to hide the sarcasm in her voice.

"He's a good, honorable man, Katherine, and, as you well know, that's something that's getting harder and harder to come by these days."

Uh-oh! She'd riled Aunt Lou. If the reproach in her aunt's voice wasn't clue enough, the use of Kate's full name was. Still, considering her experience with the man, Kate couldn't help how she felt. And beyond her personal interaction with Cullen, she'd seen enough corruption inside the boundaries of the law to make her leery of someone who sounded so squeaky clean, no matter what kind of endorsement he might get from her aunt.

Still, her aunt was no fool when it came to judging people, so maybe Cullen McGyver was everything she said he was—at least in his professional life. Maybe he was one of the good guys, worth protecting. That didn't make the idea of doing the protecting any more palatable, especially since they had a past…of sorts.

"Sorry," she said, with just the right amount of contrition. "Can't the police provide some protection?" she asked, looking for some wiggle room by suggesting the most logical answer to Cullen McGyver's problem.

Louella laughed. "Even if they had the manpower, which they claim they don't, Cullen won't hear of having—how was it he put it?—a seven-foot wrestler type tagging along behind him."

Kate swung her long bare legs to the top of the cluttered desk, knowing she had to ask the question that was uppermost on her mind. "So how does he feel about having an almost six-foot woman tagging along behind him?" *How does he feel about having me tagging along behind him?*

"He wasn't crazy about that, either, mainly because he doesn't want everyone to know what's going on."

Right. Kate figured that Cullen was probably about as eager to hire her as she was to accept the job. Actually, though, the reason he'd given her aunt for his reluctance wasn't a bad one, especially since Aunt Lou had no idea that there was anything but a brief, professional relationship between the two of them.

"He doesn't want to get the media stirred up," her aunt continued, in blithe ignorance. "That's why I suggested you. I told him that if you took the job instead of a man, we could hide the fact that you're there for his protection by letting the world believe you're his current love interest."

Kate's tentative, grudging interest evaporated. She lowered her feet and the chair to the floor. Her aunt's tone was matter-of-fact, but Kate knew from experience that tone could be deceiving. "Hold on just a minute here, Aunt Lou. Is this another of your matchmaking schemes?"

"Of course it isn't! Why would you even think such

a thing?'' There was no disguising the hurt in her aunt's voice.

"Maybe because you have been known to try your hand at it before.''

"The man is in genuine trouble, Kate,'' Louella said in an injured tone.

"That's good, because if he isn't and you're just trying to fix me up with an eligible male, I'm definitely not interested in this gig.''

"Fix you up with Cullen?'' Her aunt gave a trill of silvery laughter.

"What's so funny?''

Louella giggled again. "The idea of you and Cullen as a *real* couple. Oh, that's too rich! No offense, honey, but you're not his type at all.''

Kate frowned, a bit miffed her aunt considered her so undesirable but curious as to why. "Oh? What is his type?''

"Petite. Socially polished. Classy dresser.''

Well, that certainly shed light on why he took what he wanted from her and then went on his merry way, Kate thought. Outside the bedroom, she wasn't his type. She'd been okay for a few nights of fun and frolicking, but when it came to permanent relationships, the handsome prosecutor went for the dewy-eyed fashion-plate type, which left out Kate, who despised dressing up and whose only concession to fashion was to buy the most up-to-date running shoes.

She breathed a sigh of relief. Or was that disappointment? "That lets me out, thank goodness.''

"Oh, don't sound so put out, Katherine. You have good manners and you clean up very nicely.''

"Thank you, Aunt Lou,'' Kate said, not missing the

fact that her aunt hadn't said anything about the fact that Kate was anything but a classy dresser.

"Now that we have that cleared up, will you please consider the offer? As a favor to me?"

Kate felt her resolve weakening.

"I did tell you he's prepared to give you five thousand up front, plus six hundred a week and expenses, didn't I?" Louella said, dangling the right kind of carrot in front of Kate's nose.

"Five thousand!" Five thousand was more than she'd made the past three months.

Are you really considering putting yourself into a situation you know could be disastrous not only for Cullen McGyver, but for yourself, your own mental health— never mind the potential damage to your ego and your heart—just to get out of a financial bind?

You bet she was. It was galling to think she could be bought, but sometimes life had a way of bringing a person to his knees. "What expenses?" she asked.

"An apartment for the duration of the job and a new wardrobe."

"Are you sure this guy is legit?" Kate asked, astonished by his apparent generosity. "I mean, how can he afford all this on a prosecutor's salary?"

"Old money. His mother's family was Texas oil, I believe, and his father was in timber."

That explained it. "Why do I need a new wardrobe? Since I'm not his type, it isn't like anything I do would impress him."

"You'll be dressing for the public, honey. Cullen is a very eligible man with a very active social life. Once he gets over his injuries, he'll be on the go again. Why, he brought the highest bid at the bachelor auction last year.

And if you're pretending to be his current love interest, you'll have to go along with him to certain events.''

"Wonderful," Kate said, her voice drenched with sarcasm.

"I know it isn't your bag—or whatever the current saying is—but you're a great actress, which is why you were so good at undercover work and why you'll be so good at this.''

"I don't know," Kate hedged. "I'd have to turn over all my clients to a friend of mine, and some of them won't be too happy about that.''

She heard her aunt sigh. "I know it's a big decision, but will you at least fly up and talk to him?''

Maybe it was time to confront him, Kate thought. Maybe Aunt Lou was right. Maybe she did tend to hide from the past instead of dealing with it head-on. Maybe it was time to face Cullen McGyver and tell him exactly what she thought of him for running out on her. But... "I can't afford the ticket.''

"Cullen said he'd buy the ticket, if you'll come.''

My, my, our Mr. McGyver was thorough, wasn't he? Kate sighed. Since he was paying for everything, what could she lose by having a little chat with him? "He's thought of everything, it seems," Kate observed.

"He tried," Louella said.

"Okay, then. Why don't you see if you can get me a flight out early tomorrow?''

"How about this afternoon at two-fifteen?''

Kate closed her eyes and gave her head a slow shake of disbelief. Aunt Lou's habit of doing everything full steam ahead was well documented through the years as well as it was often a source of irritation. "You've already bought the ticket?''

"Well, yes, Kate, I did," her aunt admitted. "I thought

it would be a good way to get to spend some time with you, if nothing else.''

Kate felt as if she were being swept along by a gigantic tidal wave. Unlike her aunt, who was known for her impulsiveness, Kate didn't like to be rushed. Normally, she liked to think things through, look at them from every conceivable angle, weigh the pros and cons so she wouldn't make any mistakes. *Which is why you hesitated a fraction of a second too long and allowed that scumbag to kill your partner.*

She wouldn't think about Raul. She couldn't afford to. This job with Cullen had the potential to get her out of her current financial bind, and that was all that mattered. Kate sat up straight in the chair and squared her shoulders. ''Looks like I'll see you this afternoon, then.''

''I'll meet you at the airport. We can have dinner, and you can talk to Cullen tomorrow.''

''Sounds great!'' Kate said with far more enthusiasm than she was feeling. She got her ticket information, told her aunt goodbye, hung up and scrambled to her feet. She'd better get moving if she hoped to be on time for her flight.

As she showered and packed, Kate kept asking herself if she'd lost her mind by even remotely considering her aunt's suggestion. She justified her decision to go to Arkansas by telling herself she hadn't committed to anything. A job interview was only a way to see if the potential position was workable. *And it's a chance to see Cullen again.*

Kate scolded herself for thinking about Cullen. She should concentrate on the job, not the man. Unfortunately, the two were inextricably bound. Going to Arkansas and meeting with him face-to-face was important if she was seriously considering the job. A lot could be earned from not only questioning a person, but his or her body language and attitude. By looking him in the eye, she'd be able to see exactly where she stood with him. *Forget the personal angle, Kate. You need the money, and this is a heck of a job opportunity.* Going to see him was the right thing, both on a personal and professional level. By talking with him, she hoped she could put part of her painful past behind her, where it belonged, if she wanted to do a good job protecting him in the future, which she should not forget was the important consideration here. No matter how good the money might be, there were a lot of factors to consider, the most important being her gut reaction to how Cullen McGyver felt about her playing a significant role in his life.

Besides, it was Friday, and another lonely weekend loomed ahead of her. The weekend trip would break the monotony of her life, and, as her aunt suggested, it was a chance for them to spend some time together.

As promised, Aunt Louella was there to meet Kate when she got off the plane several hours later. Enveloped in a warm embrace that smelled of White Shoulders, her aunt's signature scent, Kate was overcome with a rush of nostalgia and love. Until her now-deceased uncle had been transferred to Little Rock eleven years ago, Louella had been the mother whom leukemia had taken from Kate at the age of ten.

"I've missed you," she said, blinking back tears. "I never realize just how much until I see you."

"I miss you, too, honey," Louella said, reaching up and patting Kate's cheek. "Are you hungry?"

"Starving." Kate had always had a healthy appetite. Fortunately, she also had a wonderful metabolism.

Louella chuckled. "Some things never change. Where do you want to eat?"

"You choose. I'm not familiar with the area."

"Let's get your suitcase while I think."

They started toward the baggage claim area. "I miss Uncle Bert," Kate said suddenly. It was her uncle, gone four years, who'd always fetched the luggage.

"So do I."

"He was a sweetheart," Kate said. "Too bad there aren't any more out there like him."

"Oh, there are a few," her aunt said. "They're rare, but they're out there. You just have to look hard for them, and you, young lady, haven't had nearly enough dates since you and Lane broke up to even hope to find yourself a good one."

"Sort of like kissing a lot of frogs to find the prince, huh?" Kate said with a smile.

"Exactly."

"How about you?" Kate asked, skirting a woman pushing a stroller for twins.

"What about me?" Louella asked with a sideways glance.

"Are you dating anyone?"

Louella laughed. "I'm too old for that nonsense."

"You most certainly aren't," Kate said, her tone indignant. "You're the youngest person your age I've ever known. And you're pretty and smart and—"

"And not interested." Her aunt broke in as they passed a book and magazine store. "Oh, look! There's the new Dean Koontz."

"Stop changing the subject."

"I'm not!" Louella's face wore an indignant expression.

"Of course you are," Kate said with a grin. "Let's be honest. Dating is just too stressful, isn't it?"

"I wouldn't know, but I'm sure it must be. Unfortunately, it's the best way I know to find the right man."

"Yeah? Well, someone needs to come up with a better way."

Louella smiled. "Maybe they will. Which reminds me. Cullen's sister called and said they'll be releasing him from the hospital early in the morning. She's taking him straight to their farm to recuperate. She wants us to drive down there and spend the weekend."

Kate stifled the urge to scream. She'd come for a job interview, not to hobnob with Cullen and his sister. She was tired. She was worried about paying her upcoming bills. The last thing she wanted to do was spend the weekend fraternizing with strangers. Furthermore, she didn't like the way her aunt had made the segue from finding a better way to meet a man to Cullen McGyver. She knew her aunt. Kate didn't doubt that Cullen was in some sort of trouble, but Aunt Lou was not above trying to kill two birds with one stone, even if one was a glorious peacock and the other was a drab little wren.

Chapter Three

The next morning, after devouring a home-cooked, fat-laden country breakfast complete with her aunt's feath-erlight buttermilk biscuits, Kate and Louella loaded the car and headed for the McGyver Thoroughbred farm. After seething half the night, Kate had come to grips with the fact that her interview with Cullen had somehow changed to a weekend visit. There was nothing she could do about the situation. She'd come this far, she could certainly play nice for a couple of days. After all, if she was hired for the position of bodyguard, she'd be expected to hobnob with Arkansas's finest. That settled, she'd fallen into an uneasy sleep filled with fragmented, erotic dreams.

Now, headed down the interstate with Louella's assurance that the drive to the farm would take at least two hours, Kate leaned her head against the window and promptly fell asleep.

* * *

"This is the road."

Kate, who had been dozing, opened her eyes and saw that they were turning off the highway onto a narrow asphalt lane. Black Angus cattle dotted the pasture to the right, and ten or so horses grazed in the gently rolling fields to the left. Stands of hardwood and pine trees marked the horizon. Recently painted white board fence helped delineate the roadway that led to a white two-story house with a porch wrapped around three sides.

The house sat amidst at least ten trees, one of them an ancient magnolia. An old-style red barn sat back from the house, along with several outbuildings. Her brief association with Cullen had led Kate to imagine something more grandiose, something less down-to-earth. She was as pleased as she was surprised at having her expectations overturned.

Louella pulled her car to a stop in front of the house. She'd barely gotten the engine turned off when a pretty, dark-haired woman fairly burst through the front door and down the porch steps.

"There's Meghan!" Louella exclaimed.

Despite the woman's apparel of jeans and sweater, Kate got the impression of class and wealth. Maybe it was the perfection of Meghan's dark, chin-length haircut or the patrician sculpting of her features. Whatever it was, it gave Kate an instant feeling of inferiority. She hadn't bothered getting her hair cut since Raul's death. Impressing people with her looks wasn't a priority, and it was easier to catch her hair up in a ponytail or twist it up. She'd worn a new pantsuit for her initial meeting with Cullen and his sister. Now she wished she'd taken the time to get her nails done and put on a little more makeup.

Any notions Kate might have had about her hostess being stuck-up went by the wayside when, without any hesitation, she took Kate's aunt into a warm embrace.

"Did you have any trouble finding us?" Meghan asked.

"None," Louella said. "How's Cullen?"

"The drive really tired him, and he was in a fair amount of pain, so I gave him something to help him rest."

There was no disguising the concern in Cullen's sister's eyes. She was worried about her brother, and she was there to make certain that his best interests were carried out.

Her concern for her employer satisfied, Louella made the introductions. "Meghan, this is my niece, Katherine Labiche from New Orleans. Katie, this is Cullen's sister, Meghan Longstreet. Meghan's a trauma doctor at Baptist Memorial in Little Rock."

Smiling, Meghan turned to Kate, who felt the full force of the woman's intelligence in her all-encompassing gaze. Kate was taking in her hostess, too, from the faded jeans with a hole in the thigh to the dusty-rose cashmere sweater. Only someone like Meghan Longstreet could carry off the classically casual look, which, Kate surmised, was why Meghan had given the impression of class and wealth even though her overall look was supposed to appear informal.

An interesting woman, Kate thought. Meghan Longstreet looked more like a socialite gone slumming for the weekend than a professional. But if she was part of a trauma team, she had to be good. Kate took the woman's proffered hand and found her handshake firm and cool. "It's a pleasure meeting you," Kate said.

"You, too," Meghan replied with a smile.

Though her demeanor was pleasant and her body language wasn't stilted in any way, Kate noticed that, for an instant, the smile didn't quite reach Meghan Longstreet's eyes. Kate also noticed that there was a bit of something else in those brown eyes. Concern? Was her hostess already worried that Kate couldn't handle the job? Or was it the idea of making her over to fit the role that was causing the anxiety?

"Cullen raved about the work you did for him in New Orleans," Meghan said with a smile.

"Really?" The statement took Kate aback and ended her evaluation of her hostess. If he'd been so impressed, why hadn't he contacted her? Simple. Being impressed with someone's work didn't necessarily equate to being impressed with the person.

"Really. What name do you go by?" Meghan asked. "Katherine?" She bounced an amused glance from Louella to Kate. "Somehow you don't look like a Katie."

Kate couldn't help the slight smile that claimed her lips. "Aunt Lou has called me Katie since I was a baby. I'm just plain Kate to most people."

"Then Kate it will be," Meghan said. "You know, you're nothing like what I expected from your résumé."

"What did you expect?" Kate asked, uncertain what to say.

"I don't know. Someone plain, I guess. Unattractive." Meghan smiled. "Maybe even someone…burlier. You're none of that."

"There's nothing plain about my Katie," Louella interjected. "Except maybe her name."

Kate laughed along with Meghan, surprised by the backhanded compliment. "I try to make myself as inconspicuous as a six-foot redhead can," she said with a self-deprecating smile. "A look of anonymity helps when you're tailing someone and trying to blend into a crowd."

"I imagine so," Meghan said thoughtfully. She made a sweeping gesture toward the house. "Let's go on in. I'll show you to your rooms and give you some time to get settled in. I'll have someone bring up your bags. Greg—the man who's agreed to do some cooking while you're here—can't come in until tomorrow, so I'm fixing lunch and won't be able to give you the nickel tour. Just make yourselves at home. There are a couple of quarter horses if you ride, and a fully equipped weight room with a hot tub. By the way, lunch is at eleven thirty, dinner's at six, and we don't dress unless it's a special occasion." She paused to take a breath, smiled and said, "That was quite a speech, wasn't it?"

"I think you covered everything," Louella said as they stepped onto the porch. "Did Dan come?"

Meghan gave a shake of her head and pushed open the door. "I left him with the girls. Under the circumstances, I thought it might be better if, when they meet Kate for the first time, it was with her ensconced in her role as their uncle's girlfriend."

"Your brother may not want me for the job," Kate reminded.

Meghan offered her a wry smile and gestured toward the stairs. "He doesn't want anyone for the job." A note of steel crept into her voice. "But this is one time my brother is outnumbered."

Kate's room was lovely, done in old-fashioned tone-on-tone wallpaper in cream and green with creamy lace curtains and accessories in soft hues of green, pink and darker rose that appealed to Kate's love of the traditional. She unpacked her few belongings and relegated them to their appropriate places. Then, hoping to kill some time before the noon meal, she changed into jeans, touched up her pink lip gloss and took the pins from her hair, letting it flow over her shoulders and down her back.

That done, she perused the small stack of books on the bedside table and went to the window, where she watched a mare with a huge belly graze on sparse patches of green grass. If anyone had asked, she'd have admitted that her mind was less on the horse than on her upcoming meeting with Cullen. Would he make it to lunch, or would she be granted a brief reprieve?

The thought of meeting him face-to-face sent her springing to her feet in a sudden rush of nervous panic. She paced to the door and back, knowing that her bout of nerves was based on her fear of seeing Cullen again after almost two years. But it wasn't fear of seeing him that made her stomach churn sickeningly. It was more a fear of what she'd see in his eyes.

She told herself to forget about the past. Clearly, Cullen had. She'd come to interview for a job, period. She would be polite, friendly and professional. She'd just be herself—whoever that was these days. Unable to stand being alone with her thoughts, she left the room and headed down the stairs. Maybe Meghan could use some help in the kitchen.

"Don't! Don't stop!"

The soft plea was punctuated with wet kisses and groaned huskily into his ear, more a soft exhalation of breath than actual words. Kate's arms were around his neck. His body pressed hers into the softness of the mattress, their heated flesh fused together by a thin film of perspiration and a primitive passion.

"I have to slow down or die," he said with a weary

chuckle, pulling away far enough to look into her partially closed eyes. A fiery tendril of damp hair lay against her cheek. Smiling a tired smile of masculine satiation, he brushed it back with a single finger. ''Did anyone ever tell you that you need to learn to pace yourself, Ms. Labiche?''

''What's the matter, counselor?'' she taunted, moving seductively beneath him. ''Can't keep up?''

He moved against her with a slow, deep stroke. ''I can keep it up as long as you can.''

''Promises, promises...''

He shut off her pseudocomplaints with a hard, hungry kiss. Then, other than moans and groans, neither of them spoke for a very long time.

Later, when sensation eased enough to allow rational thought, he brushed back her hair. ''When I hired you, I never dreamed anything like this would happen.''

''Me, either,'' Kate confessed. ''Why did it?''

He feathered a kiss along the line of her jaw. ''Because I've never seen anyone so alive in my entire life?'' It was more a question than a statement. ''Because I couldn't help myself?''

''Neither can I,'' Kate said, her hands working their particular brand of magic.

''Ah, Kate, Kate,'' he murmured, realizing that maybe he wasn't as tired as he'd thought....

''Kate...'' The name was on his lips when the phone rang, shattering the enchantment. Peering through a groggy haze from the medication Meghan had given him, he reached automatically for the receiver, only to be reminded of his situation by a sharp, stabbing pain. Thankfully, the ringing stopped. Meghan must have picked it up in some other part of the house. He heard a click and the soft purring of the central heat that began to blow its warm breath over him. He smelled something cooking and heard the sounds of a muted conversation, probably a television. Louella, he thought. Or Kate.

Kate. Memories of the sexually charged dream came rushing back, along with an almost painful physical need he hadn't assuaged in longer than he could remember. Kate. His one slip since losing Joanie. The one woman he'd become involved with whom he hadn't been able to banish from his mind. The one woman whose company had filled him with an unexpected eagerness to stop dwelling on the past and get back to living his life. The one woman whose incredible ability to give everything— both emotionally and sexually—had given him so much pleasure and satisfaction that the guilt he'd felt for abandoning his mourning for Joanie had threatened to be his undoing.

Confused, angry, uncertain how to cope, he'd simply left her and come back to his life where he'd thrown himself into his work in an effort to try to forget the four days and three nights that might possibly have been the most intensely satisfying of his life.

Why had he reacted so strongly to her?

I've never seen anyone so alive in my entire life... because I couldn't help myself.

The words from the dream—from the reality—were true. But the need to make love with Kate had had more to do with the fact that ever since he'd lost Joanie less than a year earlier, he'd felt half-alive and was beginning to fear he'd never feel any other way. Drowning in sorrow, able to function only when he was immersed in work, he'd bowed to Louella's wishes and agreed to use Kate for some investigative work he'd needed done on a particularly nasty environmental case. He'd flown to New

Orleans and met Kate, and the rest, as they say, was history.

He wasn't proud of the way he'd left her, alone in her bed without a word of goodbye or explanation. But at the time, his conviction that he was being disloyal to what he and Joanie had shared had been stronger than his fledgling feelings for Kate. He'd loved Joanie. Losing her had been the end of life as he'd known it. The end of happiness, of hope. Being with Kate had teased him with the notion that those feelings were within reach, but a nagging feeling that he was being unfaithful to the love he and Joanie had shared had forced him to leave and goaded him into a determination to forget Kate and everything she'd made him feel. How could he miss Joanie so much, how could he have loved her so deeply and still find so much promise and pleasure in another woman's arms?

Leaving had seemed the only way to salvage his image of himself and his core beliefs, but he'd quickly learned that forgetting Kate was far easier said than done, and his efforts were still failures even after almost two years. The irritating, maddening inability to put her from his mind did have one plus. It made it easier to say no to long-term relationships with the other women who flocked to him, each hoping to be the one to bring him to heel, take him out of circulation and get him to the altar. And there had been women the past two years. Not many, and all easily forgettable when compared to the incomparable Kate.

Now, unexpectedly, she was back in his life, and all because some crazy had taken a potshot at him. He was glad to be out of the hospital, eager for his life to get back to normal and more than anxious to get back to work. Unfortunately, after considering all the evidence and talking to Buddy, the sheriff's department had reluctantly come to the same conclusion as Meghan—someone wanted to do him harm. That established, they said they were dedicated to following up any leads that might come along. They also agreed to his laying low awhile and with Louella's suggestion that having a woman bodyguard pose as Cullen's current love interest would keep the perp from becoming suspicious while they tried to figure out who he was and put him behind bars.

So here he was, hiding out in the country, waiting to see Kate again, wondering how he would feel when he did…wondering how she felt about the whole thing. Would she consider acting as his bodyguard just another job, or would it be something more? Something special?

Bodyguard. He lifted his right hand and covered his eyes. Dear lord! The whole idea of expecting a woman—Kate or any other—to step between him and a bullet was not only ridiculous, it was downright offensive. Raised by Southern parents, he'd been brought up with the old-fashioned notion that women were physically the weaker sex. Not only did men do the heavy work, they did their utmost to protect women. Somehow, it seemed alien to him that any woman would find that objectionable.

He gave a snarl of irritation and rolled to his side, disregarding the accompanying pain. He pushed himself to his elbow and then to a sitting position, grunting at the pain, which in a few days' time had mutated from excruciating to something almost bearable. He glanced at the clock and saw that it was almost lunchtime. For the first time since the shooting, he actually felt the rumblings of hunger. A good sign that he was on the road to recovery. He slid his feet into some slippers and headed downstairs to see if there was any way to hurry the meal along.

* * *

Uncertain where to find her hostess, Kate was poking her head into various rooms when she stumbled onto the library. Her immediate impressions were of wood and leather. Burgundy and deep green. Old, classy decor. Quiet tastefulness. Always a book lover, she stepped inside to check out the offerings.

A grouping of photos on the mantel caught her attention, and she paused to look them over. There was an older couple who, judging from their looks, must have been the elder McGyvers. There was a snapshot of a much younger Meghan in a University of Arkansas cheerleading outfit and Cullen in his basketball uniform. There were pictures of them in high school graduation gowns, holding diplomas and wearing wide smiles. There was an eight-by-ten of Meghan and Dan on their wedding day and one of Cullen standing beside Joanie, a petite woman with auburn hair who wore a Victorian-style wedding gown.

With delft-blue eyes, rich auburn hair and a soft smile, Joanie McGyver was achingly beautiful. Soft. The word seemed to say all that needed saying about Cullen's dead wife. Wondering what she'd really been like, Kate reached for a snapshot of a clearly pregnant Joanie who Kate knew had died along with her baby in childbirth. She was smiling and smoothing the maternity smock over her distended abdomen, proud of the proof of her femininity. Intuitively, Kate knew it was one of the last pictures taken before Joanie McGyver's death. Feeling a sorrow she didn't understand, Kate gripped the photo and stared into the likeness of Joanie McGyver's eyes as if she hoped to find some answers there.

All she saw was a happiness that brought a lump to her throat. It was a happiness she understood well, but not fully, having been granted a mere sampling of what it must have been like to be loved by Cullen.

"Pretty, wasn't she?"

The sound of his voice—deep, smooth and somehow matter-of-fact—caused Kate to give a guilty jump. She gripped the photo tighter to steady the sudden trembling in her hands, a trembling that was rapidly spreading throughout her body as she tried to mentally ready herself for her first look at him in nearly two years. She forced herself to turn and face him. A sigh slipped from her lips. She'd forgotten just how handsome he was, she thought, regarding him with all the wary consideration she would a dangerous situation before putting herself into the middle of it.

He stood in the doorway with an elegant Pierce Brosnan-like nonchalance, wearing jeans and a soft knit shirt, one arm in a sling. His dark hair was cut stylishly short. He had a strong jaw, an aristocratic nose and a firm chin. A mouth designed solely for driving a woman wild. She should know. Another involuntary sigh escaped her.

Unable to bear his sharp scrutiny any longer, she turned and set the photo of his dead wife in its place. "Yes," she said, turning to face him.

"Yes, what?" he asked with a frown.

Had he forgotten his question so soon, then? "Yes, she was a very beautiful woman," she said to remind him. "It's easy to see why you loved her."

Cullen shook his head. "How she looked had nothing to do with why I loved her."

Of course not. Joanie McGyver was no doubt the perfect woman. After all, didn't Cullen lead a perfect, flawless life? One with no problems his wealth, charm and intelligence couldn't overcome?

"I'm surprised you came," he said, derailing the turn of her thoughts.

She gave a little shrug. "I'm surprised you asked me to."

"It was Louella's idea."

"Ah," Kate said with a slow nod of understanding. "Clearly she had no idea that we didn't exactly part on good terms."

For the first time since she'd turned to face him, she thought she saw a crack in his control, an indefinable something in his smoky blue eyes. He rallied quickly, as all good lawyers must.

"I thought we parted on excellent terms," he said, hooking the thumb of his good hand into the front pocket of his jeans. "No regrets, no recriminations, no promises we couldn't keep."

"No goodbyes," Kate added with a hint of bitterness.

"Would goodbye have changed anything?" he asked. "It was what it was."

"And what exactly was it?" Kate prodded.

"A moment out of time. Laughter. Talk. Two lonely, hurting people looking for a way to heal themselves."

Which, Kate supposed, pretty much summed it up, at least from a man's point of view. So in that respect, he was right.

"I suppose you're right," she admitted grudgingly. "Goodbye wouldn't have changed anything."

Especially since it was clear that all she'd meant to him was a few days and nights of diversion from his pain and loneliness. Nor would a lengthy, sorrow-filled parting have changed the fact that she had been on the verge of falling in love with him, something she had never expected to do so quickly after Lane's desertion. Which just went to show you how irrational a woman's heart could be. But she'd learned her second lesson in love well, and since that time, she'd taken great pains to build a tough barricade around her heart. Twice burned, she wouldn't be so easily taken in a third time.

"So do you have a problem with the job offer considering our...brief past history?" he asked.

Kate raised her chin to a degree just shy of haughty and forced her lips into a derisive smile. "I came, didn't I?"

Cullen gave a slow nod. "Indeed you did."

Good grief! Cullen chided himself. Had Kate noticed the double entendre? And what on earth had prompted him to reply with such a provocative comeback to an innocent question? Was it that looking at her standing there in tight-fitting jeans and a short-cropped sweater had him recalling a time when he'd stripped a similar sweater over her head and peeled another pair of jeans down her long, shapely legs? Maybe it was the challenge in her eyes, a look that said even though she'd taken him to task for it, she didn't give a hoot in hell what he thought of her or that he'd left her without a word of goodbye.

Always one who loved a challenge, Cullen found he was still fascinated by her go-to-Hades attitude, which was one of the things that had drawn him to her when they'd first met. But Kate hadn't come to satisfy any unresolved sexual feelings he might still have for her. She'd come because she was good at what she did, and he needed her in a completely different way.

"Aunt Louella says someone tried to off you," she said, abandoning the personal tone of their conversation and getting to the real reason for her presence.

"Off me? Did anyone ever tell you that you have a

real way with words?'' he asked, a wry smile lifting one corner of his mouth.

"That makes two of us, then," she said. The expression in her eyes said she wished she could call the comment back, since it was a reference to their past relationship.

Determined not to heed the tiny voice that whispered he'd been a fool to walk out of this woman's apartment without a backward glance, Cullen ignored the provocative comment. "You're right. The general consensus of the authorities seems to be that I'm not the most popular guy in town."

"And it's also the general consensus that the best way to protect you is to hire a woman bodyguard to pretend to be your latest…love interest, right?"

"Right."

Kate rested her weight on one leg and crossed her arms over her breasts, looking him up and down with a gaze of cool calculation. "And how does your current real love interest feel about having someone usurp her place, even as a temporary pretense?"

"There is no current love interest," he said, his gaze holding hers.

Surprise and doubt filled her eyes. "I find that hard to believe."

"Try harder," he quipped, with another of those insincere smiles. Good lord, he'd forgotten how exasperating she could be.

She heaved a great sigh. "Okay, then," she said, moving her hands to her hips. "That's one obstacle out of the way. How about I throw your question back at you?"

Cullen raised his eyebrows in question.

"How do you feel about having me around twenty-

'our hours a day, seven days a week considering our...
brief past history?"

"Honestly?"

"Honesty is nice in any relationship," she said with a slow nod.

Cullen wondered if she was aware that her words might be construed as a dig. Again, he let it pass without comment. Lord, he thought, his emotions somewhere between exasperation and relish, it would be a challenge having her around all the time...especially since he couldn't stop himself from recalling the way she felt in his arms, the way her mouth tasted, the throaty way she said his name in the throes of passion.

He cleared his throat and pushed away the tantalizing memories. "Then, honestly, I don't like the idea of having you or any other woman around all the time. The idea of expecting a woman to protect me goes against everything I believe in."

"You're old-fashioned, counselor."

"In some respects, I guess I am," he agreed.

"So," she said in a no-nonsense tone. "Back to the question. You don't want any woman as a bodyguard, but you have to have one. How do you feel about it being me?"

Afraid of revealing too much of the conflicting feelings warring inside him, Cullen said, "I suppose having someone else would make it easier on us both, but I have no doubt about your ability to do the job, if you take it."

She dropped her arms to her sides. "So you're officially offering me the position, then?"

"Don't be coy, Kate," he said, an edge of irritation sharpening his voice. "It doesn't become you. You know as well as I do that when Louella called, the job was yours if you wanted it."

"That isn't what she said."

"Never mind what she said. You know me."

"Actually, counselor, I don't."

He swore, the epithet taking her by surprise. "This isn't going to work if we keep taking potshots at each other. And it won't work if we keep bringing up the past."

"Then I guess it isn't going to work," she snapped, "because, unlike you, I can't turn my feelings on and off like a water tap."

"You're still angry because I didn't wake you to say goodbye?" he asked incredulously, knowing that he'd hit the problem on the head and knowing he was guilty as charged.

"You're damn right I'm angry!" she snarled. "And don't try to act as if you wouldn't feel the same way if the shoe were on the other foot."

"So how can I make amends?" he asked, holding out his good arm in supplication. "An apology? I'm sorry. It was unforgivable of me. I'll never do it again."

"You're darn right you won't," she said with stark finality. "And it was unforgivable. The coward's way out."

"Three nights doesn't mean I owe you any explanations for my actions," he said, his voice cold.

"You're right. It doesn't. Excuse me for thinking you were an honorable man."

"It was sex, Kate," he said bluntly, but the heat of anger had left his voice. "Great, no-strings sex. I knew it wouldn't work, for a variety of reasons, and I thought my leaving would be an easy way out for us both. Now can we just get past it and move on?"

"Sure," Kate quipped. "Why not? I'm a woman of the times."

"Why don't you stow the attitude for a minute and tell me why you're even considering this job when it's obvious that you still have a lot of anger bottled up against me."

"Because business is slow, and if what Aunt Lou told me is true, the money is good."

"Whatever Louella said you can take to the bank. Literally."

"Good," Kate said with a tight smile. "You got yourself a bodyguard."

"Good," Cullen replied, but he wasn't sure it was. Almost everything about the redhead standing in front of him rubbed him the wrong way.

"Do you have any idea how long this gig will last?" she asked, cutting into his thoughts with brutal bluntness.

"I don't have any way of knowing that," he told her. "But if things have died down in, say, three or four months and they still haven't pinned the shooting on anyone, we'll call it quits and you can go back to New Orleans. If we catch the perp in a couple of weeks you can go back with a generous severance check."

"Fair enough," Kate said, nodding. She looked uncomfortable suddenly. "You do know why I quit the force almost two years ago?" she asked, changing the subject without warning.

"Of course I know. Louella told me when she first asked me to consider you for the Landry case."

"And you don't have any doubt about my ability to do the job?"

"Why?" he asked, frowning. "Because of what happened to your partner?"

"What happened to Raul was no small thing," she reminded him.

"No, but it's the sort of thing that happens when you

have a job like yours. Every cop knows it can happen to him at any time. Raul knew it.''

She gave a deep sigh and shook her head. ''Doesn't it make you just a little bit worried that I stood by, shaking in my boots, and let my partner take a bullet?''

''I'm not overly concerned about it.''

''Yeah, well, that's another reason I hesitate taking a position that has the potential to put me in a similar situation. And as smart as everyone says you are, it seems to me that you'd have a few reservations yourself.''

''Look, as I see it, we'll spend most of our time here, not in the city. No one knows where I am, and we'll take precautions so that, with luck, no one will find out. This bodyguard thing is just an added safeguard in case there is a leak somewhere. I honestly don't anticipate any situations where your fears will be put to the test.''

''Then why put up so much money to hire someone?''

Cullen smiled. ''I was a Boy Scout. And I believe my success as a prosecutor comes from trying to think of all the angles and being prepared for any contingency. Everyone I've talked to thinks you can handle the situation, and I'm a big believer in the idea that we should face our fears.''

She shook her head. ''You sound like Aunt Louella.''

''She's a wise woman,'' Cullen said. ''Maybe I should be asking you a question.''

''What?''

''Let's say history repeats itself and something happens to me. Would it send you completely over the edge, or could you get past it?''

Her face drained of color, and the haunted look came into her eyes for a fraction of a second. Then she tossed her hair and gave a smile of pure sarcasm, a trait he was learning she adopted when she was reluctant to let her true feelings show. "Oh, I'd get over it," she drawled in a sarcastic voice. "I'm not nearly as attached to you as I was to Raul."

"Good, then," he said. "I guess the job is yours. When can you start?"

"I need to go back home and tidy up a few loose ends."

"How long would it take for you to wrap things up?"

"A couple of days. I'll have to shut down my business."

"Why would you do that?"

"Laws regulating private investigators vary from state to state. It would be simpler to shut down than try to meet all the requirements in a short time."

He frowned. "What will you do when this job is over?"

"I had an offer last week to go to work for an insurance company as a fraud investigator. I think it will still be available when I'm finished here. It won't be very exciting, but the pay is good and it's steady work, which is nice when the bills roll around every month."

"I don't want you to do that just to take this job."

"I've been thinking about calling it quits for a while. This just forces my hand," she told him.

"If you're sure…"

"I'm anything but sure."

"You'll stay the weekend, as we'd planned, then. You can catch a late flight Sunday evening and come back midweek. How does that sound?"

"As if you're used to calling the shots."

Cullen gave a sigh of exasperation. "It was a suggestion, Kate. I'm not an ogre. If it takes longer, it's no problem."

"Sorry," she told him. "I guess you just bring out the worst in me."

"Ditto," he said and held out his uninjured hand. "Can we shake on it and call a truce?"

"Sure," she said, crossing the room toward him.

Cullen's hand closed around hers. Her grip was firm; her hands were soft. "Friends?"

Kate gazed into his eyes and shook her head. "I can manage the truce thing—I think. But friends? I don't think so, counselor. That would be stretching credibility a bit too much. Let's just try not to be at each other's throats, okay?"

Chapter Four

Cullen went to his room to rest after lunch. He w
feeling hungover from the pain medication and needed
some time to mull over his conversation—or was that his
confrontation?—with Kate. If he were fair, he had to take
part of the blame for the tone of their discussion. He'd
been wrong, and she'd taken him to task for it. No one,
least of all Cullen, liked being caught doing something
wrong, and he liked being taken to task for it even less.
He'd say one thing about Kate Labiche. She could give
as good as she got, a trait he'd always admired in his
judicial adversaries. The question was, would that be a
good thing during the upcoming weeks?

He raked a hand through his dark hair and cursed under
his breath. Even though he'd apologized and they'd
called a truce, he wasn't sure it would hold. There was
little doubt that hiring her was asking for trouble of one
kind or another, yet for reasons unknown—or that he was

unwilling to look at too closely—he'd folded like a soft taco when his sister and Louella had pushed him to hire her.

Those two were thrilled that Kate had accepted the job. Cullen was thrilled when he and Kate managed to make it through lunch without coming to blows. Actually, it had been fine. She knew how to behave in mixed company even though she chose to challenge him on every point of conversation when they were alone.

No, that wasn't true, either. Though they hadn't discussed the deaths of her partner or his wife, they'd spent much of their time together in New Orleans talking about their jobs, their disappointments in the system, their agreement that not enough was being done and their frustration in knowing that no matter how much they did do to get the scum off the streets, it would never be enough.

'd met in February. On Valentine's Day, in fact. lla's urging, Cullen had flown to New Orleans to do some undercover work for him, watching guys who were reportedly involved in illegal -waste dumping that carried over into Arkansas. Tracers Inc., Kate's investigation firm, was brand-new, and Raul's death and her divorce fresh enough to be sources of considerable pain. She had still been grieving for her partner and burdened with guilt because she considered his death her fault.

Cullen, still in mourning for Joanie and suffering from his own brand of guilt for her death, had been both fascinated and infuriated by Kate. He found her fascinating because she was unlike any woman he'd ever met—truly knowledgeable about the ins and outs of her job, assertive and acerbic, different from the women he was usually drawn to.

Though he often made snap judgments about people

based on first impressions and was seldom ⸻
hadn't been able to put his finger on the reason ⸻
his feelings. It would be weeks before he realized ⸻
the irritation was rooted in the fact that she was the first
woman to make him painfully aware he hadn't died with
Joanie. Kate was a woman with an edge, a type he'd
tended to steer clear of during his dating years, choosing
to date women who were softer, more feminine and less
confrontational.

Yet everything about Kate made him feel as if he were
emerging from some dark, dreamless sleep. His days,
which had been like a drab black-and-white movie since
Joanie died, were suddenly infused with vibrant color.
Everything about Kate screamed life—her lithe, physically fit body, her quick tongue, the way she looked at
him with that hint of challenge in her eyes, as if she were
telling the world to come on and try it, she was ready for
whatever life threw at her. Never one to pass up a challenge, Cullen picked up the gauntlet. He hadn't known
her twenty-four hours before he made the move.

He'd said something to her that she disagreed with.
She'd turned away, and he'd grabbed her arm and
whirled her around to face him, dragging her into his
arms and kissing her as much to punish her as because
it was something he'd wanted to do ever since he'd laid
eyes on her.

No one had been more surprised than he when things
had gotten out of hand so quickly. They'd wound up in
her bed, and for four days and three nights, he had tried
his best to infuse himself with her life force. The intensity
she made him feel was both liberating and frightening,
and while she'd made him feel more alive, he hated himself because the magnitude of the feelings she aroused

dwarfed anything he'd ever experienced with a woman, including his wife.

During the time he'd spent with Kate, the certainty that he was being disloyal to Joanie and their love was never far from his mind. It was that guilt that had sent him hightailing it out of Kate's apartment without an explanation or a goodbye. He'd known when he left that it was the cowardly thing to do, but on that particular morning, the remorse had been a tight knot of pain in his gut, and he'd known he had to end things with Kate or lose his sanity.

Back in Little Rock, he'd reminded himself that he was a healthy man and that what they'd shared was nothing but sex and that even though it was the first intimacy he'd experienced with a woman since Joanie's death, it was no real threat to his memories of her because sex wasn't the same thing as love. Taking another tack, he told himself that it was ridiculous to feel disloyal to a woman who had been dead almost a year, that what he was experiencing was a natural progression in recovering from his loss.

It had taken months for him to believe his rationalizations, longer than that for him to forgive himself for what he considered a major transgression against his wife. He'd never managed to forget Kate, even though he knew in his heart she was all wrong for him. She was nothing like the women he usually dated. Nothing at all like Joanie. And he and Joanie had had the perfect marriage....

Forget what happened in New Orleans. This is a new situation, a new game field. You need Kate and all the things you admire about her professional expertise.

True. So he should just forget their little fling and concentrate on the present. He was a professional who never let his personal feelings get in the way of a case. This situation was no different from any of a dozen he'd worked on, except that it was his life, his safety, at stake. And, despite her uncertainly about how she'd react in a standoff situation, Kate was qualified to handle the job.

He clenched the fist of his good hand. Damn! He hated this feeling of vulnerability. Hated hiding out like some common criminal. Hated the idea that someone had been watching his every move, lying in wait for the perfect opportunity to do him harm. Hated more the idea of a woman standing between him and death. But that's the way it had to be. Whether it was Kate or some other woman didn't matter. What was it his mother used to say? Oh, yeah. Better the devil you know than the one you don't.

Back in her room, Kate was having second thoughts about her decision to become Cullen's bodyguard. She'd come because her aunt had given her the hard sell, pushed a plane ticket on her and promised her the moon—well, several thousand dollars, at least. The idea of getting out of debt for doing what sounded like a cream-puff job despite the so-called threat to Cullen's life had caused her to lose her mind for a brief while.

She paced the floor, muttering under her breath, cursing her aunt, cursing Cullen, cursing the circumstances that had brought her here. Had she really thought she could forget the intimacy they'd shared? If so, the laugh was certainly on her. All it had taken was seeing him in the all-too-disturbing flesh and the memories had come rushing back, making her painfully aware that he had left finding her wanting and acutely aware that almost two years was a long time for a healthy woman to go unfulfilled.

His leaving as he had had hurt more than she could say, more than she would have ever imagined, coming as it had so soon after Lane divorcing her. In fact, considering how devastated she'd been over her divorce, she couldn't believe she'd fallen into bed with Cullen as easily as she had. Brushing elbows with every facet of life on the streets had left her with few illusions, but she was still not as liberal about sex as most women her age. Her behavior with Cullen wasn't like her at all.

But it had happened, and he'd gone on his way, and Kate had filed away a little notation in her mind that there must be something basically flawed about her, since she seemed to lack what it took to hold a man. It was several months before she saw her interlude with Cullen for what it was—two lonely, grieving people indulging in a brief fling in the hope that they could jump-start their lives. The problem with her perception was that no matter how casual an affair it was supposed to be, Kate couldn't forget him. And recognizing it for what it was didn't make his cavalier leaving any easier to take.

She still recalled those three nights in vivid detail, could still remember every word they'd spoken to each other. She still wondered why she'd fallen for his line, for his vulnerability, for him—and fall she had—knowing they were worlds apart, knowing it could never be more than it was.

And now, by a quirk of fate or a would-be killer's bullet, here she was, putting her heart in harm's way again. Her resolve wavered. Was she strong enough to spend day after day with a man she was already more than half in love with? How would she survive when the job ended? She'd agreed to stay and protect Cullen. The question now was—who would protect her?

* * *

Cullen, who hated being dependent on anything or anyone and was trying to cut back on the pain medication, had experienced a rough afternoon and opted to have dinner in his room the night before. The nagging pain and the fact that he'd dozed so much throughout the day combined to guarantee him a sleepless night. He'd tossed and turned and stared at the ceiling in an effort to hold the memories of Kate at bay, all to no avail. Like an invasive garden plant, the tormenting recollections had sneaked in at every chance. When he did manage to fall asleep, the erotic turn of his dreams had left him feeling dissatisfied and needy and angry.

He'd gotten up and dressed early, managing to make the coffee himself. He was in the kitchen watching the dark liquid drip into the glass carafe when Kate came into the room. When she saw him sitting at the table, her footsteps faltered, then, with a look of determination, she stepped into the room, her head high, a neutral expression on her face.

She was wearing black jeans and a form-fitting sweater. Her hair was twisted and caught with a clip, the slightly curly ends trailing over the French-twistlike coil. If she was wearing makeup, it was so subtle as to be imperceptible. Her mouth, which had tormented him in his dreams the previous night, held the sheen of lip gloss. It took him a moment to realize that the real difference in her was her attitude. It was gone.

''Morning,'' he said.

''Good morning.''

''Have a seat,'' he offered, indicating a chair across from him.

She sat down but she didn't meet his eyes. More and more interesting.

"Did you sleep well?" If the surprise in her eyes was anything to go by, the simple question had caught her off guard.

"Actually, I didn't. I don't sleep well away from home."

"Me, either," Cullen said, recognizing, as he had in New Orleans, that she had an attractive, distinctive voice. Low and husky. Something between Lauren Bacall and Demi Moore.

The topic of sleep apparently depleted, a silence descended over them. Outside the kitchen, a chill, capricious wind rustled the berry-bright nandina bushes that scraped the sides of the house like hundreds of irritating fingernails. The coffee sputtered to a stop.

"Look, I—"

"Look, can—"

They started speaking simultaneously and stopped in tandem.

"Ladies first," Cullen said.

She shook her head. "No. Go ahead."

"All right." Cullen rose and went to the cabinet and took down two mugs, filling them with coffee. "Cream or sugar?" he asked.

When she declined both, he continued. "I was going to ask you if we could start over. I know we called a truce yesterday, but I want you to know that there's no way I can change the past, and I have no excuse for my behavior yesterday except that this whole thing has shaken me up pretty good. No one wants to believe there are people out there who'd like to see them dead."

Kate just stared at him. A wary curiosity had replaced the guarded expression in her eyes. Not certain what to make of her silence, Cullen sat down across from her and lifted the cup. "And, as I said, I'm having a bit of a problem with the idea of using a woman for protection."

"That's a normal reaction," she said carefully, as if she were weighing each word of her reply. "And I understand. I don't hold any hard feelings about what happened yesterday."

Cullen noticed she didn't make the same disclaimer about what had happened in New Orleans. "Good," he said, glad to have the apology out of the way. "Now what was it you wanted to tell me?"

He watched as she drew in a deep breath and brought her gaze to his. He'd forgotten how unique the color of her eyes was, a light golden brown. Eyes a man could drown in, just as he could the aged whiskey their color reminded him of.

She cleared her throat. "While I can appreciate your feelings and have no problem putting what happened yesterday behind us, I have to be honest and tell you that after sleeping on it, I don't think this arrangement will work. As much as I need the money..."

Cullen blinked, wondering if he's heard correctly. "What isn't going to work?"

"Me as your bodyguard. Pretending to be your... girlfriend—" she shrugged "—or whatever."

Cullen hardly heard what she was saying. All that registered was that she wasn't going to take the job after all, something he found unacceptable suddenly. "What's changed since yesterday?"

She sighed and gave a shake of her head. "Forget yesterday. Even though you've apologized and we shook hands, I'm not sure we can get past...New Orleans."

She spoke quickly, as if she wanted to get her speech over with and move on. This was a side of Kate Cullen had never seen before. Hesitant. Uncertain. Unsure.

"Spending so much time together would be...awkward to say the least."

"You don't have to spend any time with me except when we're in public," he told her. "Will that make you happy?"

"Happy has nothing to do with it."

"Then what does?"

Kate shifted in her chair and chose to ignore the question. "Let's look at it from a different standpoint. My aunt described the kind of woman you're drawn to. I'm nothing like those women. Even with the right clothes, I won't blend into your world, and I think that would be obvious to the people who know you well. To be blunt, I don't think they'll buy it—me."

"Louella said you were a good actress, which is why you were so good at undercover work. This shouldn't be any different." Good grief! Was he out of his mind? Was he actually trying to convince her to stay when he felt the same way she did? She was right. New Orleans would get in the way. The memories would be there with them every time they were together, so why tempt fate?

Because you still want her, McGyver. Because you never got her out of your system, never got your fill of whatever it was she gave to you.

So what was he hoping here? That she'd fall back into bed with him, that they'd pick up where they'd left off? Fat chance. The lady was thoroughly angry with him over the way he'd deserted her. She was thoroughly through.

"Look," Kate said, leaning forward, an earnest expression on her face. "I'm used to dealing with the dregs of society, not the upper crust. I'm telling you that even if we didn't have New Orleans dogging our heels I won't fit in your world. Besides, I have this gut feeling that no matter how much either of us tries to be polite, we'll wind up snipping at each other, even in public."

"We'll chalk it up to lovers' spats," Cullen said

smoothly. "Love is supposed to conquer all, remember?"

"Yeah, but we both know it doesn't, and besides, it won't really be love, which will make it all the harder to be convincing."

Cullen heard the bitterness in her voice. Was she referring to her love for her former husband? Had her love for him not been enough to make him stay? Cullen suddenly found himself wondering about her ex and why he'd left. The general consensus was that law enforcement was hard on relationships. He knew plenty of male officers with more than one marriage behind them, but he'd never known a man married to a female cop before. What sort of problems were inherent to that relationship? Were they the same? Different? Lane Labiche had filed for a divorce after the shooting. Why had he suddenly decided he'd had enough?

"Cullen?" she said, snapping her fingers in front of his face. "Are you listening?"

"Thinking," he said.

"About what?"

"About why you're making such a big deal over this. You had time to think this through before you came to talk about the job, yet you did come."

"I didn't have much time," she reminded him. "Aunt Lou had already bought my plane ticket."

"No kidding?" Cullen said, surprised.

Kate nodded and took a sip of her coffee. "So I came because, quite honestly, I was desperate for the money."

"Then take the damn job, Kate," he said angrily. "I'll try to stay out of your hair, and there won't be much to do except when we go out in public. You can think of it as a sort of paid vacation in L.A."

"L.A.?" she asked, her eyebrows drawing together in a frown.

He smiled. "Lower Arkansas. That's what we locals call the area."

Giving a half smile and a shake of her head, she leaned back in the chair and folded her arms across her breasts. "Why are you doing this?"

"Doing what?"

"Trying to get me to change my mind."

Good question. "Everyone says I need a protector, and I'd just as soon it was you as anyone. And you do come highly recommended."

Even as he mouthed the glib answer, he knew it wasn't the truth. At least not the whole truth. At this point, he wasn't sure what the truth was. All he knew was that it was imperative that she take the job.

She stared into his eyes, and he could tell she was giving the situation careful consideration.

"How much did Louella tell you about what happened?" he asked, hoping to pique her interest.

"That you were shot in the woods, fell from your deer stand and cracked some ribs. That you got to your car and tried to drive for help and went into the ditch. Initially, they thought you passed out or something, but then they learned that your brake line had been cut, which, along with the strange incidence of the shooting, makes law officials think you're the target of a hit." She rattled off the incidents with admirable efficiency.

"That's pretty much it."

"Do they have any clues as to who might be behind it?" she asked.

Cullen took her interest as a good sign. He shook his head. "I've put a lot of people behind bars, and I've made my share of enemies."

"It goes with the territory," she said, nodding. "But if it's one of these people, why wait until now to try and off you?"

"That's a question we've all been asking. A friend of mine seems to think that it has something to do with my name being mentioned as a possible candidate for U.S. senator. There's nothing like running for a high-profile office to bring out the crazies with axes to grind. There's also the possibility that it's someone whose been behind bars and was recently released. It could be anyone. We were hoping you could shed some light on that particular question once you came aboard."

"So I wouldn't just be sitting around waiting for something to happen? I'll be actively working the case?"

Definite interest shone in her eyes. "I'd like for you to, yes."

Her gaze probed his, but he wasn't sure what she sought there. "You'd have to be honest with me if I start asking a lot of questions and hit a touchy spot. And you can't get mad about it if it's part of the job."

She was weakening. "I make it a habit to be honest, Kate. And I'll try to control my temper." He held her gaze. "About the bodyguard-girlfriend thing, you should know that I have an active social life with certain commitments, so we'll be going back and forth to Little Rock fairly regularly once I'm up to it."

Her mouth turned down at the corners. "Aunt Lou mentioned that. What kinds of social commitments?"

"Theater and art events. Parties. Fund-raisers. As my… current love interest, you'll be expected to attend those functions with me. I will, of course, take care of any items of clothing you may need to update your wardrobe."

He watched as her mouth curved into a crooked smile. "This is exactly what I was worried about."

"You'll be fine."

She sighed, another sign of her weakening. "I doubt I have anything that would be suitable for the kinds of events you're talking about."

"We'll take care of it as soon as possible, then. It will give us something to do while my shoulder is healing. We'll also look for an apartment for you."

"Why should you pay for an apartment I'll never use?"

"Why wouldn't you use it?"

"I can't guard you if I'm not nearby, now can I?" she asked with a lift of her eyebrows.

He hadn't thought of that. "If you stay at the house, the media will find out and assume we're living together."

The wry smile returned. "Bad for your image, huh?"

"Actually, I was thinking about your image."

She gave a negligent lift of her shoulders. "This is a job. I'll disappear when it's over, and no one will care one way or the other. Besides, the whole idea is to deter the killer. He's less apt to try something if there's another person around."

"Maybe," he said with a slow nod. "And maybe they'd have no compunction about taking out two people instead of one."

"There is that possibility," she agreed with admirable aplomb.

"There's no way you can be with me twenty-four hours a day, though."

"Why not?"

"What possible reason is there for you to follow me to work and into the courtroom?"

"Good point." She gave a thoughtful sigh. "Not even people who are really crazy about each other have that much togetherness. I suppose that all we can do is take each day as it comes and hope we can identify this creep as soon as possible."

He regarded her steadily. "It sounds as if you've changed your mind. Again."

She offered him a wry smile. "You're very persuasive, counselor, but I suppose you know that."

Cullen smiled. His ability to sway a jury was legend. "And you do need the money."

"Right," she said with a smile, "I definitely need the money."

"You aren't going to back out on me again, are you?"

"No. I won't change my mind again," she told him. "That's a promise."

What had she done? Kate asked herself a hundred times the next few days. And why had she done it? Why had she accepted the job with Cullen against her better judgment, knowing she was flirting with disaster by putting herself into such close, intimate contact with him?

The answer was simple, but she didn't want to admit it. She'd said yes because taking the job meant she would be close to him. He'd used her, hurt her, and after going through that particular pain with both him and Lane, she'd sworn she would never put herself in a position to be hurt so badly again. As Aunt Louella would say, "Never say never."

She had gone to New Orleans and farmed out all her clients, cleaned out the fridge, packed everything she thought she might need for a few weeks into her beige Ford Contour and headed to Arkansas, unable to shake the disturbing feeling that she wouldn't be coming back. She forced herself not to dwell on that thought.

The drive took longer than she expected, and she didn't arrive at the ranch until after dark. She got out of the car, opened the trunk and grabbed a couple of suitcases. Weariness dragged at her like the two pieces of luggage dragged at her arms as she climbed the steps to the porch and knocked on the door. Through the lace panel covering the window, she saw a shadowy figure exit the living room, and then light flooded the long hall. Cullen.

She tried to smile as he pulled open the door. Didn't quite manage it. He was wearing jeans and a smoky blue sweater and looked incredibly handsome, though it irked her to admit it. "Hi."

"What took you so long?" he said, without returning the salutation.

Irritation edged aside Kate's weariness. "Sorry," she said in a crisp voice. "I stopped and took a little break."

"It's no big deal, but I was starting to worry. Come on in," he said, stepping aside. "You look beat."

"Flattery will get you nowhere," Kate quipped, picking up the suitcases again. "Where shall I take these?"

"The same room you had before will be fine, and I didn't mean to offend you," he said.

It might have been her imagination, but she thought she saw a hint of red creep into his cheeks. Deciding it might be best to ignore the blush and to temper her smart mouth, Kate started up the stairs.

"I feel like a jerk," he said from behind her.

She paused and glanced over her shoulder. "Why?"

"For not being able to carry up your things."

Definitely embarrassment. "It's no big deal."

"It is for me," he grumbled. "Have you eaten?"

"No."

"Hungry?"

"Starving."

"Good. I'll be in the kitchen when you're finished. I have a casserole and salad for dinner."

"Sounds great."

Cullen turned and started down the hallway to the kitchen. As she watched him go, she realized that maybe the way to stop snipping at each other was to carry on one-word conversations. She was also thinking that she liked the way his jeans—old, faded, skintight Wranglers—fit, too. And she liked the way he moved with a sure, long-legged grace that was both elegant and sexy. *Stop it, Kate! The more you think about all that sex stuff, the harder this will be on you. Just protect Cullen the prosecutor and forget about Cullen the man.*

She turned and started up the stairs then stopped. "Where is everyone?" she asked.

"Meghan had to get back to the hospital."

"Oh." Of course. Her aunt and his sister had lives and jobs to get back to. Kate climbed the rest of the stairs, trying to come to grips with the fact that though there were bound to be hands who helped with the livestock and kept things running when Cullen and Meghan weren't around, she would be more or less alone with him for an indefinite period of time. She was suddenly thankful that they would be making those trips to Little Rock where they would be around other people. At least it would be a different sort of stress.

Ten minutes later, Kate had managed to carry everything to her room. She ran a brush through her unbound hair, noting that since it had grown out, it had no particular style. She brushed her teeth, spritzed on a clean-scented cologne and glazed her lips with a rose-tinted gloss.

Stepping back from the mirror, she surveyed her appearance with a jaded eye. Nothing spectacular here—she really needed to get her hair styled—but she looked clean and neat, which was all she needed to be for this job. It wasn't as if she was there to impress anyone. She'd already convinced her new employer that she could do the job he needed her to do. For that, she didn't need to be a fashion plate. And, as for impressing him in any other way, she'd already tried and failed.

She found Cullen in the brick-and-copper kitchen that boasted lots of windows and green plants. Two places were set at the oval oak table. Blue denim place mats were topped with ironstone spatterware, and canning-jar mugs were filled with ice. Red bandannas served as napkins. One-handed, Cullen had managed to get the casserole out of the oven without dropping it onto the polished wood floor. Resting on a bright blue trivet, it held a place of honor between the table settings, its savory, spicy aroma filling the air.

The casual serving style helped put Kate at ease. She wasn't a crystal-and-china type woman, which didn't bode well for the future when she'd have to accompany Cullen to his various social obligations. Oh, well, she'd take it one day at a time and worry about that problem when it arose.

She stepped through the doorway as Cullen took two salad plates from the refrigerator. He turned with the salads and saw her standing in the doorway. "All settled in?" he asked, setting the plates on the table.

"All carried up, at least," she told him. "This looks great. I didn't know you were so domestic."

"Actually, I barely get by. Since I wasn't sure whether or not you cooked, I decided I'd best hire someone to take care of us while we're here. I think Meghan mentioned Greg to you.''

"Yes," Kate said. "He's trustworthy, I hope."

Cullen smiled. "I've known Greg Kingsley all my life. He used to be the town's general practitioner. He's the one who bound up our hurts when we were kids. His wife was one of my mother's best friends.''

"That's a pretty good recommendation," Kate said. ''And now?''

"Greg retired about six years ago, and Maude passed away last spring. He told Meghan that since he was bored out of his mind, he'd be more than glad to keep an eye on my wounds as well as do some cooking for us. His daughter, Connie, said she'd come in a couple of times a week to do the cleaning. And before you ask, yes, he can cook. Probably better than most of the women in town.''

He smiled then, the first full-fledged smile she'd seen. The effect on Kate's resolution to keep things impersonal was immediate and devastating. Her breath caught in her throat, and the room seemed too hot suddenly. The difference it made in his looks was astounding. He was already incredibly handsome, but the upcurving of his lips and the accompanying light in his eyes gave him an approachability she'd seen only when they made love. She forced herself to take a calming breath.

"Who did you tell him I was?"

"I went by the plan. Told him that you're my girlfriend and you're staying with me while I recuperate from the hunting accident.'' Cullen gave a reminiscent chuckle, and Kate's heart took another nosedive.

"What?" Kate asked.

"Greg hardly approves of our arrangement. He gave

me a stern look, muttered something about kids and lack of commitment, said it was none of his business, but he'd expected better from me. Needless to say, I felt about seven again, and properly chastised.''

She made a gesture toward the table. ''Well, whether he approves or not, I'm glad he agreed to cook for us. This looks delicious.''

''It will be,'' Cullen said, pulling out a chair for her.

Unaccustomed to such acts from the men she'd worked with at the police station, Kate sat down, thinking that being surrounded by such gracious little things might take some getting used to. As Cullen helped her scoot the chair beneath the table as best he could, she caught a whiff of his cologne, something exotic that brought to mind sultry desert nights and dashing turbaned men on prancing Arabian horses. Thoughts that were totally taboo considering their arrangement.

Not good. She'd barely gotten settled in and she was in deep trouble emotionally. It would be a long three or four months.

Chapter Five

Kate woke early her first day on the job. Her first thought was to wonder if Cullen was already up and about. If not, should she wake him? No. It wasn't as if they had anything pressing to do. There was plenty of time during the next month or so to try to get a handle on who was behind the attempts on his life.

Dinner had gone better than she expected, probably because they were both so aware of the possibility of offending the other. Their conversation had been general, and when they finished eating, she'd helped load the dishwasher and excused herself, claiming a weariness that was all too real. She thought she'd recognized relief in Cullen's demeanor, as if he, too, were anxious for the night to be over.

She showered and donned faded jeans and a brightly colored Mardi Gras sweatshirt and went downstairs to see what she could rustle up for breakfast. By the time she reached the top of the stairs, she encountered the mingled aromas of coffee and frying bacon. Evidently, Cullen was already up. Taking a fortifying breath, Kate started down, uncertain what the day might bring but determined to give it all she had and, if Cullen resorted to his earlier sarcasm, to give as good as she got.

She pushed open the door to the kitchen and saw a tall, spare, gray-haired man standing at the stove, a mug of coffee in one hand, a fork in the other. Hearing the squeak of the door as it swung shut, he turned. His face was craggy, his nose was strong, and his smile was slow and welcoming.

"You'd be Kate," he said, putting the fork down and approaching her with an outstretched hand.

Feeling a reciprocating smile curving her lips, Kate extended her own hand. "And you'd be Dr. Kingsley."

"Greg," he said, enveloping her hand in a warm, strong grip.

"Greg."

"Have a seat while I get you some coffee."

Kate waved him away. "You don't let that bacon burn. I'll get my own coffee."

Greg smiled. Kate found a mug in the cabinet over the coffeepot and poured some of the fragrant brew while she took inventory of the breakfast ingredients sitting on the countertop. A bag of grated cheese. *Picante* sauce warming in a small pan. Another filled with refried beans.

"The Mexican casserole was wonderful last night."

"Thank you," Greg said, slanting her a sideways grin and indicating the breakfast ingredients. "I'll bet you think I can't cook anything without chilies and Jack cheese."

"I happen to like chilies and Jack cheese," Kate said.

She looked at him from beneath her lashes, then glanced at the small platter piled with bacon.

He laughed. "Be my guest."

Kate snitched a piece of bacon and carried it to the table while Greg took the last piece from the iron skillet and deftly cracked two eggs into the sizzling drippings. "Not too healthy but really good," he told her.

"I know."

"Is Cullen awake?"

"I don't know," Kate said with a shrug.

Greg gave her an over-the-shoulder look she couldn't quite decipher and began basting the eggs with the bacon grease. "So how did you and Cullen meet—you being from New Orleans and him living in Little Rock?"

The question caught Kate off guard. How soon she'd forgotten that this man had no idea why she was really at the ranch. To him, she was Cullen's girlfriend, his live-in lover. No wonder he'd given her that look when she said she wasn't sure Cullen was awake or not. Great! The first hour of her first day, and her cover was already being threatened! Kate scoured her mind for some plausible answer.

"We met at my dad's restaurant," she said at last. "Cullen came in with some friends, and I was filling in at the cash register for the evening."

"Love at first sight, huh?"

"Well," she prevaricated. "Instant interest, at least. He, uh, came back the next night—alone—and asked me if I'd like to go get a cup of coffee. I said yes, and we did and..." Her voice trailed away.

"The rest, as they say, is history."

The comment came from the doorway, where Cullen, dressed in jeans as disreputable as hers, stood regarding her with a thoughtful expression.

"Good morning," Greg said. "Sleep well?"

"So-so. How about you?" Cullen asked, striding toward Kate with a purposeful gleam in his eye. "Did you sleep well?"

"Fair," she said, watching his approach with a wary expression.

He stopped within a foot of her. "Missed me, didn't you? No one to put your cold feet on."

What on earth was he talking about? And what on earth was he doing? she asked herself as he leaned down with a little grunt of pain. His gaze met hers briefly, and there seemed to be a signal of some sort in the dark blue depths of his eyes. Scant seconds before his lips brushed hers, she realized what he was up to and jerked back with an angry gasp.

Cullen straightened with a sigh. "Uh-oh. You're still mad at me."

Mad? She opened her mouth to ask what in the world he was talking about, but he lifted his good hand to her lips, pressing lightly with his fingertips.

"No more arguing, Kat. I said I was sorry. Forgive me?"

His voice as he called her by the shortened version of her name held a husky, intimate note, and the look in his eyes could almost pass for tenderness. He raised his eyebrows. Noting the warning glint in his eyes, she realized belatedly what he was doing. He'd tried to kiss her good-morning, as any man might the woman in his life. She'd pulled away, so he was trying to cover the faux pas for the sake of their audience, the good doctor. Good Lord! This weird arrangement might be harder to pull off than she imagined, especially if it called for letting Cullen kiss her. She wasn't sure the barriers she'd erected to protect her heart could stand that sort of assault.

She shot a glance at Greg in time to see him turn to the stove. Though he was busy lifting the eggs onto a plate, she knew he'd listened to every word with avid interest. How could he not? No doubt he was wondering what Cullen was sorry about. Well, she had no idea what to say, so she'd just let him get himself out of this little scenario.

Cullen chose not to offer an explanation. Instead, she watched as he sat down opposite her and accepted the plate Greg offered.

"Ladies first," Cullen said, setting the plate in front of Kate.

She looked down in dismay. Two slices of buttered toast, three slices of bacon, two eggs smothered with hot sauce and cheese and a generous spoonful of refried beans filled the plate. Moments ago, she'd been starving. Now her appetite was almost nonexistent.

"So what do you do for a living, Kate?" Greg asked.

Kate shot a questioning glance at Cullen. What should she say? He wouldn't want her to tell Greg she was a P.I.

"Skip tracing."

"Insurance."

Cullen and Kate spoke together, their gazes clashing when they realized they'd said two entirely different things.

"Well," Greg drawled, raising his eyebrows in question. "Which is it?"

Striving for normalcy, refusing to meet the older man's gaze, Kate picked up her fork and began to cut her eggs. "I used to try to locate people who'd skipped out on things—car payments, child support, that sort of thing," she said. "But I'd just taken a job last week with an insurance company to try to help identify fraudulent claims. It's so new, I guess Cullen forgot.''

"Oh." Greg went back to cooking the eggs. "I'll bet it was hard to get the time off to come here, since it's a new job."

Kate's wide-eyed gaze begged Cullen for some help. "Actually," she lied, "they were pretty understanding."

"That's good." Greg took up the second batch of eggs and began assembling another plate, which he carried to Cullen. "So how does this long-distance dating work, anyway?" Greg asked. "Looks like it would cramp a man's style."

Kate glared at Cullen, telling him without words it was his turn to come up with something. "It does," he said. "That's why Kate finally decided to move up here."

Greg went to the coffeepot and poured himself another cup, turning to face them with a thoughtful expression on his craggy face. "I see," he said, nodding. "So the new job with the insurance company is in Little Rock, then?"

"Yes!"

"Right!"

Kate's *yes* was uttered with heartfelt relief. Cullen's *right* was vocalized in a tone that seemed to say Greg's take on the imaginary scenario was a darned good idea.

Greg cradled his mug between his bony hands and looked from Kate to Cullen and back again.

"What?" Cullen asked.

Greg's smile was grim. "Who in heck do you two think you're trying to fool? The village idiot?" Ignoring the shock on both their faces, he continued. "If Barnesville had a village idiot, he'd be the only person around who'd fall for that cockamammy story."

"I don't know what you're talking about," Cullen said, attempting to cover the misstep with bravado.

"Sure you do. And so does Kate here—" Greg cocked his thumb at Kate "—if that's her real name."

"Of course it's my real name," Kate said indignantly, feeling as if their whole plan was coming apart before their very eyes.

"Well, at least that's a start," Greg said. "Now why don't the two of you stop looking so put upon and tell me what in the hell's going on."

Five minutes later, Cullen finished the story. Greg hadn't spoken a word as he'd listened about the accident, the reasoning behind Meghan's fears and how Kate had agreed to play along as Cullen's love interest until the would-be killer was found.

"Might be a lifetime sentence," Greg said.

"What do you mean?" Cullen asked.

"The police may never find out who it is."

"They will," Kate said. If the determination in her voice had any bearing on it, they would. "Cullen and I are going to start making a list of possible suspects this morning."

"That'd be a good idea, but I have an even better one."

"What's that?" Cullen asked.

"The two of you ought to sit down and get the story about your romance straight. Nobody's going to buy it the way it is."

"He has a point," Cullen said to Kate.

Greg smiled. "I guess that explains why Kate here didn't know if you were awake or not." When she just looked at him, he said, "Correct me if I'm wrong, but there aren't a whole heap of folks who don't share a

bedroom in this day and age.'' He pointed a finger at
Cullen. ''The two of you might try a little cuddling and
kissing and stuff, too.''

''Kissing!'' Kate said, as if the whole idea were for-
eign to her. A little voice whispered that surely she'd
known that would be part of the deal. After all, she was
supposed to be Cullen's live-in girlfriend. Kissing would
certainly be a part of her act.

''Kissing,'' Greg said in a dry tone. ''You know. It's
sorta like the sleeping-together thing. When a man and
woman are considered a couple they usually do a little
hugging and kissing. It's part of that thing called
love…or lust. Whichever. But you need to do it mostly
because no one's going to believe you two are the real
thing if you act ticked off every time Cullen here gets
close to you.''

''I didn't act ticked off!''

''Yeah, sweetie, you did. And I'll bet if you look at
your palms there are grooves there from your fingernails.''

Kate looked before she thought. He was right.

''Told you.'' Wearing a satisfied smile, Greg turned to
Cullen. ''As for you, you've got to look at Kate as if you
adore her. She's the woman you love, the woman you
want to get into the sack with at every opportunity…maybe the woman you want to marry someday.
You sure as heck can't glare at her as if you'd like to
throttle her.''

''I didn't.''

Greg looked at him with that implacable expression,
then said, ''Now let's throw out those cold eggs and start
over.''

Surprisingly, Kate's appetite returned once it wasn't
necessary that she play a part. They dined on the Mexican

eggs and tried to come up with a story about their meeting, courtship and Kate's job that would pass muster with Cullen's friends and business associates.

They kept the part about meeting at Kate's father's restaurant a few months ago and added that they'd seen each other a few times when Cullen happened to be in town. It was instant interest, if not love at first sight, but after a few dates, they decided that with their living in different states, it just wouldn't work out, that they'd get over the attraction. Cullen's accident had made them both realize they were wrong, that what they felt was more than they'd first believed. He had told his sister to contact Kate as soon as he'd come around, and she'd flown up to be at his side, knowing what she felt was the real thing.

They decided that Kate should be a high school history teacher—history had been her major in college—who was taking a year's sabbatical, which would be a reasonable explanation for why she was able to drop her life in New Orleans to be with the man she loved for an extended period of time.

Greg said that the shorter the amount of time they had spent in each other's company the better. It would serve to cover the many blank places in their knowledge of each other's likes and dislikes. In the end, they determined that it wasn't a perfect plan, but that it would have to suffice.

"There's something else we need to talk about," Cullen said. "Thanksgiving is in two days, and it seems like the easiest thing for everyone would be for us to have it at the ranch, since we're already here."

"Makes sense," Greg said. "Dan and Meghan and the girls love coming here, though they don't have a chance to get away much these days."

"Right," Cullen said, nodding. "And it will give Louella and Kate a chance to be together." He looked at Greg. "Didn't I hear you say Connie and her family were spending the day with her in-laws?"

"Yep."

"Then you may as well join us rather than sit at home alone."

Greg nodded, a wry smile on his lips. "I'd be glad to join you, even though I strongly suspect you only want my presence because you need someone to cook the feast."

"That had crossed my mind," Cullen admitted with a wry smile. "What do you think, Kate? Would Louella like to come?"

"I'm sure she would," Kate said. "But I have one stipulation."

"What's that?"

"That Aunt Lou makes the dressing."

"Greg?" Cullen asked.

"I suppose that would be okay," he said, though he didn't look at all pleased about the request. "I do make a mean wild-rice dressing."

"Maybe next year?" Cullen said.

Greg nodded. "Well, now that that's settled, I guess I'll clean up the kitchen and get something out to thaw for lunch. Then I'll take a look at that shoulder."

"I'll help," Kate said, preferring to be with Greg than Cullen.

"Suit yourself."

Cullen left to call his office and the sheriff's department to see if there were any new developments. As the door swung closed behind him, Kate uttered a deep sigh.

"That bad, huh?"

Kate glanced at him out of the corner of her eye. "What?"

"Being with Cullen."

Kate picked up her plate and carried it to the sink. "It's the whole situation."

Greg scraped the breakfast remains into the garbage disposal, rinsed the plate and handed it to Kate, who put it in the dishwasher. "No," he said with a slow shake of his head. "It's more than that."

"What are you? Psychic?"

"Nope. Observant."

"If you must know—"

"I must," Greg interrupted with a grin.

"Cullen and I...we really did meet in New Orleans, but it was almost two years ago."

"And was it love at first sight?" Greg ask, looking askance at her.

Kate met his gaze with a steady one of her own. "I plead the fifth."

Greg nodded. "He's a good man, Kate. An honorable man."

Kate was grateful that he didn't pry. Her smile didn't quite reach her eyes. "So they say."

"Well, whatever the two of you feel or don't feel, I suggest that since you took the job, you work real hard to at least act like you care for each other. Like I said, no one's going to buy that there's anything between the two of you if you both act like a pair of porcupines with halitosis."

Kate couldn't help smiling at the analogy, but there was no arguing with the logic. "What can I say? You're right."

Disgusted, frustrated, furious, the man folded the newspaper section and slapped it on top of the others.

Where had McGyver disappeared to? Tracking him down at the deer lease had been no problem, everyone knew about the famous McGyver camp. And when you were unemployed, it was easy enough to stake out someone and follow them. The hard part had been waiting until he could catch McGyver alone, planning out the hit so it looked like an accident. Who'd have ever thought he'd survive?

Now, it was back to square one, and other than a brief mention of the fact that he'd been released from the hospital on Friday by the local television stations, there hadn't been so much as a word on his whereabouts. He wasn't at his home in the Heights, and he hadn't gone back to work. He was hiding out—recuperating or whatever you chose to call it—but where?

It wasn't fair that a man like McGyver should have it all—looks, loving family, celebrity, success. It wasn't fair for a man's life to be destroyed for revenge. And it wasn't fair that McGyver wouldn't accept his role in the downfall of a man's hopes and dreams…his very life. Misjudging a situation couldn't—shouldn't—have caused so much pain.

Time should have made things better, healed the wound, but it would never heal, because the man had no intention of letting it. Instead, with every passing day, the hate intensified along with his determination to see justice done.

It wasn't over. There was nothing like a success to build confidence. He'd come close to ridding the world of the arrogant, self-righteous attorney the day of the so-called hunting accident. The next time, he'd make no mistakes.

* * *

Encouraged by the fact that Greg would be around as a buffer and determined to get down to business, Kate left the kitchen and went in search of Cullen. She found him in the library, his desk chair turned so he could look out the window. She was aware of the scent of leather and a hint of cigar smoke from some past occupant as well as the faraway sounds of Greg banging around in the kitchen. It was all just a backdrop for what held her attention—the man behind the desk.

His shoulders were slumped, the arrogance—or was that confidence?—gone. Unaware that he was being watched, Kate sensed a vulnerability about him she didn't think she'd ever seen. For the first time since she'd agreed to come talk to him, she didn't feel as if she was on her guard. His physical life had been threatened, and now his whole world was in flux. She knew what it was like to have your world destroyed, your beliefs and values crushed beneath the harshness of life's realities. She knew exactly how hard it was to rebuild on those shattered illusions. Hurts lessened, scars faded, but the disenchantment would linger for a long time.

To hide a sudden surge of sympathy, she rapped on the door frame. Cullen looked toward the door almost guiltily. "Hi."

"Hi," she replied, stepping into the room. "Is everything going okay at the office?" She asked the question as much to break the ice and pull him out of his introspective mood as because she cared.

He swiveled the chair to face her. "I suppose." He held up a piece of paper. "I've been sitting here making a list of people I've prosecuted in the past who might have the psychological makeup to harm me. I can probably come up with more names if I give it some more thought."

Kate sat down across the desk from him, determined to be as professional as possible under the stressful circumstances. "It can't be pleasant knowing someone is gunning for you."

"You should know."

"Because I was a cop, you mean?" When he nodded, she shook her head. "That's different. It's the good guys against the bad. It seldom becomes personal. The grudges are usually against the defense attorneys who the bad guys feel didn't do their job well enough, or someone who snitched on them. They don't generally see the ones who put them behind bars as their enemies. I mean, if it wasn't me busting them, it'd be someone else. It's just the rules of the game."

"You consider law enforcement a game?"

She shrugged. "It's as apt a description as any. Just as there is in any game, there's a lot of strategy involved in bringing someone to justice. You know that, because having a strong strategy is vital to both a successful prosecution and defense. And there are rules—laws—whose main objective is to keep anyone from cheating. At least the law enforcement officers have rules, and they're supposed to play by them."

"Sometimes they don't."

"Sometimes they don't," she agreed. A fleeting, sarcastic smile flitted across her lips. "All in all, comparing it to a game isn't a bad correlation. Look at us. We're involved in a game to try to flush out the perp."

"You have a point," he said with a nod. "What about you?"

"What about me?"

"Did you ever break the rules?"

The smile made another brief appearance. "I've bent a few," she admitted.

"Funny. You look like a straight arrow to me."

Kate didn't want to talk about herself. "I give it my best shot," she told him. "So who's on the list?" When he looked at her with a pained expression, she said, "We have to get started on it sometime."

"I guess so." He handed her the paper.

"Dub Lambert." She met his gaze. "What did he do to make the number one spot?"

Cullen picked up a pen and began making a crosshatch design on the yellow legal pad in front of him. "He confronted me outside my house a month or so ago."

"About what?" He dropped his gaze to the paper he was doodling on and didn't answer immediately.

"You can't have any secrets from me, Cullen," she told him. "I have to know it all. The good, the bad and the ugly."

"Right," he said, nodding. He took a deep breath and looked at a spot across the room. "Dub is married to a woman named Lucy. Lucy and I had a brief thing before either of us was married. Joanie and I had broken up, and so had she and Dub. Lucy was pretty and sympathetic and…willing. I guess you could say I used her." His gaze found Kate's. "Not very commendable of me, was it?"

Outside, a cardinal perched on the windowsill and looked inside, cocking its crested head this way and that as if he, too, were curious about Kate's opinion. Though she knew it was silly, Kate was surprised at the pang of pain his admission brought. Cullen was a good-looking man. Of course there would have been women. There had no doubt been women since New Orleans.

She brushed aside the feeling and schooled her features to composure. "I'm not here to judge what you have or haven't done," she told him. "I'm here to try to protect you and to find out who's behind the attempts on your life.''

Whatever Cullen felt about her comment was hidden behind the unreadable expression in his eyes.

"How did Dub find out about the fling?"

"Lucy was pregnant when she and Dub got married. Evidently the boy had to have some tests done a year ago, during which time they found out that his blood type is different from either Lucy's or Dub's.''

Kate grimaced. "That would be a heck of a way to find out the child you thought was yours isn't.''

"It would be tough," Cullen agreed with a nod. "Especially since she used the pregnancy as a way to get Dub to the altar.''

"So...he must have put pressure on Lucy, and she told him about you," Kate theorized, after several long seconds of thought.

"Bingo." Cullen stood and turned to the window. The red bird flew to safety on a branch of the naked oak tree whose summertime leaves helped shade this side of the house. "Actually, it was a weekend thing, not a full-fledged affair," he said without turning around.

"That's splitting hairs," Kate said, trying to keep the bitterness from her voice. Cullen's situation with Lucy was too much like Kate's. "The bottom line is, you did sleep with her, and because of that, Dub believes you're the boy's biological father.''

"Yes," Cullen said, turning to face her.

Kate leaned back in her chair. "So what happened when he came to your house?"

Cullen pinched the bridge of his nose with his good hand. "He wanted money. For me to own up to my responsibilities, as he put it, or he'd go to the press.''

"Ah," Kate said. "Sounds like blackmail to me,

which tells me how disturbed he really is about the child's paternity.''

''That's what I thought.'' Cullen turned and walked around the desk as if he were too keyed up to be still.

''What did you tell him?''

''That if he wanted money, he should get a lawyer and prove his case, that he'd better not go to the press without proof, or I'd hit him with a slander suit.''

''How can you be so sure the boy isn't yours without a paternity test?''

''I'm sure.''

Kate gave him a dark look. ''And you haven't heard anything else from him?''

Cullen raked his free hand through his dark hair. ''Not a word.''

''Did you call Lucy and talk to her about it?''

''No.''

''Since she's the one who pointed the finger at you, maybe you should have done that as well as have the test.''

A muscle in Cullen's jaw tightened. ''Maybe.'' He paced to the door and turned. ''I really thought she'd get in touch, or that maybe it would just...go away.''

A naive rationale from such a worldly man, Kate thought. To him, she said, ''Things like this just don't go away as much as we might want them to.''

''I suppose not,'' he said with a heavy sigh.

She leaned forward in her chair. ''Aren't you even the slightest bit curious about whether or not the child is yours?''

''He's not,'' he said flatly. ''I may not always make the best decisions, but I'm not generally a careless person. I took precautions.''

Kate saw the dull color that crept into his cheeks. ''So

you were careful," she said with a shrug. "Accidents happen, Cullen. I imagine that a goodly percentage of the kids walking around today are here despite precautions."

"Whose side are you on, anyway?" he asked.

"There isn't any side taking to this situation," she said. "I'm just presenting the facts, which aren't necessarily palatable." Determined to get his reaction, she said, "You need to get the DNA test done."

He closed his eyes and pinched the bridge of his nose.

"How would you feel if the boy were yours?" she pressed.

The expression on his face mutated to what could only be described as stricken. "He can't be mine!" he said in a voice harsh with anguish and regret. "My son was supposed to be born in love...created from love. I was supposed to be involved in his life. For this child to be mine wouldn't be fair...to me or Joanie."

His statement told her two things. First, for all his worldliness, Cullen McGyver had a streak of the idealistic in him. Rare for a man who'd attained his level of professional stature. It also told her that he had a lot of unresolved feelings for his dead wife. No wonder he'd left her alone in New Orleans, Kate thought with a fresh burst of understanding. There was no room for another woman in his heart. Feeling as if a giant hand was squeezing her heart, Kate promised to look at this new information more carefully later. Right now she was working, and her job was to gather the information she needed to nail whoever it was who wanted to harm Cullen.

"I hate to be the bearer of more bad news, counselor," she said, a sharpness born of pain in her voice. "But life isn't always fair. If it was, my partner wouldn't be dead. So forget about fair. The fact is that there's a little boy out there who may be yours. It would behoove you to start thinking about how you'll handle the situation if he is.''

Cullen pivoted on one heel. "Don't you dare judge me!" he snapped.

"I'm not judging you," Kate argued. "I just posed a legitimate scenario. One that in my estimation needs some serious consideration, because from what I've heard, you don't seem like the kind of man who'd shirk his responsibilities, no matter how onerous they might be."

"I'm not."

The bleakness in his voice softened Kate's anger. "A DNA test could clear this whole thing up," she said.

"I know."

"But you decided against it."

"For the moment, yes."

"Which translates to, like all people in the public eye, you aren't anxious for the world to find out that you have feet of clay."

"Right. Maybe Louella mentioned that I'm thinking of running for the United States senate. You know how the media can blow this sort of thing out of proportion. With all the scandals in the past few years and all the influential people having mistresses and illegitimate babies and payoffs of one kind or another, it would be political suicide if they got wind of this or any other allegations about my character."

"Better to get it into the open now than in the middle of the campaign."

"Damn!" he said, glaring at her.

Kate shrugged.

"Okay, okay. You're right. The timing would be better

now. And it's selfish to put my career ahead of some child's life. I'll get the test done.''

''Good. If it comes back positive, other than your senate bid, I think knowing the truth would be beneficial all the way around. My feeling is that it never hurts to know where you stand.''

''You're right.''

Kate mulled over what he'd just said, concerned in spite of herself not to get emotionally involved with him again.

''What?'' Cullen prompted.

''If the hint of scandal will hurt your chances of being elected, my staying here may be a much greater problem for you than me,'' she told him.

''It can't be helped. Once this lunatic is caught, we can explain everything to the media.''

''You're the boss,'' Kate said with a shrug. ''Who knows? By the time next year's election rolls around, it may all be forgotten.''

''You're right. I'll talk to Meghan about having the test done when she gets here.''

''Good.'' Kate gave him a tight smile of approval, trying not to think of him making love with another woman. *Get back to the list, Kate. Forget about his past affairs.* Good advice if she could take it. And she may as well get used to it. There were bound to be other things in his life he didn't want made public. Bound to be other women.

Chapter Six

Kate willed away the thought of Cullen being with other women. Cullen McGyver might be a good prosecutor and a good man, but no one had nominated him for sainthood. He was still a man, with all the urges, vices and faults of men everywhere. She forced her attention back to her list.

"One more question."

"Sure."

"From what you've seen of Dub do you think he's capable of murder?"

Cullen was slow to answer. "I don't know," he said at last. "My initial impression is that he's the kind to nurture a grudge. And he's the classic bully type."

Kate made some notes on the paper. "Okay. I'll check him out. Let's move on. Who's Claude Porter?"

Cullen threw back his head and stared at the ceiling, trying to put a case with the name. "He claimed to have injured his back. Bilked his workman's comp out of thousands before the investigator caught him doing something his so-called injury would not allow him to. He was guilty. All we did was prove it. I can't see him wanting to kill me for blowing the whistle on him.''

"You never know," Kate said. "What about John Lamonti?"

"A girl's basketball coach who got a little too familiar with a couple of the girls on the team. The defense did a bang-up job—no pun intended," he said with a grim smile, "of convincing the jury it was consensual. So even though they were seventeen, he got his wrist slapped. A suspended sentence, some probation, I think."

"How long ago was that?"

"About four years ago. The last I heard he was coaching at a school in southeast Arkansas." Cullen rubbed his lower lip with the pads of his fingers and moved on to the next name. "Vincent James scammed the government out of more than a hundred thousand dollars. He kept cashing his grandmother's social security checks after she died."

"Michael Mullins?" she asked, raising her eyebrows in question.

"Michael Mullins." Cullen closed his eyes and squeezed the bridge of his nose. "Old Mike dumped all sorts of nasty chemicals in a creek for a couple of years. Killed a lot of wildlife and a herd or two of cattle. I don't remember how long he got. Not long enough, I'm sure." Cullen swore suddenly.

"What?"

His eyes found Kate's. "I do remember that he said he'd get me when he got out."

"And you don't know when that might be?" Kate said, writing furiously.

"No," Cullen said. "Sorry."

"No problem. I'll check it out." She stuck the ball-point pen behind her ear. "In fact, I'm going to do some checking on all these guys, see where they are, what they've been up to. In the meantime, you be thinking about anyone else who might have it in for you."

He nodded, and Kate got up to go.

"We should talk about my schedule, get our plans in place."

Kate's heart gave a little tumble of dismay. She'd been hoping he'd put off getting back into the mainstream of his life, at least until after the Thanksgiving holiday. So much for hopes. She shrugged. "Okay."

"I've agreed to be master of ceremonies at the Barnes-ville Christmas parade on Saturday evening after Thanks-giving. I committed to it months ago."

She frowned. "I don't know if that's wise. A parade... lots of open spaces. It would be impossible for one person to keep a watch out for any possible trouble. Besides, don't you think it's a little too soon to be out and about?"

"It's just a small-town Christmas parade," he said, "and I won't be doing anything strenuous." Irritation was causing his blue eyes to turn a stormy gray. "It isn't as if it's the Rose Bowl Parade or I'm Dick Clark."

"I understand, and I'll take it under consideration," Kate said. "What else is coming up?"

Cullen pulled a small book from his shirt pocket and flipped it open. "There's an art exhibit in Dallas the first of December."

Kate opened her mouth to speak. "It's a private show-ing," he offered, forestalling her misgivings. "It's invi-tation only, if that helps ease your mind."

"Somewhat." Actually the invitation only would eliminate people walking in off the street, Kate reasoned. Plus, there would be a lot of security at the gallery. "What else?"

"There's a party in Aledo at the home of an old friend after the exhibit."

"What old friend?"

Cullen's lips thinned, and a muscle jumped in his cheek. Clearly, he didn't like all her questions. Too bad. He'd hired her to do a job, and she'd do her best whether or not he liked the measures she took. Kate ignored the little voice that told her she liked calling the shots, liked having control. Call it payback for the way he'd treated her in New Orleans.

"Jake Lattimer."

"How many people will be attending?"

"I have no idea," he said sharply. "How could I?"

My, my, she thought, he was getting downright testy. "I'd need to see the guest list before I can okay it."

"Fine with me," he said in a cold voice. "If you can figure out how to ask for it without raising any red flags, I'd be happy for you to look it over."

"If this Jake What's-His-Name is your old friend, can't you just ask him?"

Cullen's lips curved into a thin smile. "Not without blowing our cover. No one's supposed to know you're guarding me—remember?"

Kate sat down hard. She felt like a fool.

Cullen flicked her a stony, uncompromising glance, snapped the book shut and put it back in his pocket. "That's pretty much it, except that I planned to spend Christmas with Meghan and her family. If you want to spend Christmas with your dad, I'm sure I'll be perfectly safe with Meghan and Dan."

Kate's mind whirled. This secret bodyguard thing was

a whole new ball game, one she wasn't sure she was up to playing. "Dan and Meghan live in Little Rock?"

"Yes."

She shook her head. "No way we can chance your being alone. I'll go, too. The job takes precedence over what I want and where I spend the holidays."

"You're the boss."

The words were the right ones, but the expression in his eyes was anything but accepting. He was as angry about her stance on the upcoming events as she was worried. Kate started to tell him that it would be hard enough to do the job she was hired to do without having to butt heads with him over every call she made. Of course, if she played it straight, without indulging in any little power trips, it might be easier, too. They were both going to have to give a little for the whole plan to work.

"It looks like we'll be driving into town for a shopping trip," he said, before she could find the right words to put him in his place.

The sudden change in topic threw her for a moment. "Shopping?"

"Yes. You'll need some things. For the exhibit and the party afterward."

So he planned to go despite her reservations. Fine. She'd go and do her best to protect him. If someone put a bullet in his black heart, she could always fall back on "I told you so." But an art exhibit! Kate stifled the urge to groan out loud. She hated formal dos. No matter how nice everyone said she looked, she always felt as if she were playing a part, as if she was being examined and found wanting. "I—I don't have any idea what to buy…what would be appropriate."

"I do." His smile was grim. "Don't worry. You and I will make a hell of a team. You put your life on the line for me, and I'll see to it that you're the best-dressed woman in the room. And since I'm bored out of my mind, we'll go this afternoon.''

''This afternoon?''

''As you said earlier, there's no sense putting it off.''

She sighed. ''I suppose not.''

''Good. If you'll excuse me, it's time for my medication.''

He turned, leaving Kate bemused and more worried than she'd ever admit. In the past, she was able to immerse herself in her new identity, insinuate herself into the bad guy's life...play along, gather bits and pieces of information along the way. This was different.

The difference was that not only had she been gathering information in her old job, she'd had someone else providing her with details she needed to know to make her role easier. This time she was virtually alone, flying by the seat of her pants, so to speak. No informants. No backup. Just her and Cullen and someone who wanted to see him dead.

Shopping. With an arrogant, insufferable...idiot! Kate dragged the brush through her hair with all the vengeance she might use to bludgeon a purse snatcher. Cullen had hardly spoken to her at lunch—which didn't escape Greg's notice—and now she was supposed to spend the afternoon with him trying on clothes. Having a root canal would be preferable, she thought, coiling her hair.

As she donned a charcoal-gray pantsuit and a white lightweight sweater, she tried to sooth her ruffled feathers by telling herself to let it go and reminding herself that in many ways this really was a cream-puff job. Her alter ego argued the fact that they hadn't gotten to the hard part yet. The real test would come when she and Cullen stepped out in public.

Her fury faded a bit at the thought. Not only was she angry at Cullen for his attitude, she admitted that part of her own attitude was based on pure fear. She was afraid. Not that they wouldn't be able to set aside their animosity and fool the world but that something would happen and she'd be forced into a situation similar to the one she'd faced with Raul. Forget her personal feelings. She couldn't afford to let down her guard for one minute. Not to him. Not to anyone.

Kate took a steadying breath. *You can do this.* Right. She could. During the time she'd spent packing her things in New Orleans, Louella had kept her apprised of any mention of Cullen by the media. So far, there had been nothing on the news except that he was recuperating from a hunting accident. No one would know they were shopping, so the chances of running into trouble were slim. It worried her, anyway.

She regarded herself in the mirror. She'd put on a minimum of makeup, glossed her lips and spritzed herself with her usual clean-scented cologne. With her hair pulled back in the customary knot, she decided it was the best she could do with what she had to work with.

You can do this. The words were her mantra as she went downstairs to meet Cullen. When she saw him standing near the desk, the phone at his ear, her heart sank. She paid no attention to his conversation. She was too preoccupied with the man himself, who looked like the million or so dollars he was no doubt worth in his pricey gray slacks, pale lavender shirt and sports jacket. He was freshly shaven, and his short dark hair was brushed to the side. He wore an onyx ring on his right hand and a watch on his left wrist that probably cost more than she made in months.

When he half turned and saw Kate standing in the doorway, he said, "Hold on. Talk to Kate." He held out the receiver. "It's Meghan. You need to hear this."

Kate took the phone. "What's up?"

Meghan spoke in a panicked rush. "I went by Cullen's place to get some more clothes to bring tomorrow, and I decided I should check his messages. There was one from a man that said something like, 'Saw about your accident on television. Too bad it didn't quite work. I'll be in touch again whenever you stop hiding out.'"

Kate's heart began to beat a little faster. So the perp had no idea where they were, which made her feel a bit more comfortable going shopping. However, the brief message left no doubt that the shooting was intentional.

"I didn't know what to do," Meghan said.

"You did the right thing, but you need to calm down," Kate told her. "Cullen's in no immediate danger. Can you make a copy of the tape?"

"Yes," Meghan said.

"Make a copy, give one to the cops and bring the other one here, so Cullen and I can listen to it. He can see if the voice sounds familiar."

"Good idea."

Meghan said she and her family planned on arriving by noon the next day, and Kate hung up and glanced at Cullen. There was no need expounding on the conversation. He'd heard it all.

"Ready?"

She nodded, and he tossed her the keys, since he couldn't drive on the pain medication. Kate caught them easily, and preceded him out of the room, her bearing professional, her features schooled to a calm she was far from feeling. The threat was real now, not just the product of an overactive imagination. Someone—a man— wanted Cullen dead. It was Kate's job to see that it didn't happen.

They drove to Little Rock, and following his directions, she drove to a boutique at a busy strip mall. The moment they pulled up in front of the door, which read simply Chyna's, Kate knew she was out of her league. The store was upscale, high-end, or as Aunt Lou would say, fancy schmancy. Not the sort of place Kate was likely to shop, even if she had the money. A sick, uncomfortable feeling settled in the pit of her stomach.

Cullen held the door for her and she preceded him inside. The boutique was small and decorated in a forties deco style that Kate found appealing. A saleswoman, the only employee Kate saw, approached them immediately, gave Kate the once-over, dismissed her with a single glance and homed in on Cullen, whom she obviously knew.

Cullen asked the whereabouts of Chyna, and Kate, who had wandered to a display of silk blouses, heard him say something about Joanie as she reached for the price tag attached to a teal blouse. When she saw the price, she jerked back her hand as if it might be a sin to touch it.

"I understand you're looking for a formal gown," a silky voice said from behind her. The saleswoman, probably in her fifties and dressed to the nines, offered Kate what passed for a polite smile. The problem was, it never reached her eyes.

"Uh, yes," Kate said. "I am."

The woman gestured toward the rear of the shop. "If

you'll step back here, you can see if there's anything that catches your eye.''

Kate flicked Cullen an uneasy glance and fell in step behind the woman, who offered her another counterfeit smile and said to call her Freida.

''Did you have a specific color in mind?''

Kate started to say that she didn't and realized the woman had directed the question to Cullen instead of her.

''Something pastel, I think,'' he said, the expression in his eyes far away, as if he were doing his utmost to recall another time and place.

Pastel? Kate thought with something akin to horror. She hadn't worn many pastels since she was a baby. She glanced at the saleswoman, but Freida's attention was fixed on Cullen. Kate saw an emotion she couldn't identify flicker in the woman's eyes.

''Something flowing and soft. Chiffon, maybe,'' Cullen added.

''Certainly, Mr. McGyver.'' She gave Kate a quick once-over, muttered something about her height and selected three gowns. ''Let's try these to start.''

Dutifully, Kate went into the dressing room carrying gowns of lavender chiffon, peach beadwork and mint-green satin. The woman started to follow her inside. Kate turned in the doorway, effectively blocking her. The woman stared back as if to ask what the holdup was.

''I've been dressing by myself since I was three,'' Kate said, refusing to undress in front of the snooty salesperson.

''But I—''

''I'll call you if I need you,'' Kate said with what she hoped passed for a polite smile.

Freida gave her a chilly smile in return. ''Of course.

I'll be right outside. Oh, and Mr. McGyver would like to see each gown as you try it.''

Kate nodded. Of course he would. He was footing the bill.

She tried the green slip-type gown first. While she liked the way it fit, the color made her want to hurl. She exited the small room and faced Cullen, who sat in a wingback chair, waiting. Kate bit her tongue, determined not to say anything to cause any sparks to fly between them. It was only a dress that she'd wear one time. Still, if she had to wear this dress in public, she'd quit the job, killer or no killer.

Cullen's expression was enigmatic, his forehead furrowed in concentration. At Freida's insistence, Kate made a slow pirouette. Cullen's frown deepened.

''It looks good on you,'' he said.

He actually liked it? Kate threw discretion to the wind. ''I hate it.'' The words were uncompromising. ''I'm not a minty-type girl.''

''I have to say I think she's right,'' Freida said, offering Cullen an apologetic smile. ''Let's try another one.''

The peach had a beadwork bodice and a dropped waist with a flowing skirt. The color was good with her hair, but in Kate's estimation, the beadwork was much too much.

''The color is good,'' Freida said, encouraged by the look in Cullen's eyes. ''Don't you think?''

''I feel like a Christmas bauble,'' Kate said, indicating the beadwork. Her defiant gaze met his. Cullen's eyes held a murderous glint, as if he thought she was being deliberately hard to get along with. Well, he might be footing the bill, but she'd be the one parading around in the darned dress, so she was at least going to have one she felt halfway comfortable wearing—even if it was only for one night.

"Try another one," he said.

The lavender chiffon was a disaster—from the gauzy skirt to the color. The crisscross bodice made her feel like a Mexican bandito in an old western, or maybe a Prom-Night Barbie. Gritting her teeth, Kate went out to get the opinion of her private audience.

Clearly, Cullen was perplexed about something. "Joanie had a dress similar to that one," he said, frowning at the memory.

Just as she suspected. He'd given Freida instructions to show Kate dresses in styles and colors that his dead wife might have worn. Well, Mr. McGyver needed to realize right up front that she had no intention of being turned into a Joanie McGyver clone.

"Let me see the back," he told her.

"No." Kate wasn't sure who looked the most surprised by her refusal, Cullen or Freida.

"I'm not Joanie, and I won't let you try to turn me into her." Though the words were softly spoken, they were said loud enough for Freida to hear the bit of steel in them. The saleswoman cast Cullen a look that seemed to ask what she should do. Kate wouldn't have been surprised to see her start wringing her hands.

Both were saved when a feminine voice said, "No! No! No! Good grief, Freida! What are you trying to do to this poor thing?"

Cullen and Freida the Frigid turned. Kate's gaze flew to the diminutive café-au-lait-skinned woman in a forties retro-style suit who crossed the boutique like a tiny tempest.

"Hello, Chyna," Cullen said, smiling.

Ah. The absentee owner. Kate heard the pleasure in

his voice. Petite, curvy and achingly beautiful, with huge brown eyes, a sexy mouth and a short and sassy haircut, the boutique owner was everything red-haired, too-tall Kate had ever longed to be.

"Hello, partner!" Chyna said with a wide smile before she leaned over and dropped a kiss to Cullen's cheek.

Partner? What was going on?

Chyna eyed the sling supporting Cullen's arm. "What on earth happened to you?"

"Don't you listen to the news?"

"Sugar, I make the news," Chyna said with a wink.

"Indeed you do," he said with a laugh. "I got in the way of a careless hunter. No big deal."

Chyna turned her attention to Kate. "The man gets shot and he says it's no big deal." She extended her hand. "Hi. I'm Chyna Talmadge. And you are?"

"Kate. Kate Labiche."

"Kate Labiche," Chyna said. "Cullen's...?" She let the question hang as she glanced from Kate to Cullen.

"Why, I'm the love of his life," Kate supplied in her most sugary New Orleans accent and what she hoped was a convincing smile at Cullen. She didn't miss the flash of irritation in his eyes.

Chyna slanted Cullen a pleased look. "Well, it's about darn time, if I do say so. A man can't play the field forever."

"Kate has certainly put a stop to that," he said with an amiable smile.

Yeah, Kate thought. Me and an unknown killer.

Chyna raised her perfectly arched eyebrows. "Must be serious if you're shopping for clothes."

The look in Cullen's eyes was teasing. "Serious enough."

Kate watched the lighthearted banter between the two

friends with something akin to envy. She'd never had many close friends, and the ones she did have had moved across the country or were still part of the NOPD, which meant she seldom saw them now.

Turning her back on Cullen, Chyna gave her full attention to Kate, cocking her head this way and that as she gestured for Kate to make another full turn for her benefit.

"You're from New Orleans, aren't you?" Chyna said in a conversational tone, though her attention was clearly focused on the gown Kate was wearing.

"Yes."

"Thought so. You've got the accent." Chyna turned to Freida. "Why on earth would you put her in lavender?"

"Mr. McGyver said pastels," the saleswoman said in defense.

Chyna put her beringed hands on her slender hips. "Mr. McGyver said? May I remind you that you're the expert. Never put a woman into something you know won't become her. Your job is to sell her on what will. Or in this case, to sell him."

Freida visibly wilted beneath the criticism, though even to Kate, it seemed delivered in as much a kidding tone as a derogatory one.

"What else have you tried?" Chyna asked Kate.

When Kate described the other two dresses Chyna wrinkled her nose in distaste. "The peach color with the green's style would have worked, but I think I know what will be better even than that." She turned to Cullen with lifted eyebrows and waggled a scarlet-tipped finger at him. "You're trying to turn her into Joanie, sweet cheeks, and Joanie, she ain't."

Scarlet color suffused Cullen's cheeks. So Chyna had

figured it out, too. Strangely, Kate didn't feel any elation at knowing she'd been right, only a strange sense of sorrow.

Seeing the expression in Kate's eyes, Chyna said, "Don't take any offense, Kate from New Orleans. Joanie McGyver was one of my best friends. If it weren't for her, I would never have had a chance to open this place. All I meant is that Joanie was soft and sweet. There's nothing soft and sweet about you."

Kate wasn't sure she'd ever known anyone so outspoken.

"But that's okay," Chyna hastened to add, patting Kate's arm as she hustled her toward the dressing room. "I'm not too sweet myself. If you'll notice, a lot of things that are hard to get or are an acquired taste are often those things that are pretty darn special.

"Now let me go get this killer gown for you to try. I designed it myself, and I guarantee it will knock Cullen McGyver's socks off."

"Yeah, right." The cynicism Kate heard in her voice was expected. The pang of something closely akin to regret wasn't. There was no time to analyze the feeling.

"What's wrong?" Chyna asked with a lifted brow. "Wrong piece of clothing to get off your man?"

This woman was sharp, Kate thought. Not much got by her. "I plead the fifth," she drawled, doing her best to play the part she'd assumed.

She was still trying to figure out why the idea of her inability to impress Cullen as a woman should bother her when Chyna returned with the gown and Kate slipped into it.

It was perfect. Kate was surprised and pleased at the difference the color and style made in the way she looked and more stunned by the way the dress made her feel.

Chic. Sexy. Desirable. Things she hadn't felt in a long time, if ever.

Sewn of something soft and clingy, shimmery and stretchy in a soft sage-green, the dress had a deep draped neck. Sleek and sensual, it hung loosely from the tips of her breasts and skimmed her hips while a slit on both sides revealed a length of creamy thigh with every step she took. While the front gave a demure sophisticated look, the back was bare to a point just below her waist. The whole thing was topped off by a collarless jacket in black velvet that was cut short in front but had a longer gathered back that covered the deeply draped back of the dress. It was demure yet bold. Nicely naughty. A dress that inspired confidence and power.

Kate's reflection mirrored the excitement in her eyes and the flush of color on her cheeks. She felt as Cinderella must have under the supervision of her fairy godmother. The parallel didn't end there. Kate knew that when they caught the person behind the attacks on Cullen, the clock would officially strike twelve and she'd wake up in her rags, back in her office, tracing skips for a living while Prince Charming carried on his perfect life with one of the kingdom's true princesses. Still, she had an unspecified time to enjoy, and she would try to make the most of it.

Chyna—who looked nothing like anyone's interpretation of a fairy godmother—was standing back to evaluate the results of her handiwork. She caught the reflected expression in Kate's eyes. "Oh, yeah, baby," she said with a satisfied grin and a throaty purr. She gave Kate a little push. "Well, go on and let's see what your man has to say."

Kate opened her mouth to say that Cullen wasn't her man, remembering just in time that this was all a ruse to keep Cullen safe and that Chyna, their first test in the world outside the ranch, was buying into it. Which was good. Then why, she asked herself as she made her way to the front of the shop, was she suddenly so depressed?

Cullen was still torqued from Kate's and Chyna's comments about his trying to make Kate into Joanie. What made him angriest was that they were right. He had tried to put Kate into styles and colors that would have been perfect for Joanie but did nothing for Kate's more dramatic look. As Kate had, Chyna had recognized it the minute she'd arrived.

Joanie and Chyna had been college friends, an unlikely duo who had gone into business after graduation. Chyna had had a flair for design, and Joanie had a trust fund. Cullen had met Joanie at the shop—then in another location—while with another woman. As today, Chyna had been gone, and Joanie was watching the front. It had been love at first sight.

It still amazed him that the two women had gotten along so well. On the outside, Chyna was breezy, flighty. Inside, she was shrewd, creative and a force to be reckoned with when it came to matching style, color and fabric as well as when it came to getting her ideas marketed. She was not only a whiz at design, but had a real knack at reading a woman's first impression and translating that impression into the right combination of clothes and accessories.

Joanie had been the quiet one, the businessperson, the one who kept Chyna's feet on the ground and the books on the fiscal straight and narrow. Her favorite saying was that they had to crawl before they walked. Since Joanie's death, that job had fallen to Cullen, and he had to say that Chyna's business acumen had come a long way in the last three years. It would soon merge with her other skills. A year ago, she'd convinced Cullen that it was time the one shop became two, and so far the expansion was working out incredibly well.

He was beginning to get antsy waiting when he saw Kate emerge from the dressing room and come toward him, her head high, her shoulders erect, a black velvet jacket dangling from her fingertips. With the classic simplicity of her hairstyle, stunning was the only word that came to mind. The unusual soft sage hue did wonderful things for her complexion and her hair. The dress clung, dipped, revealed. Tantalized. Desire—sudden, unexpected, unwanted—burst throughout him like a Fourth of July fireworks display, making his heart race, his nerve endings sizzle with awareness and his head spin as if he'd had too much to drink.

"Well?" Chyna said.

He was so wrapped up in Kate's metamorphosis, Chyna's self-satisfied smile didn't even register.

"What do you think?"

What he thought was that he wanted to smooth his hands up and down Kate's arms and see if they were as silky as he remembered. Wanted to press his lips to each and every one of the golden freckles that were scattered over her shoulders and upper breasts...an impossible task. He'd already tried. Wanted to slide his hands over her hips and feel the softness of the fabric that clung to the firmness of her body as they struggled to get closer...

The startling craving stunned him in its intensity, leaving him dismayed, embarrassed and angry. Speechless. He dragged his gaze from Kate to Chyna, whose smile had faded to a frown. "I thought you'd like it, but if you don't—"

"I do like it." His voice held an uncharacteristic huskiness. His gaze moved to Kate against his will.

"Try on the jacket, sugar," Chyna said, a pleased expression in her eyes.

Kate complied and made another pirouette. Though he had no idea why, Cullen knew the dress was perfect. "We'll take it. And whatever else she needs to go with it."

When they were finished, Kate was in possession of not only shoes and underthings to go with the gown but a brown suit and several pairs of slacks and coordinating shirts. Chyna told Cullen he could have the clothes at cost—she had to keep the accountant happy. When she gave him the total, Kate, who was standing next to him, gasped.

Still wrestling with his feelings, Cullen allowed his gaze to find hers as he slid his platinum American Express onto the counter. "Is something wrong?"

"I— It's just...I...I can't accept these," she stammered. "It's too much."

"Don't worry your pretty head. He can afford it," Chyna said in a droll voice.

Fully aware that they had a role to play but completely unaware of the hint of desire that still smoldered in his eyes, Cullen let his gaze move over her features. Couldn't stop it from lingering on her mouth. He saw the confusion in her eyes disappear beneath a sudden understanding as he lifted his hand and trailed his knuckles over the crest of her cheek and the tips of his fingers down the sweet-curving line of her jaw to the fullness of her parted lips.

The feelings he'd harbored since he'd first seen her standing in the library holding Joanie's picture—forbidden, hidden, squelched at every opportunity—could no longer be denied. He wanted to kiss her. The thought was less surprising than it was fatalistic.

"Chyna's right," he said, a slight smile curving his mouth. "I can afford it, so let me do this for you."

Kate's eyes widened in surprise at what she saw in his. She gave a halfhearted shake of her head, but his fingers closed over her chin, holding her firmly but gently as he lowered his head. He paused, their mouths a breath away from touching.

"Besides," he said, the huskiness back in his voice, "the gown looks as if Chyna created it just for you. It would be a sin for anyone else to have it."

That said, he closed the space between their lips and felt the reciprocal jolt all the way to his soul. Her mouth was softer than he recalled, much softer than the mouth of a woman as acerbic as she was should be. Sweeter than his favorite sangria. He fought the urge to drink their sweetness longer, managing to confine the kiss to a brief but firm touch and the slightest touch of his tongue to the seam of her lips.

Feeling slightly dazed and more than a little awestruck, he raised his head. Kate's eyelashes drifted upward. Her golden-hued eyes mirrored a dazed confusion. Except for the romantic music coming from the hidden speakers located throughout the store, complete silence filled the room.

"He's right, sugar," Chyna said, shattering the stillness. "It's perfect for you. I must have had you in mind when I designed that dress."

Still wearing a somewhat stunned expression, Kate turned toward Chyna and tried to smile. "Thanks."

"Sure. Here you go, handsome." With a wink, Chyna handed the bags to Cullen and the boxes to Kate, since he only had one usable hand.

"Thanks, Chyna."

"As I live and breathe! Is that who I think it is?"

They were turning to leave when the husky feminine voice halted them. When Cullen saw the smartly dressed woman bearing down on them, his heart sank. Tracy Cunningham was a woman he'd dated briefly, one who had been hell-bent on getting him to the altar. When he'd had to get borderline ugly with her to make her understand that his interest wasn't that deep, she'd responded by spreading rumors about how he'd led her on and dumped her, leaving her with a broken heart. She was beautiful, clever, catty and an inveterate gossip, whether or not people believed her. If there was a hint of success, or a breath of scandal in the state, Tracy was the first to know about it. He heard Chyna's soft groan of dismay.

"It is!" Tracy cried. "Cullen McGyver, in the flesh." As expected, she went through the fake kiss routine, pressing each rouged cheek to his and kissing the air with her scarlet-painted lips.

"So how have you been?" Without waiting for his answer, she asked, "I heard about the hunting accident on the news."

"I'm fine, thanks," he said, determined to be polite if it killed him. To treat her the way he'd like to would only invite more untrue stories.

"Ms. Cunningham." Chyna, who must have sensed the tension coiled inside Cullen, stepped into the breech. "I guess you came to look at that silk blouse I was telling you about?"

"Yes, I did," Tracy said, without even looking at her.

"I'll get it," Chyna said.

Tracy shifted her attention from Cullen to Kate. "Aren't you going to introduce us, Cullen?"

Cullen had no choice but to do just that. "Kate, honey,

this is Tracy Cunningham, an old friend of mine. Tracy, this is Katherine Labiche. The new lady in my life.''

Kate's eyes widened imperceptibly. ''It's a pleasure meeting you, Ms. Cunningham.''

''Likewise, I'm sure,'' Tracy said, dismissing Kate with a glance. ''Where have you been keeping yourself?'' she asked, taking Cullen's uninjured arm in both her hands.

What could he say? *Hiding out until they find the person who tried to kill me?* Hardly. He went for the general, the most logical and, he hoped, the least damaging. ''I've spent some time away recuperating. The family is spending Thanksgiving at the ranch. Meghan needs the time away from the hospital.''

''She's all right, then?''

''She's wonderful.''

''Good.'' Tracy's gaze kept moving from the shopping boxes and bags to Kate's face and then back to Cullen. He could almost see the cogs turning in her brain, trying to size up Kate's potential to hold him, wondering exactly how serious he was about her and probably concluding that they were sleeping together, since he was buying her clothes. Cullen had no intention of satisfying her curiosity. Let her think what she would.

''Here's the blouse, Ms. Cunningham,'' Chyna said.

Cullen could have kissed her. ''We won't keep you, Tracy,'' he said, the epitome of politeness as he took Kate's arm. ''We really have to run. The family is descending on us tomorrow, and we have some other stops to make.''

''Oh!'' Tracy said, with a little moue of disappointment. ''I was hoping we could catch up on what's been going on with your life over lunch.''

''Another time,'' Cullen said. ''Ready, Kate?''

She nodded.

He started toward the door.

"It was good seeing you," Tracy said, though the considering glint in her eyes said otherwise.

"You, too," he replied, with a wave. As Kate preceded him from the store, he realized that lying could become habit-forming.

Chapter Seven

Neither Kate nor Cullen spoke as they made their way to the car. She kept thinking of the expression in his eyes when he'd introduced her as the new woman in his life. She'd have to tell Greg what a fantastic job Cullen had done with his role. If she hadn't known he was playing a part, she might have believed that the tenderness she'd seen on his face was the real thing. Following the kiss, it had been very convincing. But she knew from experience that just because he could act convincing didn't mean the feelings he projected were real. What counted was that Tracy seemed to find it as persuasive as Kate had.

Tracy. Kate recalled the unexpected feeling of something that closely resembled jealousy when Cullen had introduced the catty woman as an old friend. Okay, it was jealousy. Just how old a friend was Tracy? Had they been an item before or after Joanie? How good a friend had she been?

None of your business, Kate, and don't forget it. Don't start taking this lovey-dovey stuff to heart. You're only playacting, remember?

Tracy didn't know it was all part of the job. What would she tell Cullen's friends about the woman she'd seen him buying clothes for? The thought left Kate with a definitely uncomfortable feeling, which she dismissed. It didn't matter that Cullen's friends might consider her a kept woman. After all, that was the plan.

Recalling the hungry expression in Tracy's eyes as she'd looked Cullen up and down, the jealousy returned. Absurd. Even though they'd shared the most intimate of acts, Kate hardly knew the man. There was no way the animosity she felt for Tracy Cunningham could be jealousy—could it?

She glanced at Cullen, who was looking out the side window. He was definitely a handsome man, and it was clear that he didn't like the situation any more than she did. But what she was doing was necessary, and she needed to do her best to make it as stress free as possible. For instance, Cullen had just dropped a bundle on some clothes for her, and she hadn't been appropriately thankful for his generosity, something she needed to correct.

"Thank you for the clothes." The words were right, but the tone was definitely stilted.

"My pleasure. The gown is sensational on you. You'll knock 'em dead at the gallery."

Kate experienced a little thrill of pleasure and no small amount of surprise at the compliment. "I'll settle for not embarrassing you."

"No chance of that."

Again, the unexpected praise took her by surprise. She

flicked him a glance and saw that he was regarding her with a brooding expression in his eyes.

"I hate that we ran into Tracy," he said, leaning his head against the seat. "God knows what she'll tell people, but there's no sense fretting about it. There's nothing we can do to stop her."

"No." She gave him another sideways glance.

"What?"

"How good a friend was Tracy Cunningham, anyway?"

Kate sighed. She hadn't meant to ask the question. It just sort of slipped out. So much for good intentions.

"Not as good as she'd like to have been."

"Could that have been because you led her to believe things were more than they were?" Kate asked, trying to draw a parallel to her own experience with Cullen.

"I never led her on, if that's what you're asking." His voice had taken on a definite chill. He turned his head to look out the side window.

"Did you sleep with her?"

Glancing over again, she saw his chest rise in a sigh. He cut his gaze back to her. Before she returned her attention to the traffic, she saw the amusement in the cobalt depths of his eyes. "What's the matter, Kate? Jealous?"

Kate forced a laugh. "Curious."

"I know you don't think I'm the most honest man in the world, but give me some credit. The woman is a piranha. She didn't take kindly to my rejection."

Relieved, Kate concentrated on her driving. If she kept her mouth shut, maybe they could make it home without coming to blows. She'd think about something else.

"Did you have to kiss me in the boutique?" Again,

the unplanned question spilled from her lips without her meaning it to.

From the corner of her eye, she saw him lift his good shoulder in a negligent shrug. "It seemed like the appropriate thing to do under the circumstances. We are supposed to convince the world that we're a couple."

"I know. I just..." Her voice trailed away. What could she say that wouldn't give away her feelings?

"I know it may be tough on you, but it's part of the job, so you'll just have to grin and bear it. Actually, if I remember correctly, you used to like my kissing you." There was no denying the mockery in his voice.

Kate flicked him a startled glance. It was the first time he'd deliberately brought up their New Orleans relationship. Unable to think of a snappy comeback, she kept her gaze on the traffic. She'd liked them, all right. That was the problem. And she suspected he knew it.

"Hungry?" Cullen asked out of the blue.

Kate was hungry, but she wasn't sure she was up to making conversation over lunch, especially with her mind in such turmoil. Still, why not? There was no difference in sitting with Cullen in a restaurant or a car.

"I could eat something," she said.

"I know a good Italian place."

"Fine."

He gave her directions to the nearest restaurant, and Kate did her best to concentrate on getting them there in one piece instead of thinking about Tracy Cunningham or the way her heart raced when Cullen had kissed her.

Cullen couldn't rake up much sympathy for Kate's feelings of dismay when he was having his own problems with the kiss and his reaction to it. There had been women since New Orleans. Not a lot, but some. Pretty women. Sweet women. Willing women. Women who were often chosen because something about them reminded him of his dead wife, chosen in hopes that they could erase the guilt and fill the emptiness inside him, chosen in an effort to wipe out the memories of a red-haired enchantress. None had.

Kate was no clone of his dead wife. She was like no woman he'd ever known. An original. He'd known it the first time he'd seen her. If he compared Kate to other women, he'd have to say they were wired for 110, while she was 220. Sweet and proper ladies as opposed to pure, raw woman. She'd angered him in New Orleans. Irritated him. Impressed him. Yet somehow, without even trying, she'd made him want to embrace life again before he'd felt he should. And now, here she was, back in his life, making the past two years seem lifeless and insipid, making him want to experience everything he knew life had to offer.

Maybe it's knowing that someone wants to end your life that is suddenly making you feel so unfulfilled. Maybe. Maybe it was the combination of that and Kate's arrival. All he knew was that the moment he kissed her in the boutique, he knew he had never stopped wanting her. Even though he suspected that she might feel the same way, he knew he'd have a heck of a time breaking down the barriers she'd erected between them. Kate Labiche wasn't the kind of woman who would give a man a second chance to make a fool of her...even if his leaving had been prompted by his sense of self-preservation.

Kate didn't know how Cullen fared throughout the night, but she hardly slept a wink. Feeling his lips on hers brought back memories she'd tried hard to forget. That, combined with the knowledge that she was jealous of his old girlfriends, made her realize that becoming part of Cullen's life had put her heart in jeopardy, just as she'd feared.

She had loved Lane with all her heart, and his defection and the ultimate divorce had devastated her. Cullen had come into her life before the ink had dried on the divorce papers, and, though he wasn't the kind of man she usually went for, she'd been unable to resist his advances. He was handsome and polished, far too pretty. Kate liked her men more rugged—men's men. He was a public figure; she liked her privacy. He had been raised rich; her background was one of hardworking, middle-class values in a home where self-employment often meant chicken one day and feathers the next.

But he'd wanted her and, at the time, that had been of vital importance, since she was feeling less than desirable and needed to bolster her feelings of self-esteem, which Lane's demand for a divorce had trampled in the dust. She'd needed to know she was still attractive, desirable. Wanted. Cullen had made her feel all that. For a few days.

Since then, he had been the only man to get close to her. Their brief ill-timed affair coming so close on the heels of her divorce had pretty much been the defining moment of her life. She dated infrequently and always made it clear that she was looking for neither a one-night stand nor a serious relationship. She was more of a dinner-and-movie kind of date. It was simpler to lead a more or less monastic life than to engage and disengage oneself from a string of relationships. Kisses had become rare in her life, which she knew was part of the problem.

The kiss was just a ploy, Kate. He needed to make your relationship look like the real thing for Chyna and for Tracy. It's all part of the game. He said so himself.

She knew that maintaining the illusion of a serious relationship was critical to their plan of protection, she'd known the risk to her heart when she accepted the job. Somehow, she hadn't expected things to become so intense so quickly. She was smart enough to realize that it would only get worse the longer the deception continued. But she'd taken the job, and she had no alternative but to see it through.

Oh, you have options, Kate. You could pack up and leave. Her psyche called her a chicken for not doing just that, but the other half of her argued that Cullen truly did need protection and that it would be a character-building exercise to stay, endure and overcome. Right. Considering the potential for her to come out of the whole thing with a broken heart, it was a pitiful argument, but for the moment, she had no intention of packing her bags and heading back to Louisiana.

The night wore on. She took a shower and washed her hair and sat in a chair near the window and looked at the moonlit night, imagining Cullen's enemy on the loose and trying to visualize a potential attack. Where might the man hide? The outbuildings? The ground-hugging magnolia tree? What would her first reaction be?

Kate knew she was borrowing trouble, something Aunt Lou had warned against from her childhood. Unless you were a novelist, playing what-if was an exercise in futility. Finally, sometime in the wee hours of the morning, she managed to forget the threat and the kiss and succumbed to the welcome embrace of Morpheus.

Kate slapped the snooze button when the alarm went off at seven and didn't open her eyes until almost eight. She was usually finishing breakfast by now. Thankful she'd showered during the night, she splashed cold water on her face, brushed her teeth, clipped back her hair and pulled on a sweatshirt and a pair of jeans, longing for a few more hours' sleep. Her aunt and Cullen's family would be arriving soon. Life would be hectic the next few days.

Greg was in the kitchen putting some dishes in the dishwasher when she entered the kitchen, which was filled with the wonderful aroma of cinnamon and apples. Cullen was nowhere to be seen.

Greg smiled at her over his shoulder. "'Bout time you came down," he drawled. "If you'd slept any longer, the sun would've warped your ribs."

"I had a rough night."

"It happens. How about some of my cinnamon-walnut waffles with maple syrup and warm applesauce on the side?"

"That sounds wonderful," she said, taking a mug from the cabinet and pouring herself a cup of coffee. "Where's Cullen?"

"He ate and went to get the paper."

The house was too far from the main road for the paper to be thrown in the yard, but there was a tube next to the mailbox on the highway for the carrier. The problem was that the tube was half a mile from the house.

"You let him go alone?" Kate asked, aghast.

Greg shrugged and picked up the bowl of batter. "I asked him if he thought it was a good idea, and he told me he was a grown man and didn't need a baby-sitter to fetch the paper. Said the walk would do him good."

Muttering something uncomplimentary about men and their macho inclinations, Kate slammed her mug onto the tabletop, sloshing the hot liquid over the edge.

"I heard that," Greg said with a mock ferocious narrowing of his eyes.

"Then you know I'm right," she said, wiping her hand on the leg of her jeans.

"I never argue with a woman who carries a gun."

"Smart man," Kate said, heading for the door. "Smarter than our boss, anyway. I have to go after him."

"I'm parked behind you, but the keys are in my truck. Hey!" he called to her retreating figure. "Does this mean you don't want any waffles?"

"Hold them until I get back," she yelled from the hallway.

"Will do."

Kate hit the front door running. As he'd said, Greg's keys were in his truck. She started the engine, backed up until she could turn around, then barreled down the gravel road that led to the highway. She rounded a curve and saw Cullen just ahead of her. He had the paper in hand and was walking toward the house.

She braked to a stop alongside him, slinging gravel and fishtailing slightly before straightening out the Ford. She threw the gearshift into park, and without bothering to shut off the engine wrenched open the door and leaped from the truck. Only then did she see the panicked expression on Cullen's face.

"What's wrong?" he asked, transferring the paper to his sling hand and gripping her upper arm with the other.

"What's wrong!" she cried, jerking free. "Someone out there wants you dead and you just decide to go off on your own? That makes it pretty hard for me to do my job."

Cullen didn't say anything for long seconds. She saw the concern in his eyes turn to anger, saw his lips thin and the muscle in his jaw knot. "I'm perfectly safe."

She planted her hands on her hips. "Are you?"

"No one knows where I am."

"That we know of." There was no compromise in her expression or her tone.

Cullen switched the paper to his good hand and slapped it against his jean-clad thigh in frustration. "I feel like a damn prisoner."

"Unfortunately, that pretty well sums up the situation." When he had no ready comeback, she gestured toward the truck. "Get in. I'll drive you back to the house."

Cullen fumed all the way to the house, occasionally giving Kate a look that, if it could kill, would have sent her to the grave. By the time they pulled in front of the house, his temper had cooled enough for him to realize she was right, which sent his frustration level to an all-time high.

When they entered the kitchen, sensing the tension between them, Greg remained silent and set about pouring the waffle batter into the iron. Without a word, Kate sat down and cupped her coffee mug between her palms, her attitude daring anyone to say something to her.

Ignoring her as best he could, Cullen unbanded the paper, abandoning the front pages for the section containing Arkansas news. It didn't take long for him to find what he was looking for, what he'd hoped he wouldn't find.

"Prosecutor Possible Victim." The headlines pretty much said it all. He read the offering anyway.

An anonymous source came forward yesterday with information that sheds doubt on the Clark County sheriff's office's presumption that the recent hunting accident involving Little Rock prosecutor Cullen McGyver was accidental. Authorities are checking out the information before officially changing their position on the case. In another unrelated development, it has been learned that Prosecutor McGyver is recuperating at his family ranch.

The article went on to recap the events surrounding the shooting and Cullen's attempt to drive himself to the hospital. It ended with the note that his success at putting law violators away had no doubt made several enemies. He swore.

"What?" Kate asked, looking up sharply.

Cullen folded the section of newspaper into quarters and handed it to her. "Lower right-hand corner."

Kate read the piece and looked at Cullen as if to say I told you so, even though she refrained from vocalizing the thought.

"Anyone with average intelligence can find out where you are with a little digging around," she said.

"I'm aware of that." His tone was sharper than he intended, but Kate seemed unfazed by it. Cullen scraped back his chair and poured himself some more coffee.

Greg set a plate filled with a waffle and some sausage patties in front of Kate, who reached for the bowl of warm applesauce. "May I?" he asked, indicating the paper.

"Sure," she said, handing him the newspaper.

The phone rang, and Cullen, who was nearest, reached for it. "McGyver."

"Hi." Meghan.

"Hi, yourself," he said, feeling his mood lighten perceptibly. "What's up?"

"Have you seen the paper?"

"Yeah, we just read it," he told her.

"Do you have any idea who could have given out any information about the accident?"

"None," Cullen said, leaning against the cabinet top. "I might be wrong, but the part about me recuperating at the ranch probably came from Tracy Cunningham."

"Tracy Cunningham?"

"Yeah. Kate and I ran into her yesterday at Chyna's while we were looking for a gown for Kate to wear to the art show. Tracy had heard about the accident and asked where I'd been keeping myself. I tried to prevaricate by saying we were spending Thanksgiving at the ranch."

Meghan groaned.

"I know. She'd like nothing better than to cause me misery, but since she had no idea that I'm in hiding, she probably just made an innocent comment to one of her cronies and by the end of the day, it wound up in some media person's hands. There's nothing we can do about it."

"I suppose not," Meghan said. "The same story was on one of the local TV channels, with a bit of a twist."

"What kind of twist?"

"Whoever talked knew about the brake line and had figured out how slim the chances are of your being shot the way you were."

Cullen was silent while he thought about that. Finally he said, "Maybe you and Dan should stay at home for Thanksgiving. Things could get rough here, if the perp decides to head this way."

He heard Meghan sigh. "We'll take our chances. No way this guy is going to ruin my holiday." She sighed again. "I hate to add to your burden, but Lucy left a message on your machine, too."

Cullen mouthed a silent curse and pinched the bridge of his nose. "What does she want?"

"She says Dub is going to get a lawyer."

"Wonderful! No!" he said, stopping her when she started to tell him something else. "I don't want to hear it right now. It would be next to impossible to do anything before the holiday, anyway. Just bring that tape, too, and we'll see if we can figure out what to do. Since I can't talk you out of coming, what time should we expect you?"

"As soon as I can get Lindsay and Marley up and around. We should be there by noon."

"Good. We'll see you then. Be careful driving down."

"We will. You be careful, too."

Cullen heard the worry in her voice. "Always."

He turned off the phone before she could say anything else. "That was Meghan," he said unnecessarily. "She said that the same story was on the news this morning but with details that seemed to disprove the accident theory."

"What kind of details?" Kate asked, pushing her plate aside.

"My whereabouts at the time of the shooting. The fact that the brake line was cut."

"But who would say anything?" Greg asked.

"Who knows?" Kate said. "It could be anyone with access to the information. No matter how hard you try to keep the lid on something, someone invariably talks."

Cullen sighed. She was right. All it took was for one person to let their feelings be known about a subject, and the next thing you knew, there was a full-fledged investigation or scandal afoot. All too familiar with the workings of the media, he expected more speculation about the incident before the day was over. The newshounds had been thrown a bone, and now they smelled blood. It was just a matter of time before someone else thought of some other tidbit or seemingly innocent fact, and like a nasty fungus, the whole thing would mushroom out of control. That's when the real fun would begin.

"So what do you think?" he asked.

"I think it's amazing that someone didn't say something sooner," Kate told him.

Cullen turned to face her. "This is going to impact the investigation, isn't it?

"To some degree. The sheriff will continue to do whatever it is he's doing," she said. "And so will you and I. The only damage that's really done is that now the perp has a general idea where you are and that we're on to him. There's nothing we can do about the former, unless you want to move somewhere else."

"No, thank you."

She nodded. "There are two possible reactions he might have now that he knows we know this is for real."

"What?"

"You tell me."

Though her refusal to speculate irritated him, Cullen realized why she did it. He was relying too much on her take of the situation and had stopped thinking for himself, which had been fine at first, while he was in pain and unable to think straight. But he was growing stronger every day, and it was time he stopped reacting to what was happening to him and started putting himself in a more active, defensive role.

"If he knows the cops are looking for him, he might assume that I'll be more aware of what's going on around me, more prepared to act. He might even think I have some sort of protection from the police. Taking all that into consideration, he might decide it's too risky to make another attempt on my life, even though he knows the cops don't have any concrete evidence.''

"Right."

''The other scenario is that he's fully aware of all this and too angry or crazy to care about anything but taking me out. So he keeps coming.''

''Very good, counselor,'' Kate said with a slight smile. ''We have to be prepared for either contingency. We do have the edge on him in one way.''

''What's that?'' Cullen asked.

''He has no idea that a woman is your protection.''

''True. And right now, other than to pinpoint exactly where I'm staying, he and the media have found out all there is to know.''

Kate laughed, a short, humorless sound. ''You should know better than to shortchange the media. What else did Meghan say?'' Kate asked. ''What tape did you want her to bring?''

''She thought she should check my messages again this morning on her way to work—just in case. There was nothing from the man, but there was a message from Lucy Lambert.''

Cullen could almost see the wheels turning inside Kate's pretty head. She cast a look at Greg and then met Cullen's gaze. He gave an imperceptible shake of his head.

''Oh,'' she said noncommittally. ''When are they coming?''

Cullen looked at the older man, who was fixing himself a plate. If Greg sensed that he was deliberately being cut out of the information loop, he didn't let it show.

''She said they'd be here by noon,'' Cullen said in answer to Kate's question. ''But knowing the girls, they may not manage it. What about Louella?''

"She said she'd be here early this morning," Kate told him. "I think she wants to make some pies and bake the cornbread for her dressing or something."

Greg, who hadn't taken kindly to the idea of someone coming to share KP duties with him for the holiday, muttered something under his breath.

"What did you say?" Cullen asked.

Greg turned to face them. "No offense, Kate. I'm sure your aunt is a fine woman, but I'm not sure this kitchen is big enough for us both."

"She is a fine woman," Kate said. "And I'm sure the two of you will get along with no problems."

"Maybe I should just stay at home."

"No way," Cullen said emphatically. "You're not going to spend Thanksgiving by yourself. You're a reasonable man, and Louella is as good as gold. The two of you will get along just fine." Cullen pushed himself away from the cabinets. "I'm going to go call the sheriff's department and see why they haven't been keeping me informed about what's going on. And yes, before you ask, I promise not to leave the house without telling you. Or should I say that I won't leave without asking permission?"

"Say whatever you want," Kate said. "Just make sure you do it."

He sketched a little salute. "Yes ma'am."

Kate watched him leave the room, then jumped up and followed him into the hallway. "Cullen!"

He turned.

"What about Lucy Lambert?"

"Her message said she needed to talk to me. Dub is going to get an attorney."

Kate blew out a frustrated breath. "For what purpose?"

"I don't know. I told Meg I didn't want to hear about it until they get here."

"Right. No sense ruining the whole day." She stood thoughtfully for a moment. "I'm wondering if there's someplace I can go to get in a little target practice."

"Target practice?"

"Yeah, target practice. I like to stay sharp."

"Now?"

"If you don't mind," she said, nodding. "Considering that word is out that someone is out to get you, I'd feel better with a few rounds under my belt."

"Okay," he said, nodding. "Let me call and chew on the sheriff's department for a while, then I'll take you to a good spot."

"How long?"

"I'll meet you at the car in about ten minutes."

True to his word, he joined her ten minutes later and they headed for a remote corner of the ranch. Cullen, who had overcome Kate's objections to his going along with the argument that he wasn't doing anything anyway, sat in the passenger seat while she drove.

"What did the sheriff's department say?" she asked.

"The usual song and dance that they were working all their leads but they didn't have anything new to offer so they hadn't called. They were sorry someone squealed to the media, but that might be a good thing, since the perp might feel the pressure and slip up."

"Yada, yada, yada," Kate said.

"Exactly."

"Where are we going?" Kate asked.

"To an old gravel pit."

Cullen explained that when the rock had given out twenty years earlier, his dad had done his best to repair the wounded earth, moving dirt, filling in, planting trees and grass for pasture.

"Has the land been in your family a long time?" Kate said, wanting to learn more about this man who'd breached her defenses so easily.

"Since right after the Civil War," Cullen said. "The house we're living in is over a hundred years old. According to the records we have it only cost five hundred dollars to build."

"You've got to be kidding!"

"That was a fortune back then," Cullen said.

Without meaning to, he'd reminded her of the difference in their social and financial backgrounds.

"Oil money, right?" Kate said and heard the edge in her voice.

Cullen gave her a thoughtful look. "Back then it was timber. The oil came later."

"What's it like being raised with money?"

"I wouldn't know. I wasn't aware that we had any until I was a teenager. Meghan and I were brought up right here and we lived a fairly simple life. Oh, we had horses to ride and we may have had more new clothes when school started, but my parents loved this place and the people, and they'd have died before they did anything to alienate themselves and us from the people around us."

"Not ones to put on the dog, huh?"

"Definitely not. What about you?" Cullen asked. "What was it like being raised in the city?"

"I grew up in an apartment. The area wasn't bad, but it wasn't the best, either. I saw my share of the ugly things people do. My mom and dad put everything they had into getting the restaurant up and running, and almost every penny they made went back into it so they could make it better, bigger, more what the tourists wanted. My mom died when I was ten. The following year a dish washer my dad had fired came back after hours and set fire to the restaurant, which was sort of a mixed blessing.''

''How's that?''

''We were always insurance poor. As terrible as it was to lose everything, it enabled him to build a bigger, better place.''

''And the other part of the mixed blessing?''

''That's what made me decide to go into law enforcement.''

''And where is the dish washer now?'' Cullen asked.

''He died in prison from a heart attack.''

''Your dad's place is certainly a success now.''

''It isn't Commander's Palace, but he does okay.''

Cullen saw the tilt of her chin. No wonder she was so proud and prickly, he thought. She'd had to scrabble for everything that had ever come her way. And no doubt her hardcase attitude came from living in a hard world. Better to get your bluff in before someone beat you to it…or beat you up.

''Take a right here,'' he said. The road, little more than a rutted path that wound through some trees, led to a huge hilly pasture where young horses munched on sprigs of still-green grass.

''This was a gravel pit?'' Kate asked.

''Yeah.''

The results weren't bad. There was a large, extremely deep, irregularly shaped pond bordered here and there with stands of pine and the more slow-growing oak trees. It was a pretty spot, and in another ten years it would look even more natural.

''He did a good job,'' Kate said, nodding in approval.

"I think so. The pond is stocked with catfish and bass, if you like fishing."

"Never been. I was raised on concrete, remember?"

"Then we'll have to do that one afternoon."

"Sounds fun."

"Are you going to make me bait your hooks?" he joked.

"From the looks of your arm, I may be baiting yours." She shot the words back with a smile. It occurred to Cullen that it was the first time since she'd arrived that they were both behaving in a normal way. The first time the past hadn't intruded.

She pointed to a ridge of hills, some man-made, some natural, all of them providing a perfect place to set up a target. "Is this where you had in mind?"

Cullen nodded. The lady was definitely all business. He watched as she set up a series of three traditional paper targets and walked to where he stood.

"Let's back up some," she said. Approximately twenty yards from the target, she stopped, took a weapon from the waistband of her jeans and slammed in a magazine.

"A Glock?" Cullen teased, wanting to hold on to the easiness of the moment. "I thought an old cop like you would prefer a .38."

"Times change," she said, assuming a shooter's stance and taking a couple of slow, easy breaths. "Not enough stopping power, especially if you're up against someone hopped up on drugs. And the Glock's lighter. Even with a loaded seventeen-round magazine, it weighs less than two pounds."

Before Cullen could reply, she got off six fast rounds. The trio of weanlings grazing in the pasture bolted in fright, running at breakneck speed and skidding to a stop just inches before they would have crashed into the fence that banded the gravel road. Kate turned slightly, shot six more times then finished the last target with five remaining shots.

Cullen was still reeling from the quick decisiveness of her actions when she lowered her arms, shook back her hair in an unintentionally provocative gesture and said, "You want to make yourself useful and go check and see how I did?"

"Sure."

Too stunned by the professionalism of her performance to be offended, he crossed the grassy expanse. None of the shots was outside a four-inch circle. He was impressed by her skill and pleased that she was on his side. If she'd been the one to target him in the woods, he wouldn't be standing there.

He looked at her standing in the middle of the pasture, legs slightly apart, her long red hair blowing in the slight breeze and her tall, slender body encased in jeans and a sweater. She looked more like a college girl than like a woman who could nail a man at seventy feet.

At that moment, he wanted nothing more than to go to her and kiss her, to force her to the ground and make love to her. But that would only lead to more trouble. He sighed and picked up the targets. What was it about a challenge he found so fascinating?

"Well?" she said, when he was a few feet away.

Cullen held up one of the bull's-eyes so she could see the results of her handiwork. "He's dead."

There was a flicker of something in her eyes he couldn't define. Her smile was brief, cool. Satisfied. "Good."

Chapter Eight

As he did every morning before going off to his pitiful, demeaning excuse for a job, the man watched the morning news, hoping, praying for a bit of information he could use as a sign. So far, nothing. When the image of the pretty dark-haired anchor's face was replaced with a commercial for a jewelry store, he switched channels on the off chance there was something on another station.

The man ran his fingertip along the top of a small framed photo of a smiling woman. He'd loved her so much, but Cullen McGyver had ruined everything. She was gone—everything he held dear was gone. He couldn't get it back, and it was all McGyver's fault. What was it the Bible said? An eye for an eye? It was past time for McGyver to pay.

"In a late-breaking story about the Cullen McGyver shooting, Miles Gentry is outside a hospital in Arkadelphia with a nurse who was there when the Little Rock prosecutor was admitted. Miles?''

The anchorwoman's voice brought the man back from the pain of his memories. Wearing an expression of wary anticipation, he reached for the remote control to turn up the volume. Miles Gentry, a polished-looking young man no doubt straight out of college, was talking to a young-ish woman outside the hospital. The name that flashed onto the bottom of the screen said Sara Jerome, LPN. Under the careful guidance of the reporter, it was established that the nurse had indeed been on duty when Cullen McGyver had been brought to the emergency room.

When asked if she believed the shooting was accidental, the nurse expressed reservations. At the reporter's urging, she sketched a few specifics about where Cullen was at the time of the shooting, the trajectory of the bullet and the fact that it was quite a coincidence that of all the woods around, the bullet had found possibly the only human target in the area.

''So under those circumstances, you feel it more likely that the shooting was intentional?'' Miles probed.

''Let me just say that I've seen a lot of hunting accidents and a couple of hunting-related deaths. Something about this just doesn't feel right.''

The reporter thanked the woman, and they cut back to the station.

Encouraged, the man from the woods switched to his original channel. The commercial had ended, and some-one in the field was interviewing a young man who didn't look as if he was over nineteen years old. The man was an employee from Buddy's Maintenance and Repair, who told the reporter that he'd helped repair Cullen

McGyver's Jeep and that the brake line had definitely been cut.

My, my, everyone was talking suddenly.

The reporter, this one a young woman, thanked the young man and told the camera that Buddy Perkins, the owner of the auto repair shop, had declined to comment. She went on to say that this information had caused the sheriff's department to take another look at the shooting accident that had taken place nine days earlier.

"And, from another source, we've learned that Cullen McGyver, who dropped out of sight after being released from the hospital, has been recuperating at his family's ranch in southwest Arkansas."

The man sat up straighter. He wished he could push rewind and replay that last bit of information, just to make certain he'd heard correctly. Cullen McGyver at his family's ranch? The man began to laugh, shaking his head in disbelief. Oh, this was too rich! While he had fretted and stewed over McGyver's whereabouts, he'd been right under his nose.

The reporter ended the segment with a commentary about Cullen's string of successful convictions and his possible bid for a senate seat in the next year's election. The man wiped his eyes on the sleeve of his shirt. After all this time, someone had finally put two and two together and come up with the right answer. The fact that the law now suspected foul play turned the heat up on him a little, gave more of a sense of urgency to the situation. On the other hand, he knew where McGyver was. That one morsel of information balanced out the fact that for all intents and purposes, he himself was now a hunted man.

* * *

When Cullen and Kate returned from her shooting practice, Cullen went to his room to rest until lunch. Kate was glad to see him go, though she suspected that his retreat had more to do with putting some distance between them than with his needing to rest. He was getting stronger by the day, thank goodness.

Needing something to occupy her until everyone arrived, she headed for the kitchen to see if she could help Greg. She was just coming down the stairs when she heard a car door slam. Kate opened the front door to see Louella striding up the walk, a wide smile on her face. Her aunt looked pretty in tan jeans and a Thanksgiving sweatshirt she'd decorated herself.

"You should have called to tell me you were leaving so I'd be here in case you needed me," Kate chided.

"My car is in excellent condition, and I have my cell phone." Louella gave Kate a conciliatory hug. "But thanks for being concerned."

"Come on into the kitchen and meet Greg. I think I heard him come back from the grocery store a few minutes ago.

"Greg? He's the doctor, right?" Louella said, falling into step with Kate.

"Retired," Kate corrected. "He's a widower and a darn good cook."

Louella's forehead puckered into a frown. "Is he territorial about the kitchen?"

Kate thought it wiser not to mention Greg's reservations. She had enough problems without that. Let the two cooks slug it out. "I guess we'll just have to see, won't we?" she said, smiling.

Greg was popping an iron skillet filled with golden

cornbread into the oven when they entered the kitchen. "I see you're back," Kate said.

"Bruised and battered but back," he said, as he closed the oven door. "I don't know what in the heck gets into women when they go to the grocery store. They get macho and militant. Some woman actually tried to grab a dozen eggs out of my hands." He turned, and when his gaze lighted on Louella, his smile faded and his color rose.

Uh-oh. "Greg, this is my aunt, Louella Stephens." Kate turned toward her aunt and saw that Louella had that narrowed-eye look she adopted when she was in serious contemplation about a person or situation. "Aunt Lou, this is Greg Kingsley. He's our temporary cook and fill-in physician."

Surprisingly, Aunt Lou's plump features split into a wide smile as she extended her hand. "It's a pleasure to meet you, Greg."

Gentleman that he was, Greg had no choice but to take her proffered hand. Louella covered his hand with both of hers. "I understand that we'll have kitchen duty together for the next couple of days, and I just want you to know that I think it's a generous man who'll let someone into his prized domain. And I promise not to grab anything out of your hands."

"I...well, I, uh...," Greg stammered.

Clearly embarrassed at her aunt having heard his harangue about women shoppers and surprised by her meeting the potential problem head-on, Greg was at a loss for words for the first time since Kate had met him.

Aunt Lou beamed at him. "All joking aside, I promise to stay out of your way as much as possible," she said, sketching an *X* over her heart. "And I must say your reputation precedes you. I'm hoping to pick up a few tips while I'm here.''

''Oh, well, it's very kind of you to say so, Louella, but I doubt if I can teach you anything, and I don't think we'll have a problem at all sharing the kitchen,'' Greg said.

Kate coughed to hide a smile. What else could he say? Aunt Lou, who looked prettier and younger than any woman her age had a right to, had disarmed him as effectively as an explosions expert defusing a bomb. She'd confronted the problem, offered a sincere apology for any inconvenience the situation might cause and flattered him, all in one fell swoop. For Greg to have responded in any other way would have made him look like a churlish lout.

''Please,'' her aunt said, releasing his hand with a little pat. ''Call me Lou.'' She sniffed. ''Is that vegetable soup I smell?''

''It is.''

''Mm,'' Louella said. ''One of my favorites. Especially with cornbread.''

''I hope you like it.''

''I'm sure I will.'' Louella glanced at the cabinet top where various and sundry Thanksgiving necessities sat waiting. ''Is there anything I can do to help?''

The bemused expression in Greg's eyes disappeared beneath a sudden show of competence. ''Oh, no!'' he said, waving her and the offer aside. ''It's too close to lunch to start anything. Besides, you're a guest. Just have a seat. Would you like some coffee? I made a fresh pot when I got back from the store.''

''That would be lovely,'' Louella told him with another of those wide smiles.

If Kate hadn't known the crusty doctor better, she'd have sworn he blushed. Aunt Lou had him rattled. He'd gone from speechlessness to chattering. She watched as he poured her aunt a cup of coffee, fetched the half-and-half from the fridge and a spoon from the drawer.

"Thank you, Greg," Louella said with another of those winsome smiles. She doctored her coffee and gave her full attention to Kate who had to get her own coffee. "When are Meghan and Dan arriving?"

"They said they'd be here by lunchtime," Kate said.

"Wonderful. It's been ages since I've seen the girls."

"Do you have kids, Lou?" Greg asked.

"Unfortunately, my late husband, Bert, and I were never able to have children," she said. "Kate's the daughter we never had." She reached out and gave Kate's hand a pat. "And no one could ask for a better one."

"I can believe that," Greg said, to Kate's surprise.

"What about you, Greg?"

"I have a son in the military. He's stationed in Alaska. My daughter lives here, but she's with her husband's family for the holiday, so you all got stuck with me."

"Stuck with you!" Louella said. "Hardly. I think you'll be a wonderful addition to our gathering."

No wonder Cullen valued her aunt as an employee, Kate thought. Talk about the iron fist in the velvet glove! Her aunt was priceless. Wonderful. And unless Kate's intuition was entirely off base, Greg thought so, too.

Forty minutes later, there was a commotion at the front door, the sound of girlish voices announcing the arrival of Meghan and her family. Cullen, who heard the disturbance, came downstairs and ushered them to the kitchen where there was the usual flurry of hellos and introductions.

Meghan's husband, Dan, was big and burly and looked like a prizefighter. In reality he was a successful accountant who had been on the college boxing team. Their daughters, Lindsay and Marley, thirteen and fifteen respectively, were pretty, vivacious and outgoing.

After lunch, the girls saddled up a couple of the mares and headed off to explore the ranch. Dan carried in the luggage and went to watch the last of a football game. Kate and Cullen planned to go to the library to listen to the tapes Meghan had brought from Cullen's answering machine.

"Enjoy," she said in a wry tone as she handed the tapes to Kate.

"Aren't you staying?" Cullen asked.

Meghan shook her head. "I promised Dan I'd watch the game with him. Oh! I almost I forgot! He saw some coverage on at least two stations while I was in the shower this morning."

"Anything new?" Kate asked.

"Yeah," Meghan said, nodding. "One reporter was talking to a kid who works for Buddy who said the brake line had been cut, and the other was interviewing a trauma nurse at the hospital who supposedly had reservations about your shoulder wound even before the story about the brakes hit the news. Dan can tell you more about it." Her gaze found Cullen's. "I'm getting scared."

"Why?"

"I'm afraid that with all this sudden flurry of interest, some clever news reporter, as well as the creep who wants to hurt you, will dig deep enough to find out where the ranch is.''

Cullen gave her arm a comforting pat. "Kate and I have already discussed that angle. It's just a matter of time, which is why she wanted to do a little target practice.''

"If I thought it was Tracy who blew the whistle, I'd throttle her with my bare hands," Meghan said through gritted teeth.

"No sense crying over spilled milk, sis. The damage is done. The only thing we can do now is be as prepared as possible in case something does come up.''

"I guess you're right." Meghan cocked her head toward Kate, a teasing glint in her eyes. "So how was she as a marksman?" she asked, hoping to lighten the mood.

"Like I told her, if she'd been at the other end of that .308, I wouldn't be here to tell about it.''

"I like hearing that," Meghan said.

"It was a comforting sight," Cullen admitted. He brushed his sister's cheek with a kiss. "Stop worrying and go watch the game. I'm in good hands.''

"Yeah, I think you are," Meghan said. With another smile, she turned and left the room.

Cullen turned to Kate, a considering gleam in his eyes that made her uncomfortable.

"Shall we listen to the tapes?" she said, turning and heading for the library. "All this flattery will go to my head.''

They listened to the first tape, hoping to find some clue as to who the anonymous caller might be. The man's voice was soft, controlled, his message without emotion either in content or delivery. Kate's first reaction was that he was what was generally considered an organized criminal, one who methodically planned and executed his crime, giving considerable thought to leaving as few clues as possible. This theory was carried further by the man's seeming willingness to play a waiting game.

They played the tape a second time, and Kate heard a background noise she had missed before. "What's that?"

"What?" Cullen asked.

She backed up the tape and they listened again.

"It sounds like a horse whinnying in the distance."

"You're right. It does," Cullen said, a glimmer of excitement in his blue eyes. "Does this mean our guy lives on a horse ranch?"

"It might," Kate said, tempering her own thrill of discovery with prudence. "I'll check all the names on our list and see if any of them have an association with any place that might have horses." She shrugged. "Then, of course, there's the off chance the tape picked up something from TV."

"Do you have to be so practical?" Cullen asked.

"Just playing devil's advocate."

"And doing a darn good job of it." He played the message again, his forehead furrowed in concentration. "The voice sounds familiar."

"It probably is," Kate told him. "Since we're going on the assumption that the person out to get you is someone who feels you've wronged them in some way, I'd say there's a ninety-nine-percent chance that you've spoken with him on more than one occasion. What's important is whether or not you get a name or face to connect with the voice."

"Sorry," he apologized. "Maybe it'll come to me."

"Let's hope." She put the Lucy Lambert tape into the cassette player. "Let's see what Lucy has to say."

The voice sounded young and nervous. "Cullen. This is Lucy. I called because I thought you should know that I've left Dub. He's gone crazy since he found out about us…and Tyler. He's planning to get a lawyer to hit you up for child support, or as he calls it, reimbursement for five years of child care that came out of his pocket.

"I figured that with your career in high gear with the senate bid and everything, that you'd probably rather stay out of court." There was a pause. "I just thought you'd want to know. And listen, I'm really sorry." There was a click and silence.

Frowning, Cullen stared at the recorder as if he hoped it might spew forth some information that could help them. "Play it again."

Kate crossed her arms and tapped her lips with her index finger as they listened to the message again. When it was finished, she sighed. "When you first told me what was on the tape I thought it was a not-so-subtle blackmail hint. Now I'm not so sure."

"Why?" Cullen asked.

"Listen to her. She sounds as if she's been crying. And she apologizes."

"Why do you think she called, then?" Cullen asked.

"I think she's telling you Dub's plan, but I don't think she's implying that they'll keep quiet and stay out of court if you pay up. Call it a gut feeling, but I think she called to forewarn you, to give you the chance to trump his hand. Instead of calling to extort money, she's warning you."

"We can't know that for sure," Cullen said.

"We can if I ask her. Do you have any idea where she'd go if she left Dub?"

"Probably back to her parents."

"And where is that?" Kate asked.

"I don't know. I always assumed in the Little Rock area. Her name was Newman when I knew her. I guess the thing to do is see if Meghan remembers seeing the name Newman on my caller ID."

"Now you're thinking like a cop," Kate said, a pleased smile on her face.

"Osmosis," he said, returning her smile.

"You haven't been close enough for osmosis," Kate quipped.

"Regrettably."

As soon as the brief exchange was spoken they both realized that they'd passed through some unspoken barrier. As he had at the shooting range, Cullen realized that, trouble or not, he wished there could be more between them, that he'd answered her casual observation with the truth.

The moment passed. Tearing her gaze from him, Kate looked at the notes she was taking. Cullen stood abruptly. "I'll go ask Meghan about the caller ID."

"Good." He was almost at the door when her question stopped him. "What does your gut say? Do you think it's Dub?" Cullen thought about that. "I can't be one hundred percent, but I don't think so. As I remember it, Dub's voice is a lot deeper."

"Hm," Kate said thoughtfully. "There's always the chance that if Dub is the caller, he disguised his voice for the call."

"So I'll see if Lucy is at her dad's, get the number from information, call up the lady and see what she has to say."

"Tell her that you aren't going to be blackmailed and see what her reaction is. And then you tell her you don't think the child is yours and that you want DNA testing done to prove it one way or the other. Set up a time and a doctor's office or hospital to meet at, so you can find out the truth one way or the other.''

Cullen sketched a smart salute that brought a blush to Kate's face. ''Yes, ma'am.'' Then he turned and left the room.

Kate was going over her notes when someone knocked on the door. Louella stood there, a smudge of flour on her cheek, a piece of paper in her hand, which she offered to Kate. ''I hate to bother you, but I just remembered that I have some information about your list of suspects.''

There was a lot to be learned about a suspect through legal channels as well as the various and sundry methods of subterfuge used by P.I.s to get information from unsuspecting friends and relatives. Because of her role as Cullen's office manager, Louella had access to a lot of information most people wouldn't.

''Thanks, Aunt Lou. Have a seat.''

''Oh, I have to get back to my pumpkin pies. I just wanted to give you that.''

''Are you making pecan?''

''Greg is,'' her aunt said. ''His recipe is almost exactly like mine.'' She gave a little wave. ''I hope that helps.''

''I'm sure it will,'' Kate said, watching her aunt disappear down the hall with a bemused smile on her lips. Her aunt and Greg seemed to be getting along just fine. Why couldn't she have that kind of luck with a man? Unbidden came the thought of the easy conversation she and Cullen had had on the way to the old gravel pit, of their brief teasing moment. Maybe she could survive the next few months with no significant damage to her heart.

With a determined effort, Kate pushed thoughts of Cullen from her mind and read the information her aunt had gathered. Michael Mullins, the guy who'd dumped the chemicals into the creek, had been out of prison for three months. So far as anyone could tell he was being a good boy. He'd reconciled with his wife, had a job working for his brother and never missed a meeting with his parole officer. None of which meant that he didn't have some extracurricular activities that might not be so wholesome.

Kate thought about the men on the list. From what Lucy said, her life with Dub was less than idyllic, and he had confronted Cullen. Of all the suspects, it looked like Michael Mullins and Dub Lambert had garnered the dubious title of the guys most likely. At least for now.

Meghan confirmed that the name Richard Newman had indeed been on Cullen's caller ID. Cullen got the number from information and called Lucy's parents' house only to learn from the message on the answering machine that they were gone until late Thursday, which meant there was nothing to be done before the morning following Thanksgiving.

Cullen hung up and passed the information to Kate, who said, "Another case of hurry up and wait."

Cullen was pacing the room when Dan and Meghan stuck their heads in the door. "Game's over," Dan said unnecessarily. "Why the long faces?"

"We can't get hold of Lucy Lambert until Friday."

"Then worry about it then. You two are being far too serious for a holiday."

"Dan's right," Meghan said. "There's no sense in us

all sitting here and wallowing in our misery when we're supposed to be being thankful.''

"What you need is a change of scenery,'' Dan suggested. "A night out. We can go to this little bar I discovered a couple of years ago.''

"This is a dry county—remember? Where is this bar?''

"Just across the line in Louisiana,'' Dan said. "We can have some greasy cheeseburgers and do some country-and-western dancing.'' He pulled Meghan into his arms and took a couple of dance steps. "What do you say?''

"And what about the girls?'' Meghan asked. "Do you think they'll be okay?''

"We'll rent them a couple of movies,'' Dan said. "Louella will be here to keep an eye on them. I can't imagine that the idiot who shot at Cullen would be fool enough to try to come in the house.''

"I agree,'' Kate said. "He's organized, not the type to undertake anything without a lot of planning.''

"The professional has spoken,'' Cullen said. "So, what do you say, Kate? If the girls are safe, is a night out at a little country bar too dangerous for us?''

"I'm sure it will be fine,'' Kate said in a prim voice.

"Good. Count us in,'' Cullen told Dan.

When Lindsay and Marley were approached about the plans for the evening, they had no problem with staying home and watching some chick flicks. Louella was happy to stay with them, saying she had a few more things that needed doing before she stopped for the day, and she was too tired to go gallivanting. Greg agreed with Louella but offered to take the girls to town to pick out their movies while everyone got ready.

Ten minutes later, Greg and the two teenagers were on their way. Kate followed a weary Louella up the stairs.

"So how did you and Greg make out in the kitchen today?"

Louella cast a playful smile over her shoulder. "Well, Greg and I didn't make out in the kitchen, though I must say it crossed my mind a time or two that I might like making out with him."

"Aunt Lou!"

They reached the top of the stairs. "Well, I'm no spring chicken, Katie, but I'm not dead, either," Louella said. "Greg is a very attractive man. And he's smart and funny, and we got along very nicely, thank you. In fact, he's the first man since Bert died who has interested me at all."

"That's good," Kate said. Then added, "I think."

"What does that mean?"

"I was worried about the two of you getting along, now I'm going to have to worry about the kitchen help accusing my aunt of sexual harassment."

Louella gave Kate's arm a playful slap. "Oh, you!" They laughed.

"Do you think Greg returns the feeling?" Kate asked.

The expression in Louella's eyes could be called nothing but smug satisfaction. "I caught him looking at me a couple of times with this sort of...I don't know. The best description might be irritated admiration."

"And what is that, exactly?" Kate asked, placing her hands on her hips.

"Well, he likes me, finds me attractive, but he doesn't like the fact that he does."

Strangely, the explanation made a lot of sense to Kate. The feeling her aunt described was exactly how she felt about Cullen.

Cullen, Kate, Dan and Meghan piled into the Longstreets' SUV and drove the twenty-odd miles to the Midnight Cowboy. The club was loud, dimly lit and smoke-filled. Kate felt as if she'd stepped back in time. Certainly to a time before you were asked whether you preferred smoking or nonsmoking. People—both men and women—were clad in boots and Wranglers, the signature brand of the true cowboy. No hip-hugger bell-bottom jeans here.

They found a table near the back of the room, not far from the jukebox that was cranking out something by Trisha Yearwood. Cullen who after getting Meghan's permission left his sling at home, pulled out a chair for Kate. Dan did the same for Meghan, who made some comment about the smoke.

"Can we please just let down our hair and not be PC for one night?" Dan asked. "I'm going to live it up and have a greasy cheeseburger with jalapeños, some cheese and chili fries and a couple of beers—forget I ever heard the word cholesterol."

Meghan gave a delicate shudder and regarded the menu written on a huge blackboard above the bar. "I'll just have a bowl of chili."

"How about you?" Cullen asked Kate.

"I'm with Dan, sans beer. I'll have a Coke instead." Cullen's order mimicked Kate's and Dan's.

The waitress came and they gave her their order. While they waited for it to be brought out, Dan questioned Kate about her time as a New Orleans cop and quizzed her about what it was like working as a private detective. She sensed that both Meghan and Cullen were listening to her answers with an avid interest.

The waitress, wearing a pair of skintight jeans and a blouse tied at her midriff, brought their order with the instruction that her name was Pam and to call her if they needed anything else. The food was surprisingly good—cholesterol notwithstanding—the chili homemade, the French fries freshly cut and the hamburger charbroiled to a satisfying juiciness.

When they finished, Kate proclaimed that she was probably too full to dance, even if she knew how, which she didn't. Aghast at the very thought, Dan looked to Cullen.

"I don't think I'd be much good at teaching her with just one good arm," he said. "Sorry."

Dan looked from Cullen to Meghan. "I suppose it's up to me to give Kate a crash course, assuming you don't mind my giving another beautiful woman a spin on the dance floor."

"Be my guest," Meghan said with a gesture toward the small polished area.

The next few minutes passed in a flurry of hastily assimilated and clumsily executed dance steps, but by the time they made it through a couple more songs, Kate was getting the hang of the sometimes intricate steps, kicks and spins. She learned to just let herself relax and let Dan guide her into their next move. When, some fifteen minutes later, he led her back to the table with a series of spins, he announced that she was ready for the big time.

Panting, he downed half his lukewarm beer and with a wink took Meghan's hand and led her to the dance floor, where they proceeded to make everyone else look bad as they danced to a song about pillow talkin' and dream walkin'. Meghan smiled saucily at her husband, and his reciprocal grin said that he adored her.

"They're crazy about each other, aren't they?"

"Totally."

"They look as if they've been dancing together forever."

"This is definitely not their first rodeo," Cullen said. "They've been dancing together since college. The problem is that they don't often have the chance to get away since they both have such successful careers."

"They should make time," Kate said, a wistfulness she was unaware of tingeing her voice.

"You say that with authority," Cullen said, raising his glass to his lips.

Kate's smile was bittersweet. "Yeah? Well, I have the divorce papers to prove my point."

"Despite the horrific divorce numbers in this country, and despite the fact that you have a divorce in your past, the institution of marriage is a fine one if two people really love each other and are willing to work at it," Cullen said. "Don't let what happened to you bitter you on marriage, Kate."

Surprised both by the comment and what looked like concern in his eyes, Kate could think of no snappy reply. Hoping to shift the conversation away from the personal, she was about to say something about Dan's idea of getting away being a good one when a giant of a man approached the table. Other than his size, there was nothing about him to cause alarm. In fact, compared to about half the other men in the bar, he looked pretty upstanding.

"How 'bout a dance?"

Kate had no idea what she expected, but a dance request wasn't it. She glanced at Cullen to gauge his response only to see that his face wore an impassive expression. Why shouldn't she dance with another man? Cullen couldn't perform the moves, and she *had* come out tonight to have a good time. She sneaked another quick look at the stranger and decided he was harmless.

"Sure," she said rising. "Why not?"

The man led her onto the small dance floor and pulled her into a loose embrace. "What's your name?" he asked.

"Kate. What's yours?"

"Brutus."

He said it deadpan, but his eyes twinkled with an unholy glee. Kate figured he was expecting her to deny the name. "Brutus," she said with a nod. "It fits."

To her surprise, he threw back his head and roared with laughter. Kate cast a glance at the table. From the frown on Cullen's face, she'd say he wasn't amused.

"Where you from, Kate? You don't sound like an Arky."

"New Orleans."

He grinned, hugged her closer and purred, "The Big Easy."

Kate gave his chest a gentle push. "The city, not me."

Brutus relaxed his hold and frowned at her. "Beg pardon?"

"The city is the big easy. I'm not."

Another deep roll of laughter erupted from Brutus and he spun her wildly around the dance floor. They passed Dan and Meghan, who gave her a questioning and worried look, respectively.

"You dance pretty good country and western for a city girl who's just learnin'."

''Thanks. You aren't bad yourself.''

Brutus cocked his head toward Cullen. ''That guy your boyfriend?''

Okay. Time to start playing the role she was hired to play. ''He is.''

''He treat you pretty good?''

She nodded. ''For the most part,'' she managed with a straight face. ''He spends too much time working to suit me, but other than that...''

Brutus looked from Cullen to Kate. ''How come he ain't dancin' with you?''

Kate sent Cullen a brilliant smile and blew him a kiss. He frowned. ''Poor baby,'' she cooed. ''He broke a couple of ribs in a car accident recently,'' she said to Brutus with a smoothness that surprised even her. Not exactly a lie. Hey, this fake girlfriend thing was a lot easier that she expected.

They were executing a series of twirls when Brutus asked, ''Maybe it's none of my business, but since I've takin' a liking to you, I have to ask. Do you love the guy?''

Chapter Nine

Kate stumbled and felt her partner's arms close more tightly around her. "Sorry," she murmured, feeling her face flame and her stomach churn sickeningly from the unexpected question. "I haven't quite gotten the hang of this yet."

"You're doin' fine," Brutus said, giving her another twirl that sent her already spinning head whirling dizzily. When she faced him once more, he said, "So?"

"So...I'm flattered that you're interested," Kate said, hoping to ignore his question.

"But?" Brutus prodded.

"But what?"

"You love the guy, right?"

Love Cullen? The very idea was ridiculous. But even as she thought it, she knew the joke was on her. Of course she loved him, which, bottom line, was why she'd accepted the job. She'd suspected it for two years, but had managed to hide the truth behind her anger. When her anger threatened to fail her, she fell back on denial, convincing herself that there was no way she could have fallen—really fallen—so fast and hard after what Lane had done to her. It had been passion. Desire. But now, with Brutus forcing the issue, forcing her to take a good hard look into her heart, she couldn't deny it any longer.

Whatever had motivated Cullen—forgetfulness or a good time—he had managed to infiltrate the most tender places of her heart, the parts that in spite of the damage done by Lane wanted to believe in love and happy endings. What wasn't so easy to understand was why she'd let Cullen get so close so fast. She might have been better off asking herself how she could have stopped him.

With her heart pounding so hard she thought it might be heard over the music, Kate forced herself to meet Brutus's questioning gaze. "You know, Brutus," she said, her voice mirroring her disbelief as well as her misery, "I believe I do."

Brutus gave a grunt that could have meant anything, and the song ended. "I'll say this. He's a lucky guy and a real fool if he leaves a woman like you alone."

The sincerity in his voice said a lot about the man. "Why, thank you, Brutus," Kate said in a gentle voice. "I'll be sure to tell him."

"I'll tell him myself." With a swagger born from an innate confidence, the giant sauntered toward the table where Cullen sat. Kate followed uneasily, visions of mayhem flashing before her eyes, yet other than cause a scene herself, there was nothing she could do to stop her new champion. Cullen didn't seem like the type to take criticism in stride, not even constructive criticism.

* * *

Cullen sat and seethed as the big man and Kate boot scooted around the dance floor. Whatever she was saying to him must be hilarious if the man's booming laughter was anything to go by. Cullen gritted his teeth. The big oaf was holding her way too tightly, and Kate was making a damn fool of herself.

She's just having a good time. It's not her fault you're jealous because she's having more fun with a stranger than she does with you.

The realization that he was jealous hit him with all the force of the bullet that had knocked him off the tree stand. Jealous? Hardly. Jealous implied a certain state of mind Cullen wasn't ready to admit. Why would he feel possessive or jealous of Kate?

Because since the first time you set eyes on her, she's had the ability to arouse you by just walking across a floor. Guilt aside, you've wanted her since you first met her, you wanted her when you left her in New Orleans, and you want her now. You resent any other man who touches her. You were even jealous of Dan, for cryin' out loud, and you know he's crazy about your sister.

Even as Cullen tried to come to terms with his feelings, he knew he was ignoring their deeper significance, things he wasn't ready to admit. The song ended and Kate and her partner stood in the middle of the polished floor for a few seconds, talking. Finally the man started toward Cullen, a determined gleam in his eye. Angry and not fully understanding why, all Cullen could think of was that he wasn't in any condition for a barroom brawl. He'd have to call on his skill at rhetoric to smooth over whatever had set the Paul Bunyan type off.

The big man stopped at the table. "Brutus Vickers," he said, extending his hand to Cullen.

Taking the gesture as one of goodwill, Cullen shook the man's hand without hesitation. His grip was firm without being crushing. "Cullen McGyver."

"Good to meet you," Brutus said, hooking his thumbs in his pockets. "I just wanted to come and tell you that you got yourself a good little woman here."

Cullen's gaze shifted to Kate who stood a pace behind her new champion, her face white with dread, her arms crossed over her breasts.

"I know that," Cullen said, knowing as he spoke the words that at least part of it was true. Kate was a good woman. But she wasn't his. Not really.

"You ought not leave a woman like her alone so much."

He flicked an irritated glance at Kate. What had she told the man, anyway? "I really don't think that's any of your business."

"Maybe not," Brutus said in a smooth voice. "But there are a lot of lonely men out there who'd be only too glad to take her off your hands." With that, he turned and walked away.

Angry, but relieved that the encounter had ended as it had, Cullen watched him go. Kate started to sit down. Cullen reached out with his bad arm to stop her. He felt the twinge of pain deep inside his shoulder.

Eyes wide, Kate looked down at the hand on her elbow and then back at his face. He gave a sharp pull, drawing her into the vee of his legs.

"What are you doing?" she said softly, trying to pull free.

"Playing the part. Trying to do what the man suggested." He ground the words out through teeth gritted in pain. "Trying to take better care of you, pay you more attention.

Astonishment filled her face. "Don't let anything Brutus said upset you. He's just a guy I danced with."

"Yeah," he said in a low, angry voice. "And it looked as if you were having a heck of a time."

Kate's forehead puckered into a frown. "What is this, Cullen? You—you're not jealous, are you?"

Cullen couldn't think of a reply that wouldn't incriminate him. "Sit down," he commanded.

"What?"

"Sit down!" He jerked on her hand, and other than make a scene, she had no choice but to sit down on his thigh. Immediately, his senses were awash in the scent of her. He was drowning in her nearness. Unsure what part of his actions and words were for show and which were real and needing something to hold on to, he circled her waist with his bad arm, catching his thumb in the loop of her jeans. He rested his good hand on her denim-clad knee and ran it up and down her thigh, recalling the smooth feel of her flesh beneath his palm, recalling a lot of things he'd be better off forgetting.

Kate's eyes looked like those of a doe caught in the lights of an oncoming car. "Don't take this personally," she said, her voice a bit on the breathless side, "but I think you're taking this girlfriend stuff too seriously." She started to stand. He tightened his hand on her thigh.

Confusion and uncertainty and something else he couldn't quite put his finger on replaced the impudence in her eyes. He lifted his hand to the back of her neck and drew her face closer.

"Cullen?" Her voice was soft, questioning. "Don't!"

"Shh." Urgent. Needy.

"You don't have to do this." Her head moved in a sideways motion of negativity.

"I really think I do." He exerted more pressure, and

their lips met softly. Clung with a hunger they both remembered with vivid clarity. Only the vague realization that they were in a public place kept Cullen from making a complete fool of himself. He forced himself to end the kiss after just a few seconds. When he pulled back, he saw Brutus Vickers watching from across the room.

Cullen shifted his glance to Kate. Her eyes held more than a little confusion. He wanted to kiss her again, but he wasn't at all confused. He knew exactly why he wanted to taste her mouth again, and it had nothing to do with their pretend relationship. It had to do with hunger and need and a growing desire.

"Good job."

The sound of Dan's voice jolted Cullen to the moment. Kate leaped from his lap, her face flushed with hot color. "What?"

"I said that the two of you are doing a really good job with this relationship thing you have going on. Anyone who just happened to be watching would never guess it was all just for show."

Cullen raised his beer to his lips to hide their sarcastic twist. *That's the problem, Dan. I'm not so sure if it is.*

They stayed another hour and a half, and even though she danced and laughed and joked, acting as if she were having the time of her life, Kate's thoughts kept straying to more serious things whenever they had the chance. Like now. Dan and Meghan were on the dance floor, and Cullen had gone to the men's room. It was a perfect time for Brutus's challenging question about whether or not she loved Cullen to surface. The query had caught her off guard and hit her with a reality she'd rather not have faced. But face it she must. Not only face it, but figure out some way to deal with it. Loving Cullen would only

bring heartache and disaster, because even though he
might want her—and there was little doubt he did—wanting was a far cry from caring, and lust was a long way
from love.

She couldn't say she hadn't been warned. Her aunt had
told her she wasn't Cullen's type, that his type was the
socialite debutante, only older and more polished. She
was just plain Kate, pretty enough by most standards,
smart enough by others, but definitely not in the Mc-
Gyver league. Kate gave a heavy sigh. The problem was
that she'd been warned too late, like closing the gate after
the livestock got out. By the time Aunt Lou had told her
about Cullen's preference in women, the damage was already done. She'd already fallen in love with him.

She was still pondering her predicament when Dan and
Meghan and Cullen all returned to the table at the same
time.

"I'm bushed," Meghan said to no one in particular.
"I say we call it a night."

"Me, too," Cullen said.

"Party poopers," Dan said. "I suppose you want to
go home, too?" he asked Kate.

"I am a little tired."

"Okay," he said with a sigh of disappointment. "Let's
load up."

The drive to the ranch was more or less a silent one.
Meghan sat close to Dan, who put his arm around her.
Cullen and Kate sat in the far corners of the back seat,
as aware of each other as they would have been if they
were sharing the space with a cobra.

When Dan shut off the engine, Kate was the first one
out of the car. The front door was unlocked, and she went
inside without waiting for the others, following the
sounds of the television to the living room. Lindsay and

Marley were stretched out on their stomachs with floor pillows. Engrossed in some teenage angst flick, they called a listless greeting over their shoulders. Louella and Greg were nowhere to be seen.

Kate made her way through the house to the kitchen and found the two older people at the table, two glasses of white wine and a plate of snack crackers and cheese sitting between them. Her aunt's hand lay near the cheese plate, and Greg's big hand covered Louella's.

Hearing the sound at the door, Louella looked up, a pretty pink staining her plump cheeks. She smiled but seemed in no big hurry to withdraw her hand from beneath the former doctor's. "Hello, dear. Where is everyone?"

"Checking with the girls, probably," Kate said, going to the cabinet for a glass.

"They've been angels. So sweet and polite. Did you have a good time?"

"Yeah," Kate said, filling the glass with ice from the front door of the fridge. "It was something different. I learned how to country-and-western dance."

"That sounds like fun," Louella said.

Looking a little embarrassed, Greg asked, "Would you like a glass of wine, Kate?"

"No, thanks. I was just a little dry. I think I'll go on up."

"I should be going, too," he said, rising. "It's late, and we have a full day tomorrow."

"What time will you get here in the morning?" Louella asked.

Greg squinted his eyes in thought. "It's a big turkey. If we plan to eat at straight-up noon and have plenty of time to bake the dressing and things, we should get ol' Tom in by five-thirty."

Louella smiled. "I'll have the coffee on."

"You don't have to do that," Greg said, but the pleased expression on his face couldn't be denied.

Louella gave his hand one of her little pats. "I know I don't have to. I want to."

If possible, Greg's smile grew even broader. "See you in the morning, then."

Louella nodded. "'Night."

Kate put her hands on her hips as she and her aunt watched him go. "Okay," she said as the muted sounds of Greg's parting conversation with the rest of the family filtered through the walls of the old house. "What's going on?"

"Nothing's going on," Louella said. "Nothing but the beginnings of a wonderful friendship. And, if things go as well as I expect them to, something more lasting."

"Aren't you going a little fast with this romance?" Kate asked, in an incredulous voice. "I mean, Greg seems like a wonderful man, but you've only known him a day."

Louella's smile was sweet, her face reflecting an inner certainty. "When it's right, it's right, Katie. And when it's right, you know it."

Stunned by her aunt's decisiveness, Kate couldn't help feeling pleased nonetheless. Louella deserved some happiness, and if she could find it with a nice man like Greg Kingsley, then so be it. However, though she didn't want to admit it, Kate felt a bit jealous that happiness was within reach for her aunt and so very far for herself.

Thanksgiving passed in a blur of rich and plentiful food and an afternoon filled with laughter and family board games. Dan beat everyone at Scrabble, Kate and Lindsay whipped the others at Pictionary, and Cullen and

Kate surprised the group and even themselves by winning at Compatibility. Though he took part in the games, Cullen seemed more than unusually quiet throughout the day, something she was fast learning was sometimes the norm for him.

Her aunt and Greg Kingsley acted as young as the two teenagers, and Kate intercepted not only several meaningful glances between the two older people but several questioning looks from the Longstreets and Cullen. If anyone asked her about the budding relationship, she supposed she could pass on her aunt's "when it's right, it's right" comment.

Kate called her dad at midafternoon, after the rush at the restaurant was likely to have passed. James Labiche told her he was glad she'd called, asked her how the new job was going and said he hoped he could see her at Christmastime. Kate had told him the truth behind her job, knowing that he would need to be clued in about her new history-teacher background in case someone came asking about her. Kate, who usually saw her dad several times a week, hung up feeling a little depressed. She missed him and hated being away from him, especially on a holiday.

At dinnertime, they gorged themselves on leftovers—even though at lunch they'd sworn they couldn't eat for a year. Feeling full and mellow and content, they cleaned up the dishes, and Greg took his leave. Louella went upstairs to her room, and the Longstreets and Cullen joined the teenagers, who were watching a movie. Claiming she'd been too sedentary since she'd arrived, Kate changed into some exercise clothes, topped them with sweats and went to the exercise room to work out.

She'd been in the weight room no more than ten minutes when there was a sharp rapping on the door.

Before she could answer, Cullen stepped inside. Surprised, Kate stood frozen in her spot. His gaze, intense, searching, raked her from her jaunty ponytail to her bare feet, lingering on her exposed midriff and the long length of her legs, encased to midthigh with stretchy gray fabric.

Kate saw his cobalt-blue eyes darken to navy, watched in confusion and anticipation as their expression mutated to a sudden, naked need. She sucked in a sharp breath and felt a reciprocal need quiver to life inside her. Wordlessly, he started across the small expanse separating them. Kate realized the trembling in her hands had more to do with her reaction to the man walking toward her than it did with exertion and lowered the dumbbells she'd been using to the weight bench. She started to reach for the towel lying there, but Cullen beat her to it.

His fingers brushed hers as his fist closed over the soft Egyptian cotton. She straightened slowly, aware of the potency of his nearness, certain she could feel the heat of his body. She lifted her lashes, flicking a quick glance his way, and saw that his face was just inches from hers. The expression in his eyes was indisputable desire. Panicked, knowing she was in danger of more heartbreak, she straightened with an awkward jerking motion and took a step back, away from his nearness. To give in to the emotions raging in his eyes and through her body would be foolish, and she'd sworn when he left her that she wouldn't be played the fool again.

"What do you want?" she asked, finding her voice at last.

"You," he said, holding out the towel.

His voice was cool, steady, unhesitating. Kate's gasp of surprise filled the silence of the room. Grateful for any diversion, searching her mind for some sort of glib come-

back, she grabbed the towel and dabbed it over her per-
spiring face, the better to block out the intensity in his
eyes.

She felt the warmth of his hand on her upper arm and
froze. Slowly, she lowered the towel. Afraid to breathe,
afraid to move, she stood there, hypnotized by the hunger
she saw in his eyes, bewitched by the warm masculine
scent that drifted over her, a scent that washed away all
logical thought and hinted of daring and delicious things.

If you love him, why shouldn't you? The tiny voice
argued with her reason. Okay, so she loved him, which
meant she was in about as deep as she could get. Unlike
the first time she'd become involved with him, she knew
what to expect. There would be no surprises. She knew
she wasn't his type, knew he had no plans for a permanent relationship. Knowing all that up front, having no
preconceived notions, no grand expectations, accepting
whatever he offered with her eyes wide-open, there was
no way she could get hurt any worse, was there?

She shook her head, knowing she was fooling herself,
knowing deep down that it was only a token refusal, just
as she knew from the determination in Cullen's eyes that
he recognized that her rejection was as bogus as their
pretend love affair.

His hand skimmed over her shoulder to her neck, drifting up to capture her chin between the gentle vise of his
thumb and fingers. Her heart threatened to run away, yet
conversely, she felt lethargic, unable to move. He dipped
his head. His strong features blurred before her eyes.
Fine, she thought, letting her lashes glide downward. She
didn't need to see, anyway. All she needed was to feel....

...his lips on hers, warm and open, moving confi-
dently, devouring her mouth with a hunger the kiss at the
honky-tonk had only flirted with. Without meaning to,
without realizing what she was doing, Kate dropped the

towel she held. One hand grabbed a belt loop; the other slipped to the back of his head to hold him close.

His kiss deepened, mutating to a gentle assault. Her mouth parted wider, taking the bold thrust of his tongue. The hand at her throat slid down...molding, shaping. The other moved up, sliding beneath the stretchy fabric, his fingers warm against her bare flesh.

His touch was more delicious than she recalled. Maybe because it had been so long. Her body burned with need, ached with a hunger so intense it pushed away the tatters of her ability to reason. There was no use fighting it, not when she wanted it so badly.

For long moments, their mouths fused in a ravenous joining. Then his hands slid down, urging her closer to the heat and toughness of him. Kate needed no encouragement. She pressed against him, shaping her aching femininity to his hard masculinity, struggling for a closeness she knew would never be close enough. His groan of need threatened to send her into cardiac arrest. Heady, so heady, the knowledge that she had this power over him. Never mind that the power was a two-way street.

His mouth forsook hers to press tiny wet kisses against her neck. She gave a little cry, her fingers gripping... clinging. The sounds of their breathing, heavy, labored, filled the room. The last time Kate had felt so feminine, so desirable, so needy was the first time she and Cullen had made love. Or was it the last time?

"I want you, Kat," Cullen murmured against her throat, his voice low and husky.

"Yes," she said in a feverish whisper. "Please."

Without a word, he reached out and looped a finger through the scrunchie that held her hair, tugging it loose. Kate shook her head, and fiery hair tumbled to her shoulders. Cullen grasped the bottom of her sports top and tugged upward, grimacing with pain. Seeing the look on his face, Kate brushed his hands aside, ripped the top off and tossed it to the floor, disregarding the small voice inside her that whispered that her heart was in danger and for her to be careful.

It was far too late for warnings. Too late for anything but feeling....

She was beautiful, he thought. Kate stood before him, a look of vulnerable defiance in her eyes as he drank in the shape and symmetry of her unbound breasts and the creamy flesh of her shoulders dotted with honey-colored freckles. As he stared at her, soft color rose in her cheeks, and she crossed her arms in an involuntary gesture, trying to shield herself from the intensity of his gaze.

Cullen clasped her wrists, forcing her hands to her sides. Then, his gaze locked with hers, he reached out, testing the incredible softness of her flesh. Her breath caught sharply, her eyes closed, and she sank her teeth into her bottom lip. He kissed her then, coaxing her lips apart with gentle persuasion as he slid his hands to her back, easing her toward the sofa that sat against the wall.

It was tricky with his throbbing ribs and the pain in his shoulder. Tricky and awkward. Tender. Strangely adventurous and remarkably creative. When he couldn't get an article of clothing off, Kate helped, her eager fingers incredibly nimble at undoing buttons, incredibly quick with zippers. Incredibly inventive as she touched him. When supporting himself was impossible, she changed places with him, took the lead, leaving him with little to do but sit back and enjoy...to give himself over to the sheer sensation.

It was all he'd remembered, all he'd known it would

be, something he knew he could never get enough of. Too long abstinent, it was over far too quickly.

Afterward, she sat still and immovable, one leg on either side of him, her head thrown forward onto his shoulder while their heartbeats slowed and he breathed in the scent of her hair and tried to comprehend exactly what had just happened. Sex, yes. But more than sex, because Kate was more than just another woman.

You're falling in love with her.

The voice in his head whispered what his heart had refused to admit when he'd acknowledged his jealousy as he'd watched her dancing with Brutus Vickers. Cullen's eyes flew open, and the hands that were moving over her back with slow lethargy stilled. In love with her? Impossible. He admired her, was impressed with her ability to do her job. He even felt a grudging linking, despite her sharp tongue—but love? No. No way.

Why not? You can't use Joanie as an excuse anymore. It's been almost three years. He had loved Joanie, and a part of him would always love her, but he knew that since the time he'd spent with Kate, he'd moved beyond grief and his initial crippling pain. When he tried to conjure up an image of himself and Joanie, all that came to mind was Kate moving in perfect synchronization with him, her eyes gauging the depth of his need, smiling a sexy, witchy smile, sinking her teeth into her lower lip with a soft moan...a moan that he echoed as they struggled to reach fulfillment together.

The depth of feeling that image brought was unbelievable, humbling, leaving no room for past loves, past lovers or past experiences. It came to him quietly, in a moment of perfect clarity that he was over Joanie's death and had been for a while. He was ready to move on. Ready to fall in love. It was time.

* * *

Kate, who was trying to regain control of her breathing, felt the change in Cullen. A stillness, as if he was waiting for something, as if he'd just come to a startling realization. The feeling seeped into her contentment. From deep inside her, reason surfaced.

What had she done? Simple. She'd compromised her job and maybe even Cullen's safety. For what? A repeat performance with the handsome, out-of-reach lawyer? For another round of heartache? Neither love nor the fact that she'd known what she was getting into gave her the right to put Cullen in jeopardy.

She'd been hired to protect him, not to fulfill any sexual needs he—or she—might have. And now, because she'd thrown her professionalism to the wind, she may have blown the case. There was no way she could stay sharp, cool, collected, ready to protect him from unseen adversaries when she knew that every time he came near her she'd melt like a piece of chocolate in the sun. Dear sweet heaven, what had she done? What—if anything—could she do to change it?

Nothing.

The damage was done, the die cast. She had two choices—stay and brazen it out, pretending that what had happened between them was nothing but the brief fling he seemed to want. Or leave, taking her battered pride back to New Orleans. Better battered pride than a broken heart.

She felt his hand on her shoulder.

''Kat?'' His voice was a deep rumble in her ear.

She forced herself to open her eyes, made herself face his question. Her troubled gaze moved over his handsome features. What could she say? How best to end it with as little pain as possible? With no long-term effects. Brutal was better, she decided. Like ripping off a bandage quickly, feeling a sharp burst of agony instead of easing it off slowly, which only prolonged the pain.

She pulled her hand free. "This...this wasn't part of our arrangement, Cullen." She was surprised by the steadiness she heard in her voice. "You aren't paying me enough to sleep with you."

The tenderness in his eyes vanished; a low-grade anger simmered in their depths. She must not have been as much in control as she thought, because something he saw in her eyes dampened the anger almost as quickly as it had come, leaving a slight irritation in his voice. "Don't try to act like you didn't want me," he said. "I know better."

No. There was no way to deny what had happened between them. No excuses. No explanations. Or was there?

"I have no intention of denying it," she said, easing from him and turning her back on him to search for her clothes. "Let's just chalk it up as a mutual attraction, shall we?"

Kate didn't know how she could sound so detached when she felt as if her whole body might go into complete meltdown if he touched her. She found her shorts and pulled them on.

"Oh," he said with heavy sarcasm as he began to pull his clothes on. "You admit to feeling it, anyway."

"Like I said, I can hardly deny it." She forced her voice into a textbook tone. "What I meant is that there's often a...bonding that occurs between people in certain situations, even though there may be some ethical fallout. Patients fall in love with their doctors. Students with teachers. It's a proven fact that hostages even bond with their captors in various degrees. As a prosecutor, you know that as well as I do. We experienced it when we worked together in New Orleans, and obviously whatever it is is still in place.''

''You're fooling yourself, Kat,'' he told her, as he zipped his jeans and began to button his shirt.

''Kate,'' she corrected, adding, ''I don't think so.''

He shook his head. ''You're a Kat, not a Kate. Kat with the standoff attitude to discourage anyone from getting too close to you. Kat with sharp little claws that come out to scratch when they do. Like now.''

''You got close enough,'' she reminded him.

''Physically.''

''That's all you wanted.''

''Is it?''

She looked at him, hoping for clarification. He offered none, and Kate couldn't read anything more in his eyes. ''The main thing is that we can't let it continue. There's no point in it.''

''I'd think the point would be obvious,'' he said, stuffing his shirt into the waistband of his jeans as best he could. ''Mutual satisfaction.''

''I'm not into satisfaction for satisfaction's sake,'' she said with a lift of her chin. ''And I don't believe in spending a lot of energy on lost causes. I don't think you do, either.''

He crossed the space separating them, placed himself directly in front of her and planted his hands on his hips. Surprisingly, the expression on his face was one of curiosity. ''Meaning?''

Kate couldn't quite meet his eyes. ''Meaning that we both know I'm not your type of woman, so it stands to reason that whatever we just indulged in is nothing but passing lust.'' She lifted her chin, took a deep breath and raked an unsteady hand through the hair he'd tangled his hands in just moments before. ''It happened, and there's no sense us beating ourselves up over it, but to let it happen again would only make the situation more complicated and more…volatile. That's a distraction I don't need.''

He reached out and brushed the backs of his fingers down the line of her jaw. ''You're right. What's between us is volatile, and lust is definitely a part of it. I agree that continuing—'' he gave a vague wave of his hand ''—would be a distraction. And I know exactly what I feel for you, Kat. Believe me, knowing doesn't make me like it any more than you do.''

Caught off guard by the husky honesty in his voice, Kate forced herself to meet his gaze and steeled herself against the heat in his eyes. ''Then you know I'm right.''

It would be so easy to take one step toward him, she thought. So easy to wrap her arms around his neck and let the raging feelings bottled up inside her burst forth like the contents of a shaken bottle of champagne.

''That remains to be seen,'' he told her. ''But since you aren't in the right frame of mind to discuss things at the moment, I guess we'll have to take this up in more detail later. After we catch the perp.'' He leaned forward and brushed her lips with his, a gentle kiss that sent a tingle twanging through Kate's veins.

''Sweet dreams, Kat,'' he said, leaving her there, alone with her thoughts, lonelier than she'd been since she'd awakened to find he'd left with no goodbye.

Chapter Ten

The man at the window watched Cullen McGyver and the woman dress with a combination of interest and hatred. Evidently he'd arrived too late to witness the main event, but even so, it was clear that McGyver had found another woman. So much for his undying love for his dead wife. How could he claim to be so devastated by her death—which had been an accident—that he'd gone to great lengths to seek retribution? How could he justify what had just happened with the tall red-haired woman?

Never mind. At least he knew now where McGyver was and could adjust his plans accordingly. Soon, now. He crept away from the window and sprinted from shadow to shadow across the back yard. It would all be over soon. If he couldn't have his life back, and killing Cullen McGyver would ruin all chance of that, he'd at least have the consolation of knowing that McGyver's life was over, too.

* * *

Cullen went to his room, knowing sleep was impossible. He was too disturbed by what had happened with Kate to fall into the forgetfulness he craved. Maybe disturbed was too hard a word. Upset wasn't quite right, either. Surprised. Dismayed. While words fit—he was surprised at the depths of his growing feelings for her and dismayed because she was able to brush aside what had happened so easily—neither word aptly conveyed the turmoil of his feelings, feelings that were as strong as they were undeniable, something he'd faced while they were at the bar the night before.

There was more to this than the lust she seemed so anxious to label it. That was part of it, but on top of his initial attraction he was becoming increasingly entranced with the other facets of her personality and, complex woman that she was, they were many. The job she'd once had and the traumatic experience she'd gone through with her former partner had contributed to her ability to step back and see a clearer picture, to compartmentalize the things that happened to her. There was little doubt in Cullen's mind that the job had hardened her to a degree— given her a wariness about people and things that most women didn't have—but not so much that her femininity had been exterminated. No. The toughness in her was more a mental hardiness than coarseness or a rough attitude.

Despite the differences in their backgrounds and upbringing, despite what he might or might not want, Cullen bowed to the fact that the wanting and curiosity and admiration were part of a more complicated emotion, love. He loved her.

The voice inside him whispered the truth that he'd suspected ever since he first set eyes on her. His memories of Joanie, once so vibrant and clear, had lessened in frequency and potency over the past two years. He knew the lessening of his pain and the fading of his memories was a natural, normal course of events. Man wasn't made to grieve forever. Finding love was a good thing—if he could convince Kate that what he felt was real.

It's only good if she feels the same way.

Did she? Was her insistence that what they shared was only desire spoken in truth, or was it a way for her to guard her heart? Though she seemed confident about her ability to perform the job he'd hired her to do, she was far less secure in her role as a woman. Thanks, no doubt, to the husband who had walked out on her. When the time was right, he would do his best to convince her that they could be happy together. But the time wasn't right just now. Until they locked up the person trying to kill him, he'd have to bide his time and see if he could get a better handle on what Kate was feeling.

He was stepping into the shower when he realized that he hadn't used any protection. He swore roundly. What had he been thinking? That was the problem. He hadn't been thinking, only feeling. He cursed himself to hell and back, and without warning, his thoughts turned from Kate to Lucy Lambert and her son.

He swore. He had been careful with Lucy. He found himself praying that the boy wasn't his, not because he didn't want the responsibility or because it would lessen his stature in the eyes of the public, but because it was a situation that held an inherent mental hardship on everyone involved, especially Tyler.

Cullen was a firm believer in people taking responsibility for their actions, but a weekend fling would be hard to explain to a child when it was time for him to know the truth. And that time would come, no doubt about it.

What about Kate?

Kate was different, he thought, his thoughts coming full circle. If she happened to have gotten pregnant, then he'd do the right thing. He was pretty sure he wanted to do the right thing, anyway. The problem was convincing her that he cared, making her believe that even though she wasn't like the women he usually dated, she was the woman he wanted.

After a more-or-less sleepless night, Cullen awoke tired and grumpy. Resolutely, he pushed Kate from his mind, determined to concentrate on the call to Lucy Lambert. He went downstairs and found an empty kitchen. Since they'd had a fairly late night, Greg wasn't coming until later, and Louella had volunteered to fix breakfast. Needing his caffeine, Cullen made the coffee. He'd like to have the paper to look over, but he'd learned his lesson about going off on his own.

Greg, saying there was nothing to do at his place, arrived just as the coffee was sputtering to an end. Thankfully, he came bearing the newspaper. The other adults came down soon after. The girls would probably sleep till noon, Meghan said, rolling her eyes. Teenagers.

Cullen noted that Kate looked fresh and refreshed in tan slacks and a chartreuse knit pullover, as if she'd had no problem sleeping after their romantic episode in the weight room. He let his gaze meander over her long legs and slender hips, remembering the way her flesh had felt beneath his hands, firm yet malleable, her breasts soft... like her mouth.

As hard as he tried to get her to meet his gaze, she refused to look his way. If he happened to catch her eyes on him, she quickly looked away. He felt his irritation rise. They were adults. They should be able to talk about what had happened, to accept it or move on if they decided it wasn't going anywhere, a prospect Cullen found totally unacceptable.

Maybe Kate had said all she had to say on the subject the night before. Maybe her way of dealing with what had happened was to ignore it, which might be best, since the most important thing was to get to the bottom of who was out to get him so he could get on with his life, concentrate on her.

Breakfast conversation was general, and Cullen hardly participated in it. As soon as he finished eating, he excused himself and headed for the library, anxious to contact Lucy, eager to end this charade and get on with his life.

He was rummaging through the papers on his desk when Kate stepped through the doorway.

Irritated by her ability to act so calm when just looking at her made him want her, he flicked her an angry glance and gave his attention to his task. "Do you mind shutting the door?"

"I'd leave if I could." She shot the words back. "Who put the burr under your saddle blanket?"

You. "No one." The words were almost a snarl. He raised a furious gaze to hers. "I'm just sick of being held hostage by some idiot with an ax to grind."

Kate's eyebrows lifted, and her lips twisted into a wry smile. "Not a good analogy, counselor."

Despite himself, he smiled, albeit weakly. "I'm going to call Lucy. Why don't you listen in on the extension in the room across the hall?"

"Good idea," Kate said.

Cullen took a small piece of paper from his pocket and punched in the number. A woman answered on the third ring. He recognized the voice. "Lucy? Cullen Mc-Gyver."

"Cullen!" she said in a voice hardly above a harsh whisper. "How did you find me?"

"Your dad's name came up on my caller ID."

He heard her sigh. "What do you want?"

"What do I want?" he echoed. "I want to know why you're doing this to me."

"Just a minute," she said. She put down the receiver, and he heard a door close. Heard a scrabbling sound as she picked up the receiver again. "Doing what?"

"First off, I want to know why you told Dub about me."

"Dub told you why," Lucy said. "When Tyler had to go to the hospital, his blood type wasn't like either of ours, so I told him about you and me. Dub—" she hesitated "—Dub wasn't too happy that I tricked him into marriage."

"I imagine not. But that still doesn't explain why you told him Tyler is mine."

"I had to tell him something. Give him someone's name." Her voice sounded nervous, frightened.

"So you just picked me," he stated.

"Of course I didn't just *pick* you!" Lucy cried lowly. "Unless you've forgotten, there's a good chance Tyler might be yours."

"I haven't forgotten anything," Cullen told her, his own voice taking on an edge. "I certainly haven't forgotten that I took precautions."

"Yeah, well, precautions don't always work." An undisguised bitterness crept into her voice.

Cullen rested his elbow on the desk, pinched the bridge of his nose and let her words play through his mind, trying without any luck to find a way to end this nightmare. The way things were going, he was getting no-where fast. Suddenly he sat up straight.

"You said you had to give Dub someone's name, right?"

"What?" Lucy asked, in a wary voice.

"You said there was a chance Tyler might be mine." Cullen glanced at Kate, who was watching and listening carefully.

"Yes." There was a hesitancy in Lucy's voice…almost a question.

"Who else might be the father, Lucy?"

"Wh-what do you mean?"

"You said you had to give Dub a name," Cullen repeated, hoping his implication might sink in. "You said I might be the father. But if you weren't seeing anyone but me, you'd know that for a fact, wouldn't you? Is the reason I only *might* be Tyler's father because there's someone else, someone you haven't told Dub about?"

"No!" she cried, but he heard the truth in her denial.

"You're lying, Lucy." Cullen's voice was filled with sudden certainty. "There was someone besides me while you and Dub were split up. Who is it, Lucy?"

"No one!"

"Tell me."

He heard her sob, heard the despair in her voice. "It doesn't matter, does it? What matters is that Dub worked me over pretty good when he found out about you. What do you think he'd do if he found out there was another man, too?"

Cullen's stomach tightened at the thought of Dub, who had to weigh more than two hundred pounds, hitting Lucy, who couldn't weigh more than a hundred and ten sopping wet. "Is that what you're afraid of?"

"Wouldn't you be?" she cried through her tears.

Cullen heaved a heartfelt sigh. "I understand your dilemma, Lucy, and I don't want to make this any harder on you than it already is. What you should do is tell Dub about the other man and get a restraining order against him if you think it's necessary."

"You know as well as I do that those things aren't worth the paper they're written on if someone like Dub goes on a rampage."

"If he tries to hurt you again, I'll see to it that you have the best representation in court that money can buy."

"I can't." There was real fear in her voice.

"You have to, Lucy. Try to understand my position. You're threatening to take me to court for—"

"I'm not! Dub is."

"All right," Cullen said in a placating tone. "Dub is going to take me to court to try to get money for a child I probably didn't father. From what you said on my answering machine, I got the impression that if I fight this, you'll go to the press and let them have a field day."

"No!" she cried. "Surely you know me better than that. This is all Dub's idea. I only called to try to warn you about what he planned to do."

Kate had been right. "Okay. Consider me warned. And consider my decision made."

There was no ignoring the decisiveness of his voice. "Wh-what are you going to do?"

"I'm going to have DNA testing done to find out once and for all if I'm Tyler's father. I expect you to cooperate with me in getting a blood sample from him."

"And if I don't?"

"Why wouldn't you?" Cullen said, his temper very close to the breaking point. "Don't you want to know the truth for your own peace of mind?"

"Yes," she said on a soft sob, "I do. But I don't want Dub to find out there was someone else. He might forgive me for one indiscretion—but two? I don't want him to think I'm some kind of cheap slut."

Cullen couldn't believe what he was hearing. Even after putting men like Dub Lambert behind bars for so long, even after years of hearing the heartbreaking stories from battered women, it never failed to surprise him how often they stuck up for their abuser.

"Lucy. Listen to you. You said you've left the man. Unless you're thinking of going back, why would you care what he thinks of you? You just told me he beat you. It's only a matter of time before he starts on Tyler. Is that what you want?"

She was crying again. A sound of quiet desperation. "No! None of this is his fault."

"Then help me," Cullen said in his most persuasive tone. "Let's find out the truth together. If he is mine, I'll be glad to pay support. If he isn't, then you'll both be better off knowing. And if Dub gives you any trouble, I'll personally help you go somewhere to start over. Hell, I'll help you anyway."

"Why would you do that for me?"

"Because I know you aren't cheap or a slut. Sometimes we all do things in desperation and pain and loneliness we wouldn't do otherwise."

When her crying had slowed to an occasional hiccup, Cullen set a time the following week to meet her and get the testing under way. He warned her to tell her parents what was going on and to beware of spending time alone with Dub.

"One more thing," he said when they were ready to hang up.

"Yeah?"

"You know Dub came to my house and threatened me."

"Yes. I tried to stop him, but he wouldn't listen," Lucy said.

"Do you think he's capable of doing something else?"

"Something else? Like what?" Lucy asked.

"Like trying to kill me."

He heard her sharp intake of breath. "Why do you ask?"

"I'm just trying to get a clear picture of what I'm up against," Cullen prevaricated.

"Wait!" Lucy said, a note of understanding creeping into her voice. "You were shot at. I heard about it on the news. Now they're saying it wasn't an accident. Are you asking me if I think it might have been Dub?"

"Yes."

Lucy didn't answer immediately. "Dub's a bully and a braggart," she said at last. "He's mean and he's an in-your-face kind of guy, but he only likes to pick on people who can't fight back. But kill someone? I don't think so. He's too much of a coward at heart."

As Cullen told her goodbye, he admitted that her feelings about Dub made him feel better. But only slightly. After she hung up, he heard another click and punched the button of his phone. Kate entered the room, a thoughtful expression on her face.

"Well?"

She shrugged. "I figure she's as good a judge as any as to how he'd act in a given situation. Of course, people are fooled every day about people they think they know well."

"True."

"I'm glad you're getting the DNA test done. I think you will be, too."

"Yeah," he said. She started for the door. "Where are you off to?"

She turned and raked a hand through her glorious hair, which, for some reason, she'd left unbound. "Since we have the Christmas parade tomorrow night, I'm going to go do some practice shooting—just in case. Don't leave the house until I get back."

Cullen sketched a sharp salute. "Yes, ma'am."

"Save the sarcasm, counselor."

She was in her defensive mode, her claws definitely out. "Kat?" he called, using the endearment on purpose. She glanced over her shoulder at him, her eyebrows raised in question. Was her color a little higher than normal?

"Yes?"

"You look really great today. I like the way those jeans fit."

She turned to face him, anger glinting in her eyes. "Stop it!"

"Stop what?"

"Stop trying to remind me of last night by flustering me with sexual innuendo."

He stood and rounded the desk, crossed the room and stopped within feet of her. She backed up until the door stopped her, as if she were afraid to have him touch her. Maybe she was.

"Is that what I'm doing?" he asked in an innocent voice.

"You know it is!"

Ignoring the pain in his shoulder, he placed a palm on either side of her head, imprisoning her with his nearness. "It happened, Kate," he told her in a soft, uncompromising voice. "And I have the fingernail prints on my back to prove it. Pretending to be mad won't make it go away, so I suggest you accept it for what it was, or get over it.''

"I'm not pretending to be angry. I am angry. I'm furious at myself for letting it happen.''

"Letting it happen?'' he said, pushing harder. "If my memory serves me correctly, you took the lead after a certain point.''

There was nothing she could say to that, no way to deny it. Satisfied that he'd made his point, he let his hands fall to his sides and stepped away from her. "Have a good shoot,'' he said, turning and walking toward the desk.

"And just what was it?''

The sound of her voice halted him halfway across the room. He turned, frowning. "What was what?''

"You said I should accept what happened for what it was. What, exactly, was it?'' *To you.* Though the words weren't spoken, that's what she was getting at. What had it meant to him?

Cullen let his gaze move over her in a leisurely appraisal, let it linger on her lips before settling on her gaze. He knew exactly what it was, but he wasn't quite willing to hand her his heart when he knew she was a long way from being able to accept it. "I'm still trying to figure it out myself,'' he lied. "I'll let you know when I do.''

Kate drove to the abandoned gravel pit and set up her targets, cursing Cullen and herself. If she'd hoped daylight would banish the foolishness she felt for giving in to the erotic feelings his kisses had ignited inside her, she'd been disappointed. In fact, the cold light of day had resurrected the memories she'd tried so hard to suppress throughout the night. Lathering her body in the shower had roused sensitive nerve endings.

There was a difference in the way she looked, too. A soft satisfaction in her eyes, a slight slackening in the set of her shoulders and her chin. She no longer looked as if she had a beef with the world, a chip on her shoulder. She looked like a woman who'd been thoroughly loved... a woman in love.

And she hated herself for it.

They had no future together, and they both knew it. Making love with Cullen may have jeopardized her ability to protect him. The realization that when they were together she'd be more aware of him than of her surroundings left her feeling vulnerable, something she hated most of all. If something happened to him while she was supposed to be keeping him safe, she would never get over it. And it would be a great loss for the people of the state and the laws he'd chosen to protect.

Working with her aunt on the list of suspects and talking with Meghan and Greg, Kate had come to know a lot about Cullen McGyver. He fought the cases he represented with diligence and fervor. He was an advocate for helping battered women and a supporter of victim's rights, as well as promoting harsher sentencing for sexual predators. He wanted a cleaner environment and believed there should be a crackdown on welfare and insurance fraud. He was a man who believed in every case he tried. He listened. He learned. His concern was genuine, and his honesty was above reproach.

In short, he would make a wonderful U.S. senator, a man who, despite his current predicament with Lucy, was decent, with high standards and morals. So he wasn't perfect. So he'd made mistakes. Who hadn't? The affair with Lucy, which had happened before either of them had married, would make only a small ripple in the pool of public opinion. In this day and age, the media would be hard-pressed to find a man who'd remained celibate prior to marriage. An illegitimate child was another matter altogether. Kate worried about the backlash if the DNA tests proved Tyler Lambert was Cullen's child, though she felt somewhat better since he had decided to find out the truth about the boy's paternity. And hearing Lucy's feelings about her husband's ability to take a life was also somewhat reassuring.

Though there were no concrete improvements in the status quo, Kate felt as if they were making progress. If they could eliminate Dub from their list of suspects, she'd feel a lot better about protecting Cullen when they made their debut into his life in the city…if he let her stay that long. If she could bear to stay that long.

Kate sighed. The longer she stayed, the more complicated things would become. Far from getting him out of her system, last night had only whetted her appetite. Cullen's, too, if she was any judge of things. Being with him day after day would increase the hunger and add to the complexity of the situation. It would behoove her to try harder to figure out a way to smoke out the killer so she could pack up and go back to her nice, predictable, boring life and start learning how to get over Cullen McGyver.

Giving a growl of frustration, she raised the Glock, braced it with her other arm and squeezed off several rounds. From the corner of her eye, she saw the grazing yearlings raise their heads, and as they had the other time she'd practiced, they bolted in fear, racing across the pasture as if demons were chasing them.

Kate watched in dismay. She hated upsetting them, but practicing was necessary if she was to stay sharp. She could only hope they'd get used to it. As she watched, the horses neared the fence. Most of them came to a screeching halt, but one, a bay filly, hit the board fence, sending the top board flying and taking a head-over-heels tumble. She rose almost immediately, but even from where she stood, Kate could see that the filly was limping badly.

She put the Glock on safety, tucked it into her waistband and ran to the four-wheeler she'd driven from the house. She had to let Cullen know what had happened so he could check the horse and have the fence fixed before all the horses got out. She made it to the house in a matter of minutes, pulling to a stop near the kitchen. Shutting off the ATV, she raced to the back door and barreled into the kitchen. Expecting to find Greg, Kate was surprised to find Dan rummaging around in the refrigerator.

"Where is everyone?" Kate asked.

"Greg took Louella to see his house, and Meghan and the girls went to Wal-Mart," Dan said, frowning. "What's wrong?"

"I was over at the old gravel pit practicing my shooting," Kate said breathlessly. "The gunshots spooked the fillies, and one of them ran through the fence. She's limping pretty badly."

Dan frowned and slammed the refrigerator door shut. "Sam, the guy who takes care of the horses for Meghan, is off until Monday. If you'll go tell Cullen to call the vet, I'll get a lead shank and a hammer from the barn and meet you at my truck," Dan said.

Kate raced for the door, paused and turned. "Do you know anything about horses?"

"Not much," Dan said with a shake of his head. "What I do know is that with busted ribs and a half-healed shoulder wound Cullen will be worse than useless."

Kate found Cullen in the library, several law books scattered across his desk. He was no doubt doing some research for the upcoming Jones trial.

"Call the vet," she said without preamble. "One of the fillies ran through the fence."

Cullen wasted no time looking up the closest veterinarian's number and punching it in, explaining who he was and what had happened. Luckily, the assistant said, the vet had just come in from another call. He'd be there ASAP. Cullen gave directions to the ranch, hung up and followed Kate out the door.

When Cullen, Dan and Kate arrived, only one other horse had breached the break in the fence. The two yearlings were munching on the tender grass outside the perimeter as if they hadn't been running crazily around the pasture a few moments earlier.

Dan extended one of the lead shanks to Kate. "What do I do with this?" she said, shaking her head.

"The chestnut looks pretty docile," Cullen told her. "See if you can get close enough to get hold of her bridle, then hook the snap through the ring. Dan and I will try to nab the bay."

"What if she tries to get away?" Kate asked, taking the leather lead.

"Let go, or the shank can really hurt your hands."

To Kate's surprise and unending gratitude, the filly was as easygoing as she looked. She made no objections to Kate's initial approach, though she eyed her warily. Other than the filly throwing back her head a time or two and snorting when Kate grabbed the bridle, the capture went smoothly. As she'd been instructed, Kate looped the chain through the brass ring of the bridle and snapped it shut. "What now?" she called.

Cullen, who was squatted down looking at the bay's

front legs, glanced up with a slight smile. "Put her back in the pasture. She'll step over that bottom board."

"What if she tries to get back out?" Kate asked, regarding the section of destroyed fence.

"Just stand there and see that she doesn't," Dan told her. "When I finish here, I'll tack the boards good enough to hold until Sam gets back."

Sighing, Kate led the filly through the fence. If her old buds at the NOPD could only see her now. "Is she hurt badly?" she asked, after freeing the filly.

"She's got a pretty deep cut on her chest and a nasty gash to the bone on her right shin, but nothing seems to be broken," Cullen said. "She should be fine."

"As my esteemed wife, the trauma doctor, is fond of saying, it's a long way from her heart," Dan said with a smile.

For the next several moments they let the filly graze while they waited for the vet's arrival. Finally, the sound of an approaching truck caught their attention, and a red pickup pulled to a stop behind Dan's Expedition. Two men got out, one tall and curly-haired—obviously the vet—the other stooped, bearded and wearing a baseball cap. The vet headed straight toward the injured filly, while the assistant went directly to the rear of the vehicle and began opening the stainless steel drawers and compartments, extracting the necessary equipment.

"It's a pleasure meeting you, Mr. McGyver," the tall man said, extending his hand to Cullen. "Mark Johnson, the new vet." He then offered his hand to Dan and Kate who offered their names. Then the vet cocked his head toward the man at the truck. "That's Kenny, my assistant."

Kenny, apparently absorbed in his task, gave a distracted wave. Introductions out of the way, the vet began to look the filly over, making Dan lead her so he could watch her walk, and probing the chest wound to gauge the depth of the cut. Kate, who'd seen her share of blood as a cop but couldn't bear for animals to hurt, stood back, content to let the men handle the crisis.

"We're gonna need to put in a few stitches, Kenny," the vet called to his assistant. "Get me some local and some tranq just in case she tries to go goofy on me."

The assistant brought the shots, took the shank from Dan and stepped to the opposite side, putting the horse between himself and the three men. Dan and Cullen moved out of the way.

"We can try to patch up the fence while they're working up the filly," Dan suggested. "You go get the hammer, and I'll see what we can do with what's left of these boards."

"Good idea," Cullen said, heading for the truck.

"Here's the tranquilizer," Kenny said, handing over the first syringe and some alcohol-saturated cotton balls. The vet swiped the side of the filly's neck, pressed with his thumb and, with a practiced move, slid the needle into the vein. A couple of seconds later, he pulled the needle out and gave her neck another rub with the alcohol.

The horse was so busy checking out Kenny, who was scratching her nose and between her ears, that she hardly noticed.

Smiling, Kate glanced at Cullen and Dan, who were working a few feet from her. "The top board's gonna have to be replaced," Dan said. "We can nail the one good one up—split the difference between the middle and top. It should hold until Sam gets here."

"It should," Cullen agreed.

It looked like they had the repairs under control, Kate

thought, giving her attention to the horse. The vet was injecting the local anesthetic around the bleeding chest wound. Thanks to her temperament and the tranquilizer, the filly stood perfectly still.

Thinking how good he was with the animal, Kate let her lazy gaze move to Kenny. His full attention was focused on the two men at the fence. Kate was stunned by the hostility she saw in his eyes. She felt herself stiffen and her muscles tense.

"Kenny," the vet said, holding out his hand. "I need to wash out this cut before I sew her up. Bring everything we need and some antibiotic."

"Sure thing, Doc," Kenny said pleasantly, handing the shank to the vet and ambling toward the truck.

It must have been a trick of the light or her imagination, Kate thought. There was absolutely nothing in the assistant's manner to suggest anything but an accommodating attitude. When he passed within a few feet of Kate, he ducked his head, touched the bill of his cap and gave a half smile.

Kate's uneasiness passed, and she smiled back. The strain of worrying about Cullen was getting to her. Knowing they would be going out into public soon had her more concerned than she realized. She was starting to jump at shadows, to see things that weren't really there. There was nothing at all threatening about the vet's assistant. He was just a shy old man.

Chapter Eleven

Saturday night, the last night Meghan's family would spend at the ranch, was also the night of the Barnesville Christmas parade Cullen was supposed to be part of. Darkness fell, cold and crisp and calm. Louella, Kate, Greg and Cullen rode in Greg's car. Dan drove the Longstreets'.

The stars in the nighttime sky sparkled as brightly as sunlight reflected off snow, but they were no brighter than the twinkling lights that adorned every tree and window on Main Street or the smiles of the children who waited to get a glimpse of Santa.

Kate stood near Cullen, who, as master of ceremonies and local-boy-made-good and possible U.S. senator, stood on the main thoroughfare along with the judges who would decide the winning float. The people from the community television station were there, too, set to broadcast the parade into homes across the county.

Cullen was good at his job, bantering with the TV reporter and the lady from the Chamber of Commerce. He was teasing, charming, and appeared to be a storehouse of knowledge about previous parades and local clubs and civic organizations.

Standing near him, Kate was on alert the entire time, scanning the crowd, looking for that one person who looked out of place, the one attitude or posture that seemed unlikely or contrived. Thankfully, the whole thing only lasted about forty minutes, and as Cullen had predicted, there were no incidents.

Once the parade was over, they decided to go to a small café and have a cup of hot chocolate before returning to the ranch. Cullen and Kate had taken off their coats and were looking at the menu when Meghan and her family pushed through the door, sleigh bells jangling their arrival.

"You'll never guess who I saw!" Meghan said, smiling brightly as she preceded the others to the table.

"Probably not," Cullen said.

"Grady Holmes." She turned to Kate. "Grady is an old high school friend."

"An old high school *boyfriend*," Dan corrected.

"Oh, no need to be jealous, cutie," Meghan said, blowing him a kiss. "You know you're the only guy in the world for me."

"Yeah, yeah," Dan said, but he was smiling.

"So what's Grady doing here? Isn't he practicing law in Dallas?" Cullen asked.

"He is," Meghan said, as Dan helped her get her coat off. "But he came home for Thanksgiving and doesn't have to go back until tomorrow. He asked about you," she told Cullen. "He thinks it's great that you might try for a senate seat."

"I think it's amazing that so many people are convinced I'll be a good senator when I haven't even decided for sure if I'll run or not."

"What do you mean you haven't decided whether or not you'll run?" Kate asked.

"That's what I mean," Cullen said. "I've given it a lot of thought, but I haven't made a final decision. Going to Washington would mean a lot of changes in my life."

"You don't like change, do you?" Dan asked.

"Depends on what kind of change you're talking about," Cullen said. "There are a couple of changes I can think of that would make my life a better one, but other than someone trying to kill me, I'm pretty much satisfied with the status quo."

"You're certainly good at what you do," Meghan said. "And you're impacting the state."

Cullen smiled at her. "Spoken like a true sister."

"Well, you are."

"I see the waitress coming back," Dan said. "What are you having?"

"I think I'll have a coffee and a piece of pecan pie," Meghan said.

"That sounds good," Kate concurred. "Make that two."

The waitress came, and they all placed their orders. They were talking about the parade when Meghan said, "You'll never guess who else I saw. At least I think it was him."

"I'm too tired to guess," Cullen said. "Who?"

"Kent Carlson."

The name hung in the air like a fog of mosquitoes over a bog. Even Lindsay and Marley stopped chattering.

"What am I missing here?" Kate said, her gaze moving from one adult to the other. "Who's Kent Carlson?"

"Kent Carlson is the man who killed Joanie," Cullen said in a flat, toneless voice.

Silence descended on the table. Thankfully, it was only a few seconds until the waitress brought their drinks and desserts, and a lackluster conversation started again. The talk gradually became less stilted, but it never quite reverted to its former lightheartedness. By the time they finished their desserts, they all agreed that they were exhausted but that it had been a good night, a wonderful holiday. Meghan expressed regret at having to leave the next day.

Twenty minutes later, Greg pulled into the drive behind the Longstreets and let Cullen, Kate and Louella out, telling them he'd see them first thing in the morning. The group of seven tromped into the house, shedding jackets and hats and gloves. Louella went upstairs immediately, saying she had a book she wanted to finish reading. The girls and their dad went to find something on television, and Cullen went to check the phone messages.

Distressed by his obvious anger over the mention of Kent Carlson, Kate stood irresolutely at the bottom of the stairs for a moment before following Meghan, who'd gone to the kitchen to get something for her oncoming headache.

Meghan was just swallowing the tablets when Kate reached the door. "I hate to bother you, but I want to talk to you about Cullen's reaction to your seeing...Kent, wasn't it?" Kate said.

"Yes, Kent," Meghan said, nodding. "Carlson. I should have known it would upset him. I never should have said anything, especially since I'm not even sure it was him."

"He's still in love with her, isn't he?" Kate said, uncertain that she wanted to hear the truth but needing it if she was to keep her head straight throughout the remainder of her time with Cullen.

Instead of answering, Meghan countered with a question of her own. "You're falling for my brother, aren't you?"

Kate's startled gaze flew to Meghan's.

"I'm a trained observer," Meghan said. "I've seen the way you look at him. Come to think of it, he looks at you the same way."

"It's just the close proximity," Kate said, trying to slough off the whole thing. "The whole pretend situation. It happens sometimes."

"Did it start in New Orleans?" Meghan asked. "From the look on your face, I'd say that it did, which would explain a lot of things."

"Like what?" Kate asked, curious to find out all she could about Cullen's state of mind when he'd left her.

"Why he was such a bear when he first got back, for starters. He was irritable for months. I didn't think he'd ever start dating again, but when he did, he went at it with a vengeance, almost as if he were trying to prove something to himself...or forget something."

"Like what?"

"At the time, I thought he was trying to prove that he was over Joanie's death. Now, I'm not so sure. Maybe he was trying to forget you."

Kate gave a brittle laugh. "That shouldn't have been too hard. He had no problem leaving."

"So there was something between the two of you?"

Kate nodded. "Nothing serious."

"Serious enough, I think. And it happened before Joanie was dead a year, which, knowing my brother, he'd see as some sort of character flaw."

"Why?" Kate asked with a frown.

"He loved Joanie. He would consider having any kind of relationship with a woman so soon after her death as being disloyal."

"To whom? Joanie?"

Meghan shrugged. "To her memory, to what they had together. He'd think it was too soon." She gave Kate a considering look. "Knowing there was something between the two of you also explains his initial reluctance to hire you."

Though finding out that just maybe she hadn't been as forgettable as she'd thought gave Kate's ego a little boost, she wasn't ready to believe that she'd made a lasting impact on Cullen's life. Still, she wanted to know more about this complex man who had stolen her heart, wanted to know more about Joanie, who still held so much control over him.

"Tell me about Joanie."

"What do you want to know?"

"He still loves her, doesn't he?" Kate asked her unanswered question again.

Meghan shook her head. "No. I think that for a long time he was in love with the idea of loving her. And he felt guilty. I think he still feels guilty."

"Guilty?" Kate asked. "Why?"

"Because he insisted on the two of them spending some time here for a few days. She went into labor and was dead before he arrived."

With just that bit of information, pieces of the puzzle began to take shape in Kate's mind. "You said Kent Carlson was her doctor while she was pregnant?"

Meghan shook her head. "No. Not her regular doctor. Kent was the doctor who took over Greg's practice at Webster—that's another little town not far from Barnesville. He was fresh out of med school and—"

"Kate!" Cullen's voice, filled with rage and disbelief, thundered down the hall.

She shot Meghan a concerned look, the tale she was hearing forgotten. "In the kitchen!"

Cullen burst through the door, his face ashen, his mouth tight with strain. "Come into the library. You've got to hear this."

"What is it?" she asked, following him out of the room to the library, Meghan hard on her heels.

"The killer. He knows where I am."

Kate's heart took a nosedive, but she forced herself not to let the panic rising inside her get a toehold on her common sense.

At the desk, Cullen hit the play button of the answering machine. "Hi, McGyver," a man's soft, breathy voice said. "I just thought I'd give you a call and let you know that I told you I'd find you, and I have. I know where you are, and I know what you've been doing out there in the weight room with that pretty redhead."

Kate's gaze flew to Cullen's, and her shocked gasp filled the room. She couldn't bear to bring herself to look at Meghan. Dear sweet heaven! Had the killer really watched while she and Cullen shared the most intimate of acts? She shuddered. She felt as if she'd been violated, as if what they'd shared had been cheapened, desecrated.

"Sleep tight, McGyver," the breathless voice continued. "I'll be in touch."

Kate rubbed the goose bumps that had risen on her arms at the threat in the whispery voice. Worse than the fact that this unknown man had watched her and Cullen was the knowledge that he had been that close to Cullen—close enough to finish the job he'd started in the woods—and no one, least of all Kate, had had any idea he was nearby.

"Do you recognize the voice?" Meghan asked, ignoring the comment the man had made about Cullen and Kate.

Cullen scraped a hand through his wind-tousled hair. "No. I mean, it sounds sort of familiar, but he's almost whispering, so it's hard to say for sure."

"Can you tell whether or not this is the same person who left the other message?" Kate asked, finding her voice, though it sounded hoarse and strained.

"I don't know," he said, frowning. "Maybe if I listened to them both, I could make a comparison."

"We can do that," Kate said.

They did. After comparing the two taped phone calls, all three agreed that, even though it was impossible to be certain, the two messages had been left by the same person. And, after listening to them again, Cullen still had no idea if the voice was familiar or not.

"Why didn't he do something when he had the chance?" Meghan said, inadvertently bringing up Cullen and Kate's rendezvous in the weight room.

"He's playing with us," Kate said. "Sometimes the chase holds more of a thrill than the actual kill. He wants to make Cullen sweat."

"Well, he's doing a damn good job," Cullen said.

Meghan sighed. "What do we do now?"

"Make sure all the doors are locked. I don't think he'll try anything with so many people in the house, but I can't make any guarantees. It might be best if you all went back to Little Rock tonight. I promise I won't let Cullen out of my sight."

"No madman is going to scare me out of my home," Meghan said. "The girls can sleep on a pallet in our room, and Dan can keep the shotgun beside the bed. He's a good shot."

"He is that," Cullen said. "What about Louella?"

"I'll talk to her," Kate offered. "See what she says."

Louella's attitude was pretty close to Meghan's. Kate told her she was a stubborn woman.

"Where do you think you got it?" Louella said with a smile. "It was a toss-up as to which one of us was the most bullheaded, me or your dad. Now go see about that man of yours."

Kate, who had already started down the hallway, turned and took a couple of steps toward her aunt. "What are you talking about?"

"Don't act so surprised," Louella said with an impatient shake of her head. "Anyone who isn't blind can see the way the two of you look at each other."

So much for her professional persona. If two people in one night had commented on the way she and Cullen looked at each other, it must mean she was wearing her heart on her sleeve. But what did it say about Cullen? *You can't think about that right now.* Still, she couldn't help asking. "How does he look at me?"

Louella smiled. "As if he can't make up his mind if he'd rather shake you till your teeth rattle or carry you off to the bushes and have his way with you."

Embarrassed, Kate did what she could to repair the damage of too easily telegraphing her emotions. "It's just a game, Aunt Lou," Kate said, managing a crisp, nononsense tone.

"Is it?" Louella asked. She took one of Kate's cold hands in both of hers. "He's a good man, Kate. If there's something there, don't ignore it. Don't let this chance go by. There may not be another."

Kate heard the sincerity in her aunt's voice and felt her throat tighten with emotion. As wonderful as a future with Cullen sounded, she'd passed the time in her life when she believed in fairy tales. "You said it yourself. I'm not his type. Never will be."

"Fiddlesticks!" Louella said. "Cullen is interested. More than interested. Do what any self-respecting female would do and use that to your advantage."

Kate shook her head. "It would never work. Besides, I'm not a very good marriage risk, as you well know, and I'm not too good at recovering from broken hearts." She sighed. "I'm even worse at playing the femme fatale."

"It isn't your fault Lane couldn't go the distance," Louella said. "He's the one who lost out. And as for your not being Cullen's type, well—" she shrugged "—the heart doesn't go by rules, Katie. It knows what it knows and it doesn't pay a bit of attention to your head or possible risks or anything else."

She squeezed Kate's hand. "Remember us talking about there being a better way to meet men than doing the dating scene? Well, my dear," she said with a twinkle in her eyes, "I think we've both found it. It's up to us to see how we handle it from here."

Kent Carlson lay in his solitary bed, his hands laced together beneath his head, and tried to envision the concern plaguing the folks at the McGyver ranch. McGyver's sister had seen him at the Christmas parade, and while he'd sensed a bit of recognition in her eyes, he wasn't sure she'd put two and two together. After all, he looked far different than he had three years ago. Older. Grayer. And the beard gave him a more rugged appearance than he'd once had.

He wondered if they'd listened to his newest message and if Cullen McGyver was finally taking the situation with as much seriousness as he should. And it was very

serious. Especially now that there was another woman
involved. Cullen McGyver had ruined Kent's life because
he blamed him for Joanie McGyver's death. In fact, it
had been Cullen's tearful portrayal of a man who would
never get over his loss that had been the nail in the coffin
of Kent's career, so to speak. Wasn't it interesting that
never had turned out to be only three years?

Kent let his mind travel back, as it did often, to the
night Joanie McGyver had died. Newly married and a
newly licensed general practitioner, he had taken over
Greg Kingsley's patient load. Life was good. He'd been
at home with his wife, celebrating their six months an-
niversary, when he'd gotten the call from the hospital
saying a woman had come in with what appeared to be
early labor. Kent told them he wasn't on call, but the
head RN had told him they'd had no choice but to call
him; the other doctor was taking care of a car-accident
victim.

Celia, clad in a sexy satin gown, had begged him not
to leave, but Kent had known he had no choice; he was
learning fast that Greg Kingsley's shoes were large ones
to fill. Kent had poured the last of the champagne into
his glass, drained it and left her with a lingering kiss and
a promise that he'd be back before she even missed him.

The drive to the hospital through the storm-swept night
had seemed endless as he'd struggled to keep the car on
the highway while the wind buffeted it from every side.
His mind whispered that wind was only a part of it. How
many glasses of champagne had he consumed, anyway?
Not enough to hurt. He felt on top of the world, filled
with love for his wife and a desire that throbbed hotly
through him. Invincible.

When he'd arrived at the small rural hospital, the nurse
in charge had taken one look at him, frowned and asked

if he was okay. He was fine, he'd assured her with a wide smile. Just fine. He had donned some scrubs, scrubbed and gloved up, then gone into the small room where Joanie McGyver lay.

His mind was filled with thoughts of Celia as he made his examination. It didn't take an M.D. to see that she was in a lot of pain. He listened with half an ear as she explained that she and her husband were supposed to spend the weekend at their farm, about twenty miles away. His flight from Atlanta had been detained because of the severe weather system that held the southern states in a tight grip. The pains has started an hour or so earlier, and she'd tried lying down to see if they'd ease up. When they'd shown no signs of relenting, she'd driven herself through the country highways and a raging storm to the hospital.

Kent had assured her that she was going to be fine, that he was going to give her something to stop the labor.

He mouthed the word *breech* to the nurse who followed him out of the room.

"We should call Texarkana," she said as the door closed behind them. "We're understaffed, underqualified and underequipped, doctor, and this is a situation that can get really ugly."

Anger mushroomed inside him. How dare she question his ability to do the work he'd learned to do—and learned quite well, thank you very much. He was a good doctor. A great doctor. He could certainly deliver a baby...if it came to that.

"I beg your pardon," he said, the alcohol singing sweetly through his veins. "What exactly do you mean?"

"I mean that we were understaffed *before* the wreck took most of our nurses. You're a newly licensed G.P.—"

"Who finished at the top of my class."

"I realize that. No offense, doctor, but you're far better qualified to treat a sore throat or a case of shingles than you are to deliver a preemie baby that happens to be breech!"

"Good God, woman! I'm a medical doctor, and a damn good one," he said in a low, angry voice. *I was top in my class. I can walk on water—or the medical equivalent.* "I have delivered babies before. Several, in fact. It's a fairly routine procedure." *Except that this delivery shows no sign of being routine.*

He ignored the taunting little voice that told him he was being overconfident. "In case you haven't noticed, there's a storm out there. They'd never okay the chopper to leave the ground." He placed a conciliatory hand on her arm. "We're going to do all we can to stop the labor. If that fails, there will be plenty of time to turn the baby and we'll deliver it. Do you understand?"

"I understand that even if all that goes without a hitch, we don't have the facilities to accommodate a preemie baby."

An agonized scream came from the room where Joanie McGyver lay. "A moot point, it seems." He gave the middle-aged woman a confident smile and a pat on the shoulder. "Time's a wastin', Nurse Larsen. Duty calls."

Unfortunately, things hadn't worked out as he expected them to. There was no stopping the labor. For a first baby, it came fast. Faster than he'd ever seen. Not a good situation, since the baby was breech. Joanie McGyver had needed something for the pain because she was screaming and screaming…. The anesthesiologist was on the way, and Kent had had no choice but to give her something to help with the pain.

He'd tried to turn the baby, without any luck. He

thought about a C-section and scrapped the idea. It was too late for that, too. The baby was already in the birth canal, and Joanie McGyver was screaming and screaming, despite the painkiller he'd given her.

Then, mercifully, it was finally over. The baby—a boy—was stillborn, the final blow the umbilical cord wrapped around his neck. The anesthesiologist arrived, and in an act of kindness administered what was supposed to be temporary forgetfulness to Joanie. Exhausted, stone-cold sober, his faith in his own ability shaken to the core, Kent had delivered the afterbirth, dragged off his surgical mask and left the delivery room, wanting nothing but to find forgetfulness in another bottle of champagne and the soft willingness of his wife's body....

He got into the car and turned off his cell phone. He wasn't on duty, and he'd done all and more than they should expect from him. He learned later that not long after he left the hospital Joanie McGyver started hemorrhaging and nothing was able to stop it.

According to her testimony in the wrongful death suit Cullen McGyver had brought against him, Joanie McGyver was dead before the chopper Nurse Larsen had called arrived. By that time, Kent had been back home, listening to the sexy sighing of the sax, partaking of a new bottle of champagne and the delights of his wife's body in an effort to block out the sounds of Joanie McGyver's screaming.

Cullen McGyver arrived soon after the medical team. Hearing the news of the death of his wife and son, he'd gone into a frenzy of grief that had given way to anger and accusations and eventually the lawsuit that demanded Kent's medical license be revoked. Anita Larsen's testimony that he'd been drinking had added the necessary clout to the case.

Just like that, the life he'd worked for so many long hard years had ended. Celia, who'd wanted nothing more than to be a doctor's wife, had left him long before the final blow, eager to find someone who could give her the status she so desperately needed. Kent had learned many lessons from that night, among them the solemn truth that political connections could be a powerful tool in the right hands...or the wrong ones.

When Kate left her aunt, she found that Cullen had gone to his room. She took a quick shower and blew her hair dry. Slipping on a flannel sleep shirt and some fuzzy slippers, carrying the holster for her Glock over her shoulder, she made her way down the hall to his room. She took a deep breath and rapped sharply on the door.

Cullen, his hair wet and slicked back from his face, wearing nothing but a towel around his waist, yanked open the door. Neither spoke for several seconds. Kate noticed the discoloration on his chest from his injured ribs and the pristine whiteness of the square bandage taped to his shoulder. The width of his hair-dusted chest and the narrowness of his waist. The long, hard length of his legs. Memories of Thanksgiving night burst into her mind like unwanted party guests.

"What are you doing here?" The sound of his voice broke the spell binding her.

"My job." He stared at her, the expression in his eyes a cross between consideration and a dare. "I was hired to protect you, and I told your sister I wouldn't let you out of my sight."

"I didn't think you meant it literally...not after last night."

Kate's chin lifted a fraction of an inch. "We've already established that the other night was just—"

"Don't you dare say it was a mistake," he warned, pointing a finger at her.

"It was what it was. Nothing more. But it can't happen again."

"Why?"

Kate felt hot color creep into her cheeks. "Because that man was here," she said, anger at herself sharpening her voice. "He was close enough to finish what he started before, and I had no idea he was anywhere close by because my attention was otherwise occupied." *You could have been killed, and despite my assertions that I could handle it, I'd have never forgiven myself because I hadn't done my job.*

He crossed his arms over his bare chest. "So what did you have in mind?"

She cocked her head toward the oversize chair and ottoman that sat near the bed. "That'll do."

"No," he said. "It won't." Reaching out, he grabbed her arm and dragged her into the room, shutting the door behind her. "If you stay, you sleep in the bed. With me."

Kate's heart began to thunder inside her chest, and her blood turned to molten lava. She faced him angrily, her breasts heaving. "I won't make love with you, Cullen!"

"No one asked you to."

The calm reminder drained away the anger. "All right," she told him. "Just stay on your side of the bed."

"Deal."

"Which side do you sleep on?" she asked, meeting his gaze headlong.

He pointed to the right side, and Kate rounded the queen-size bed to the other, kicking off her slippers and placing her Glock on the mahogany nightstand. Without a word, she pulled back the duvet, folding it at the foot of the bed, then crawled beneath the covers, pulling them to her chin.

Cullen watched, then turned off the overhead light and went to the highboy across the room and opened a drawer. The lamp cast a golden glow, scattering the shadows to the corners of the room. Before Kate realized what he was up to, the towel fell to the floor. The sight of his nakedness elicited a slight gasp of surprise.

"Sorry," he said over his shoulder. She wasn't sure if it was a trick of the light or if there really was a naughty gleam in his eyes. "Didn't mean to shock you, but I usually sleep in the raw. Since we're sharing a bed, I thought I'd put on some pajama bottoms rather than offend you."

"Thanks." Kate punched her pillow and rolled to her side. In a matter of seconds, she felt the bed give as Cullen sat down on the edge of the mattress and reached to turn off the bedside lamp. She felt him stretch out beside her. It might have been her imagination, but she thought she could feel the heat from his body. She could definitely smell the scent of his soap, something musky and masculine. She squeezed her eyes tightly shut. This was never going to work.

"Tell me about Joanie's death," she blurted into the darkness. There was nothing like the ghost of a dead wife to keep libidinous thoughts at bay.

Cullen didn't say anything for several seconds.

"Don't tell me it isn't any of my business," Kate added. "After New Orleans and Thanksgiving, you at least owe me that."

Culled rolled to his back. She followed suit. She knew he was staring at the ceiling in the room's darkness.

"She was pregnant. It had been a terrible pregnancy from the beginning." The words came from him slowly, as if the remembering were painful. "There was some bleeding. She had to stay in bed a lot. There were lots of problems. Terrible nausea..."

He sighed and Kate waited for him to continue. "We were going to spend the weekend here. She drove down early. My flight was delayed in Atlanta. She went into early labor and drove herself to the hospital. They called Kent Carlson to come and take care of her. He was drunk—or at least had been drinking, but he thought he could handle it. It was a breech birth, evidently the labor went very fast, and the baby was born dead. Carlson left, and Joanie began to hemorrhage. She bled to death."

Kate's fingernails dug into her palms. She felt the hot sting of tears in her eyes. "I'm sorry." Her voice sounded unsteady and small in the darkness.

"Yeah. Me, too. Women aren't supposed to die having babies in this day and age," he said.

"No."

"But I made sure he'd never kill anyone again. I saw to it that he lost his medical license."

"He should have."

Without another word, Cullen turned onto his good side, indicating that the conversation was finished. Kate lay where she was, the hot wetness of her silent tears sliding down her temples to the pillow, never more sure that in spite of the differences in their lives she'd fallen in love with him. Never more certain that she'd do whatever there was in her power to keep him safe. He deserved that, at least.

Cullen closed his eyes and listened to the soft sounds of her breathing, wondering if she was asleep or if she was thinking about the story he'd just he told her. He wanted nothing more than to turn to her and pull her into his arms, to bury himself in her and seek forgetfulness of the past and the uncertainty of his future in her warmth and heat. If it hadn't been before, it was now official. He loved her.

Chapter Twelve

When Kate opened her eyes, it took her a few seconds to realize where she was. In Cullen's room, enveloped in warmth. Disgusted with herself, she threw back the blankets. She hadn't meant to fall asleep. What kind of a bodyguard was she, anyway? She started to get up and realized there was something heavy and warm lying across her waist. She reached down to move it. The something was Cullen's arm. Her back was cradled against his chest, his thighs warm against hers.

More awake, she felt the warmth of his breath against her shoulder. Without thinking, she closed her eyes and trailed her fingertips up and down his forearm, loving the feel of the soft, dark hair and the warm heat of his flesh. Sudden hot flames of desire licked through her.

Her eyes flew open. This wasn't good. Not good at all. Too much of this could become addictive, which would be bad for her in the long run, because it was beginning to look as if the final curtain would soon come down on her gig as live-in lover. The perp knew where Cullen was and was getting closer, getting braver. It was only a matter of finding the opportune time to try to finish him off. Only a matter of time before she found out whether or not she had what it took to do her job.

Giving a little sigh, she tried to ease herself from beneath the weight of Cullen's arm. His grip tightened. "Shh." She felt his mouth move against her shoulder. "Be still."

Kate couldn't have moved if she'd wanted to. And she didn't want to. She held her breath, waiting to see what would happen next. The ringing of the phone shattered the stillness and the mood. Kate stiffened. Cullen groaned.

"Can you hand me the phone?" he asked groggily in her ear.

Kate fumbled for the receiver. Cullen took it from her and rolled to his back. "Hello."

It didn't take long to figure out he was talking with the vet, who was sending his assistant to check the filly's bandage. Kate could have cared less about the hurt horse at that moment. Without the weight of his arm across her, she felt chilled and lonely, but sanity, such as it was the past couple of days, was fast returning. Now would be the perfect time to get up, get dressed and get away from Cullen's disturbing nearness before she let something happen that shouldn't. Succumbing to his not inconsiderable persuasiveness once might be excused by claiming a moment's insanity, twice by claiming weakness. But allowing him to get too close a third time would be indefensible.

She threw back the covers and started to get up, but Cullen's hand shot out and gripped her wrist, stopping her. When she glanced at him, she saw the frown of pain on his face. He'd used his bad arm.

He mouthed the single word, "Stay."

Kate shook her head and gently disengaged her wrist from his hold. As she reached for her Glock, Cullen turned off the phone and put the receiver on the bed.

"Coward."

Kate turned to look at him. The blankets only partially covered his bare chest. Her nerve endings began to sizzle beneath the heat she saw in his eyes. "Let's just say I don't think my staying would be a wise thing to do."

A half smile curved Cullen's mouth. "Amazing. A woman who knows her limitations."

Kate couldn't think of a glib reply. She recalled doing everything she could to make her life with Lane normal, remembered him telling her that living with her was too high stress. Thought of Cullen leaving her without a goodbye. Oh, yeah. She knew her limitations.

"Well, if I can't have you for breakfast, we should get dressed and see what Greg has to offer."

"Don't," Kate snapped. She could only be strong as long as she felt in control, and her control slipped fast when Cullen turned on his considerable charm.

"Don't what?"

"Don't keep coming on to me...don't play with me!"

"What makes you think I'm playing?"

She heard the edge in his voice, saw the flash of impatience in his eyes.

Cullen pushed himself up until his back rested against the mahogany headboard. "So you think that what happened between us was just a game, something I did to pass the time?"

"Wasn't it?"

"Would you believe me if I told you you're wrong, that it meant a lot more than that to me?"

Kate wanted to believe it, but the differences and her past heartaches and disappointments made believing hard, especially counting the contrast in her and Cullen's lifestyles. "No." Cold. Firm. Unmovable.

"That sounds pretty final," he said. "Even I can understand that." He smiled at her, albeit weakly, or was that sadly? "Go on and get dressed. I'll meet you downstairs."

Without another word or another look at him, Kate picked up her Glock and left the room, wondering if she'd just made a mistake she couldn't undo, fearing in her heart that she had.

Twenty minutes later, Kate was dressed and ready to face the day, the Glock tucked inside the waistband of her jeans, nestled in the small of her back beneath her sweater. Taking a fortifying breath, she went to Cullen's room to see if he was ready to go down to breakfast. He didn't answer the knock on his door, and when she stepped inside to check, she heard the sound of the shower going full blast.

There was no sense sitting there waiting for him. He'd hate that. Surely, now that it was daylight, she could leave him alone inside the house long enough for him to take a shower and get dressed. Exhaling a frustrated breath, she left the room, closed the door behind her and headed for the kitchen.

Downstairs, she found her aunt and Greg busily preparing breakfast, working together with a precision that was amazing, considering they had only known each other five days.

"Hi, honey!" Louella said, throwing Kate a bright smile.

"Good morning, Aunt Louella. Good morning, Greg."

"Mornin,' Katie," Greg said, adopting her aunt's pet name.

"Thank goodness we had an uneventful night!" Louella said, pouring a small glass of orange juice and setting it on the table.

"Thank goodness," Kate echoed. She helped herself to a cup of coffee and took a sip. "Where is everyone?"

"Meghan went out to the barn to check on the filly. Dan and the girls wanted to make the most of their last chance to sleep in."

"I can't say I blame them," Kate said.

"How many eggs do you want?" Greg said. His big hand, clutching two eggs, hovered over a small glass bowl.

"A couple," Kate said. "If you'll hold off a minute, I need to run out and tell Meghan the vet is on the way."

"I think I saw him pull in a few minutes ago," Greg said. "But why don't you see how long Meghan will be, so I'll have an idea about how long before she's ready to eat?"

"Sure," Kate said. She topped off her coffee mug and headed for the back door, snagging a jacket off the coat rack as she passed. "When Cullen comes down, tell him I'll be back in a minute. Under no circumstances is he to leave the house unless I'm with him."

"Got it," Greg said.

Outside in the crisp, sunny morning, Kate set down her cup on the antique metal table and slipped on the jacket. Picking up her coffee, she headed toward the barn. Sure enough, there was a truck parked near the back, but it wasn't the truck the vet had been driving the day before. It was an older model with a magnetic sign on the side that said Town and Country Veterinary Clinic. Maybe Mark Johnson's other truck had broken down, she thought, as she stepped from the bright sunshine into the dimness of the barn.

For a few seconds, all she could see was darkness. The scents of hay, manure and the unmistakable smell of vitamins filled her nostrils. Then, as her eyes adjusted to the light streaming through the cracks in the old barn walls, she saw dust motes dancing in the air. Her immediate impression was that the barn was empty. There was no sign of Meghan or the vet, no sound but the snuffling of horses and the stamping of hooves. "Meghan?" she called. "Are you in here?"

No answer but the rustling of hooves, the bump of feed tubs against the wall and a soft blowing noise.

A familiar and inexplicable feeling of uneasiness pricked the back of her neck. It was the same feeling she'd had when she'd faked being a drug user to nail a dealer, the feeling she'd gotten when she walked alone into a rough club, knowing there was potential for violence all around her. The same feeling she'd experienced the day she and Raul had burst through the doors of the crack house and found death waiting to say hello.

She reminded herself that she wasn't in the city and none of those scenarios applied. She was just on edge from the phone call the night before. Mark Johnson wasn't a threat. He was the local vet. He and Meghan were probably in one of the stalls, busy rebandaging the filly.

Still, years of ingrained caution made her set down her coffee mug on the top of a bandage box and reach beneath her coat and sweater for the Glock. Even as she thumbed off the safety, a feeling of foolishness washed through her. Better to feel like a fool than to wind up dead, a small voice whispered. She was comforted by the thought that Cullen was safe inside.

Cullen had just stepped into the kitchen when the phone rang. ''Where's Kate?'' he asked, as he crossed to the ringing instrument.

''She went to the barn to see how long it would be until Meghan and the vet are finished.''

''Oh.'' Cullen snatched up the receiver. ''Hello.''

''Mr. McGyver?''

''Yes.'' Cullen recognized the voice on the other line, since he'd already heard it once that morning. The vet, Mark Johnson. ''I called to see if I can talk to Kenny a minute.''

''Kenny?'' Cullen said, the name not registering.

''Yeah. Kent Carlson, my assistant.''

Kent Carlson. The name reverberated through Cullen's head. Kent Carlson, the doctor who'd been responsible for Joanie's death. An image of the vet's helper flashed through Cullen's mind. He didn't look like the man Cullen recalled from the trial, but it could be the beard and the gray hair.

''I paged him,'' Johnson was saying, ''but he didn't call me back, and I...''

The rest of what he was saying didn't register with Cullen. He was too busy trying to assimilate the fact that Kent Carlson was working as a vet's assistant. Realizing that some sort of answer was required, Cullen assured the vet that he'd make sure Kenny called him back as soon as possible. The vet said his goodbyes, but before he could hang up, Cullen cried, ''Wait!''

''Yes?'' Politely.

''How long has he been working for you?''

"Only a few days, but don't worry about the filly. Kent came highly recommended by the vet he worked for in Hempstead County."

"Thanks," Cullen said, his mind whirling, examining the information from every angle and trying to determine if it meant anything or not. He turned off the phone and stared out the window, trying to make sense of what he'd just learned. Was it possible that the vet's assistant was the same Kent Carlson whose incompetence had killed Joanie, or was this just another of life's funny coincidences? And if they were the same person, what did it matter? What he did for a living had nothing to do with the past. It was behind them.

You'll be sorry, McGyver. Do you hear me? One day you'll be sorry for what you've done to me.

The words, spoken in a harsh whisper by Carlson as he'd left the courtroom, his career and his life in a shambles at his feet. The truth shot through Cullen with all the force of the bullet that had knocked him from the tree stand.

"Cullen? Are you all right?"

Louella's voice, sharp with concern. Without answering, he turned and ran to the library where his dad had kept his hunting rifles in a handmade gun cabinet. He pulled the .22 from the rack and grabbed the box of hollow points from the shelf. He'd load it on the way to the barn.

When he got downstairs, Meghan was there, talking ninety to nothing. "I thought you were in the barn," he said.

"I was, but I had a revelation, so I made an excuse and hightailed it back in here." She grabbed his arm. "Cullen, listen to me. It *was* Kent Carlson I saw at the parade. He's the vet's assistant. And I think he could be the person who wants to kill you.''

From across the room, Louella gave a little cry of dismay. Greg slid a comforting arm around her shoulders and pulled her close.

''I know,'' Cullen said. ''I just figured it out myself.''

Noticing the rifle, Meghan's eyes widened. ''What are you going to do?''

''Kate's out there with him. I'm going to get her.''

She grabbed his arm. ''What! Why—''

Cullen jerked free. ''I don't have time to stand here talking, Meg. I'll be damned if Kent Carlson is going to kill another woman I love.''

Like the big buck that had sashayed into the woods after hearing the doe's bleating call, with no thought for his own safety, Cullen pulled open the door and headed for the barn, concerned only about Kate.

The hair on the back of Kate's neck stood straight up. Every molecule of her being said something was wrong, and that something wasn't too hard to guess. The man who wanted Cullen dead had come to finish what he'd started less than two weeks ago. Her mind churned out the reality of the situation. The person who'd shot Cullen wasn't Dub Lambert or any of the other men she'd been checking out the past week. It was Mark Johnson's assistant, Kenny. Kent.

The look of hate she'd intercepted the day the filly was injured made sense now, as did the way he'd put the filly between himself and Cullen to keep from being recognized. How had he found out where Cullen was? Had he been in the area all along? Wasn't it incredible that he happened to be working for the vet they'd called? No, not incredible. Deliberate.

Once he'd located Cullen and set himself up at the vet's, he could afford to play a waiting game. After all, he'd waited three years. A few more weeks or even months wouldn't matter. But as luck—or fate—would have it, the filly's injury had drawn him into Cullen's orbit in a relatively short time. Kate had no doubt that he intended to finish things this morning.

Slowly, carefully, she eased down the packed dirt aisle. There was a soft scuttling sound behind her, and she whirled, pistol aimed. Just a mouse followed by a barn cat that ducked behind a feed barrel. Turning back, she saw nothing in the path ahead of her. Ahead, the aisle made a ninety-degree turn to the right, cutting the twelve stalls into two sections of six. Moving slowly, stealthily, she headed in that direction, wondering where Carlson was, wondering what he'd done with Meghan.

Adrenaline flowed through Kate like some high-powered drug. Every sense was on alert, every sound magnified. Was that a noise she heard coming from the shedrow she'd just left? She started to turn when the barn door she'd entered flew open, crashing against the wall.

"Kate!"

Cullen. Kate opened her mouth to tell him to stay put when someone—Carlson—barreled into her. She gave a little cry of surprise as she fell forward. She tried to brace the fall with her elbows and hit the hard-packed dirt with such force that the Glock went spinning into a pile of hay bales stacked along the corridor where the two aisles converged. She heard Cullen call her name again. Her jacket was grabbed from behind, and she was jerked roughly to her feet.

She opened her mouth to call out to Cullen when she felt the hardness of a gun barrel jammed against her temple. "One word and you're dead."

Though she shouldn't have been surprised to have her suspicions validated, Kate's blood ran cold. It was the voice from the answering machine.

Cullen heard the sounds of a scuffle from somewhere near the middle of the barn. Why didn't Kate answer him?

Maybe she can't. No! Nothing was going to happen to her. It couldn't! Rifle poised at his shoulder, he walked boldly down the aisle, eyes darting from one side to the other, his ears as sensitive to sound as the big buck's might have been. He was hoping to hear some noise, get a location when Kate was shoved into the central passageway, her hands above her head. Kent Carlson followed at a leisurely pace, as if he had all the time in the world to accomplish his goals.

Cullen assessed the situation with as much objectivity as he could muster considering that Kate was in the line of fire. The good news was that Carlson wasn't holding on to her, didn't have the pistol in his hand pointed at her. Instead, it was held in both hands, a shooter's grip, and trained on Cullen. The bad news was that Kate was between him and a clear shot of Carlson.

"Let her walk away, Carlson," Cullen said. "This is between you and me."

"Depends on how you look at it." He laughed, taking another step forward. Kate stayed where she was, her eyes wide, a look that hovered somewhere between fear and shock on her face. "I thought she was just another of your women, and that made me really, really angry, especially since you claimed you were so distraught over your wife's death. You'd never get over it, your life was ruined, et cetera, et cetera, ad nauseam."

Disgust dripped from Carlson's voice. "But never

wasn't quite as long as you thought, was it, counselor? Your pain only lasted three years, and in the meantime your perfect life just keeps getting better.''

"Life is what we make it," Cullen said, taking a step closer. "For most of us hurts fade. Wounds heal. Unless we keep picking off the scab.''

Carlson laughed again, a sound a bit too bright, too happy for the situation. A sound that spoke too clearly of the madness kept carefully in check. He jerked his head toward Kate. "She's a cop, isn't she?''

"No.''

"Liar.'' He stepped forward, almost close enough to Kate that he could grab her if he wanted to. She looked as if she had gone into shock, and Cullen knew she was reliving the nightmare where her partner was killed. He had to do something, say something to jolt her out of the daze.

"Kate!''

Kate, whose mind was filled with images of a New Orleans alley and Raul standing in the middle of reeking trash cans, a gun leveled at him, heard the sharp sound of Cullen's voice calling her name. Her head jerked up, like that of a wild animal who hears an unnatural sound in his environment. Memories of the past evaporated. She was once more in the very dangerous present.

She tried to assess the situation. When he'd shoved her into the shedrow, Carlson had taken his gun off her and trained it on Cullen, whom she was supposed to be protecting, keeping safe. Cullen, whom she loved. Her heart sank, and a feeling of helplessness swept through her. Just as she had been before, she was powerless, although in a different way. Her pistol was gone, and she had no means of protecting either herself or Cullen.

So what are you going to do, Kate? Just stand here and let him shoot Cullen? No. She'd stood by once and let someone she cared about die. She'd never be able to bring herself back from the edge if anything happened to Cullen. *Then think, Kate.*

A slight mewling sound from high to her left caught her attention, probably Cullen's and Carlson's, too. The dratted cat was parading along the top edge of the stall, like a tightrope walker at the big top. Clearly in no hurry, he stopped and gave the humans below him a disdainful look, then leaped down onto the dozen or so bales of hay stacked at the corner of the passageway. Kate's gaze followed the feline's graceful landing, and her heart almost stopped.

Lying in the dirt, wedged between a bale of hay and the wall of the stall, lay the Glock....

For an instant, the unexpected mewling of the cat diverted Cullen's attention from Carlson. Thankfully, the cat also distracted the former doctor for the moment. But only a moment. Before Cullen could gauge whether or not he could make any kind of shot without endangering Kate, Carlson's cold, calculating gaze turned back on him, along with the muzzle of the revolver.

At least Kate seemed alert now. She stood looking at him, her gaze calm and steady, almost as if she were trying to communicate something.

"Let her go," Cullen said again.

"I—" Without warning, Kate dove sideways toward the center aisle. As if he were watching in slow motion, Cullen observed as, in a move guided by pure instinct, Kent Carlson turned the gun on Kate. *No!*

Not stopping to consider the repercussions of what he was doing, Cullen squeezed the trigger twice and saw

Carlson flinch. Almost simultaneously, he heard the sound of another weapon reverberate through the barn, and his eardrums recoiled in agony. *Ah, Kate!*

The rifle sight still aimed at his enemy, Cullen was marginally aware of the nervous stomping and the panicked whinnying of the horses in the stalls around him. Of the cat racing in front of him, looking for safety. Of Carlson standing, looking as if his arms were too heavy to hold up his gun. All Cullen could think about was Kate.

Then, before he could shift a brief glance her way, Carlson pitched forward, falling toward the stack of hay. Cullen dropped the rifle and sprinted the short distance to where Kate lay.

She was as pale as death, but her eyes were wide-open. The Glock was clutched in a two-handed, white-knuckled grip, resting on her thigh. Blood ran freely from an inch-long groove on her cheek. Cullen's stomach clenched, and his heart missed a beat. Carlson had come close. Too close.

"Are you okay?"

She nodded and held out her hand for him to help her up. With his good arm holding her tightly against him, Cullen took the toe of his sneaker and rolled Carlson onto his back. There were two wounds in his torso. One from Cullen's rifle, one from Kate's Glock.

When Kate and Cullen emerged from the darkness of the barn into the brightness of the winter sunshine, they were greeted by the comforting sound of sirens wailing in the distance. Greg, Louella and Meghan must have seen them coming out, because the kitchen door burst open and the two women ran across the patio. Greg followed more slowly, a smile of satisfaction lighting up his face. Louella clutched Kate close, and Meghan threw her arms around her brother's neck, sobbing.

It took more than two hours before the sheriff's department finished with their questioning, the EMT crew had patched up Kate's cheek, and Carlson's body was loaded and driven to the morgue. Dan and the girls had slept through the whole thing until the sounds of shooting had awakened them. Kate's ears still rang from the booming of the three discharged weapons. The paramedic said she'd been lucky. Kent Carlson's bullet had come very close.

To say that the emotion abounding in the house was one of relief would be an understatement. The danger had passed, and no one except the bad guy had gotten killed. Mission accomplished.

Kate dragged her suitcase from beneath the bed and tossed it onto the lace coverlet. It was time to get back to her own life. Her aunt and the Longstreets were heading to Little Rock, ending their Thanksgiving vacation and settling back into their lives with no immediate worries. Kate's only concern was how she'd get through the rest of her life without Cullen.

She was taking some things from a drawer when someone knocked on the door and Cullen stuck his head inside, his gaze going unerringly to the suitcase on the bed.

"May I come in?"

The last thing she wanted was to talk to him, but she knew it was time. "Sure."

He stuck the tips of his fingers into the edges of his front pockets and cocked his head toward the suitcase. "Going somewhere?"

"Yeah." She tucked a stack of underwear into a corner of the suitcase and forced a false cheerfulness into her voice. "Time to go home. The perp's out of the picture. Game's over. We win."

"I thought I'd told you it wasn't a game for me," Cullen said, leaning against the closed door. "Not after the first day or so."

Kate wondered if the noise from the guns had indeed impaired her hearing. Her heart began to beat a little faster. "What wasn't a game?"

"None of it," he said. "Not the pretending you were the woman in my life, not what happened between us in the weight room."

Kate smoothed the sweater lying in the suitcase and turned to face him. "So it wasn't a game, wasn't just sex. What are you trying to tell me? That it was love?"

He regarded her with a steadiness that was disconcerting. "And if I said yes, what would you say?"

That she was shocked. Didn't believe him. "That the pain medicine has affected your thinking. That—"

"Why, Kate?" he interrupted. "Why is it so hard for you to believe that someone can love you?"

Why was it so hard? She tossed him the first excuse that came to mind. "Maybe because I've seen just how short-lived love can be when times get tough."

"Lane?"

"Yeah, Lane."

"He was a fool for letting a woman like you get away."

"Right. I'm such a catch I'm sure he's been kicking himself for letting me go ever since we signed the divorce papers," she said in a deliberately flip tone. "And of course, I'm just the kind of woman you've been looking for."

He laughed, and she heard the sarcasm in the sound. "No. You're nothing like the kind of woman I was looking for...if I was even looking. What man in his right mind would want a woman who argues with everything he says, a woman who has a chip on her shoulder the size of Arkansas—''

''And those are my good points,'' Kate quipped, her color high.

He did laugh then, the real thing. The effect on Kate was immediate and devastating.

''And a sense of humor, too.''

Afraid she might give in if he kept up with the cajoling tenderness, Kate slammed the partially filled suitcase shut and turned to him with a haughty look. ''I'm glad you find my shortcomings so entertaining, counselor, but...''

Something about the expression on his face silenced her—sadness, exasperation and something she couldn't put her finger on.

''Who'd want a woman who's so unsure of herself she doesn't have the sense to realize she's gorgeous and smart and very desirable?''

As she looked into his eyes, she wondered how she was supposed to defend her heart against the sincerity she saw there. For the first time since they'd started their little debate, her resolve faltered.

''I have a confession to make,'' he said, his voice filling the growing silence. He took his hands from his pockets and crossed his arms over his chest.

''Yeah?''

''I left you in New Orleans because what happened between us scared me to death.''

''Scared you?''

He nodded. ''I loved Joanie. I was devastated when she died. I could hardly make it from one day to the next. I didn't think I'd ever be happy again, was certain I'd never fall in love again, and then I went to New Orleans and in a couple of days, you turned all those beliefs up-side down.''

Kate's heart beat a ragged rhythm. ''Are you trying to make me believe that you fell in love with me in New Orleans?''

''It started then. Your energy, your attitude and the vulnerability I saw in you made me realize that I hadn't died along with Joanie. They made me realize that other people had tragedies in their lives and they didn't give up. They picked themselves up, dusted themselves off and tried again.''

His voice trailed away, and his shoulders lifted in a little shrug. ''And then there was the fantastic sex. What I felt with you was so intense that I was frightened and guilty.''

''Why would you feel guilty?''

''Because I thought I'd mourn for Joanie the rest of my life. But, as Carlson pointed out, my grief didn't last nearly as long as I expected. Less than a year, in fact. What happened between us knocked me for a loop. *You* knocked me for a loop. As crazy as it sounds, I felt as if I'd been disloyal to her, to what we had.''

Surprised by his admission, Kate stood speechless. That was exactly what Meghan had intimated. Kate thought of her own guilty feelings over Raul's death and realized that people dealt with blame in different ways. Was it any sillier for Cullen to feel guilt for wanting to rejoin the living so soon after Joanie's death than it was for Kate to keep beating herself up for something that, in all honesty, she might not have been able to prevent no matter how hard she'd tried?

He smiled, a wry, tender sort of smile. ''You don't look convinced. I know it's hard to believe. I'm having a hell of a time with it myself, but I have gotten past acknowledging that it's real.''

''What's real?'' she asked, her voice hardly above a whisper, her heart filling with a tentative hope in spite of her mind's warnings.

''What I feel for you. What I think you feel for me. The love. What I have to do...what we have to do is face our fears. It scares me to death to think of losing someone else I love. When I realized you were out there with that madman, I was terrified. But love doesn't come without risks, Kate. Neither does life.''

''I don't want to face having someone walk out on me just because things get tough,'' she told him, her heart beginning to swell with the first tentative tendrils of hope and happiness. ''I couldn't take that again.''

''I won't walk out on you. Ever.''

She wanted so much to believe it, to believe him. But she was afraid. *We have to face our fears, Katie.* Aunt Louella's voice sounded loud and clear in Kate's mind, echoing Cullen's statement. But could she do that? Life was simpler without the complications that came with loving someone and having them love you.

Do you believe it then, Kate? Do you believe he really loves you?

It was hard not to when he looked at her with such longing and need in his eyes. Hard not to when she wanted to believe it so badly. ''What about Tyler? What about that fear? What will you do if you find out he is yours?''

''Face it responsibly, with as much dignity as I can.''

The right answer. ''I won't fit into your world, your life.''

He gave a negligent shrug. ''If I'm a happily married man, my social life will decline considerably.''

Kate sucked in a shocked breath. Married. To Cullen McGyver. Surely her hearing had been affected by the gunshots. Had he really said what she thought he had? Yes. Could she trust his love that much? If she ever wanted to be truly happy again, she knew she had to, but oh, it was so hard to open herself up to be hurt again.

"I'd hate Washington."

"You know," he said thoughtfully, "I don't think I'd like it much, either. I don't think I'll run for the senate, after all." He looked at her with a steady, thoughtful expression. "Do you know what makes a gambler, Kat?" Kate shook her head. "A gambler is a quarter cool calculation, a quarter bravado, a quarter gut instinct and a quarter sheer guts. Are you a gambler?"

"I don't know." A whispered doubt.

"Sure you are. Every time you walked into a dangerous situation as a cop you were taking a gamble on the fact that you could take the bad guy."

Her heart took a painful lurch. "But I didn't take the bad guy the day Raul was killed."

"No, but that didn't stop you from taking this job and putting yourself back on the line. It didn't stop you from standing between me and someone who wanted to kill me. And it didn't keep you from making the shot today."

"We both shot him."

"See? We make a heck of a team."

Slowly, deliberately, he uncrossed his arms and straightened. Took a step toward her. Held out his hand. "Come on, Kat," he begged. "Take a gamble. Stay. If you go, I'll never get to see you in that fantastic dress."

"I'm afraid," she whispered.

"That makes two of us."

Kate stood there for long seconds, her heart beating heavily in her chest, drinking in the love she saw in his eyes, terrified of failure, terrified of losing him, losing this, maybe her last chance at love, and knowing that if she did, she'd never breathe another happy breath.

Her heart beating in her throat, she held out her hand and took that first tentative step...

*   *   *   *   *

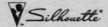

SPECIAL EDITION™

Coming in August 2002,
from Silhouette Special Edition and

CHRISTINE RIMMER,

the author who brought you the popular series

CONVENIENTLY YOURS,

brings her new series

THE SONS OF

CAITLIN
BRAVO

Starting with

HIS EXECUTIVE SWEETHEART
(SE #1485)...

One day she was the prim and proper executive assistant...
the next, Celia Tuttle fell hopelessly in love with her boss,
mogul Aaron Bravo, bachelor extraordinaire. It was clear he
was never going to return her feelings, so what was a girl to
do but get a makeover—and try to quit. Only suddenly,
was Aaron eyeing his assistant in a whole new light?

And coming in October 2002, MERCURY RISING,
also from Silhouette Special Edition.

**THE SONS OF CAITLIN BRAVO: Aaron, Cade and Will.
They thought no woman could tame them.
How wrong they were!**

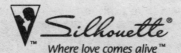

Where love comes alive™

MONTANA MAVERICKS

One of Silhouette Special Edition's most popular
series returns with three sensational stories filled
with love, small-town gossip, reunited lovers, a little
murder, hot nights and the best in romance:

HER MONTANA MAN
by Laurie Paige
(ISBN#: 0-373-24483-5)
Available August 2002

BIG SKY COWBOY
by Jennifer Mikels
(ISBN#: 0-373-24491-6)
Available September 2002

MONTANA LAWMAN
by Allison Leigh
(ISBN#: 0-373-24497-5)
Available October 2002

*True love is the only way to beat the heat
in Rumor, Montana....*

Where love comes alive™

COMING NEXT MONTH